I0699667

Trellis

Book 1 in the Alaster Trilogy

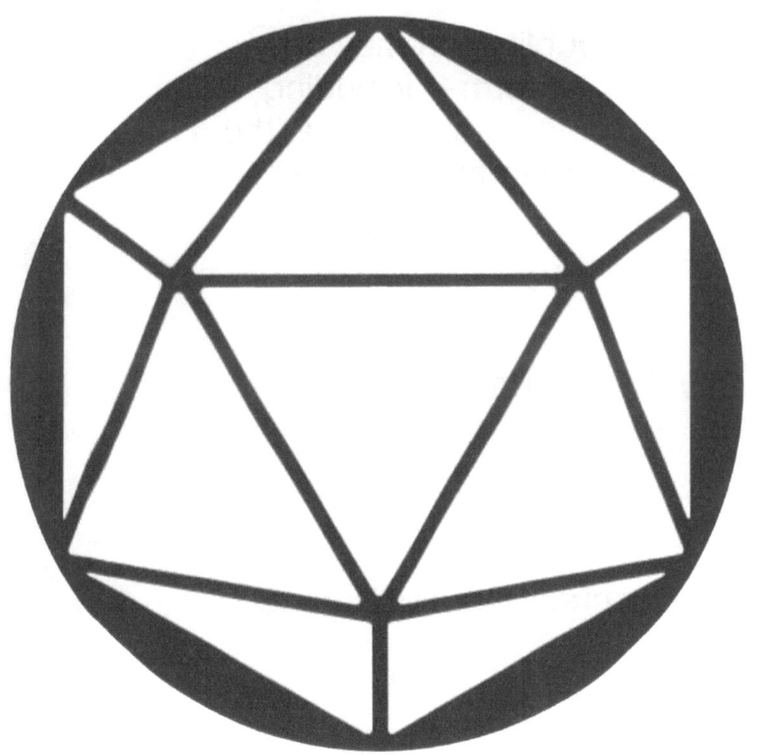

A. H. Ostmo

Trellis: Book 1 in the Alaster Trilogy

ISBN: 979-8-9874011-0-1

Library of Congress Control Number: 2022922153

https://ahostmo.com/

Cover art by Amarissa Ostmo

To Lissa, because you told me that someday I'd write a book and dedicate it to you.

Contents

Prologue: The Accident

Garridon Hamiltoni ran his right fingers across the control panel. His left hand squeezed a small pen-shaped remote. Giant screens played footage of enclosed corridors. There were no windows, only dim lights of all colors. The faintly illuminated walkways revealed community members in the different screens before Garridon and his co-worker, Emon S. Plangon.

"There it is," said Plangon, pointing to a screen.

"I don't see it," said Garridon, trying not to tense his left hand and push a button at the wrong time.

A scream sounded from the security screen.

"Water is in the phrame," Plangon urged.

Garridon stood stiff, eyes locked to the security footage of ice-cold water filling the walkway and people running to escape.

"What are you waiting for?" Plangon demanded.

"Britannica," Garridon's frozen stare didn't break as he whispered his wife's name.

Britannica Hamiltoni appeared in the corridor with a mechanical instrument in hand. Her body shoved through shin-deep water. It was like a small string connected Garridon to everything he loved as it drifted away. The remote in his hand would cut that string; it would be lost forever.

"Garridon!" Plangon couldn't wait any longer. "The area is filling with water. Close it or we'll all drown!"

Garridon couldn't unlock his eyes from Britannica's light-brown ponytail that swayed with each step she took into deeper water. Her hair glistened. It was almost like the sun's rays could reflect from her loose curls and brighten the cold atmosphere in the facility. Garridon had never actually seen the sun, but he thought the warmth of its rays might feel something like the warmth from his wife's laugh. The difference was that Garridon knew he could live without seeing the sun, but he wasn't sure he could bear life without the light of his wife's joy.

Plangon grabbed the back of Garridon's head and turned him to look at a different screen. "Your daughter is in the next phrame!"

Garridon reactively shoved Plangon away, fumbling at the realization that he could lose his daughter.

"I—" Garridon focused on the screen, "Gia— she's in training— she's not supposed to be there." Garridon's eyes shot, back-and-forth, screen-to-screen, seeing his four-year-old daughter running excitedly in front of a group of kids and also his wife wading frantically through a flooding pathway.

"We don't have time for this!" Plangon lunged for the remote. Garridon dodged Plangon, grabbing the back of Plangon's head and slamming it into a control panel before the screens. Plangon sank to the ground with a wail.

"Why is Gia there?" Garridon stepped on Plangon's chest and pushed down.

"The training has a trip to the algae fields in Phrame 22," Plangon grunted and gasped for air as Garridon released his footing.

A roar came from the security screens. Garridon turned to see a wall of water cascading through the corridor. Britannica stood before an open panel in the wall. Just before the wave of water reached her, she inserted the machine from her hand into the electrical panel. Every entrance to the flooded area sealed shut. The screens flickered before Garridon, then shut off.

All went silent.

Garridon fixated on the screens that were the only way of knowing what happened to his wife, but all he could see was his own reflection.

Chapter 1: Underwater Constellations

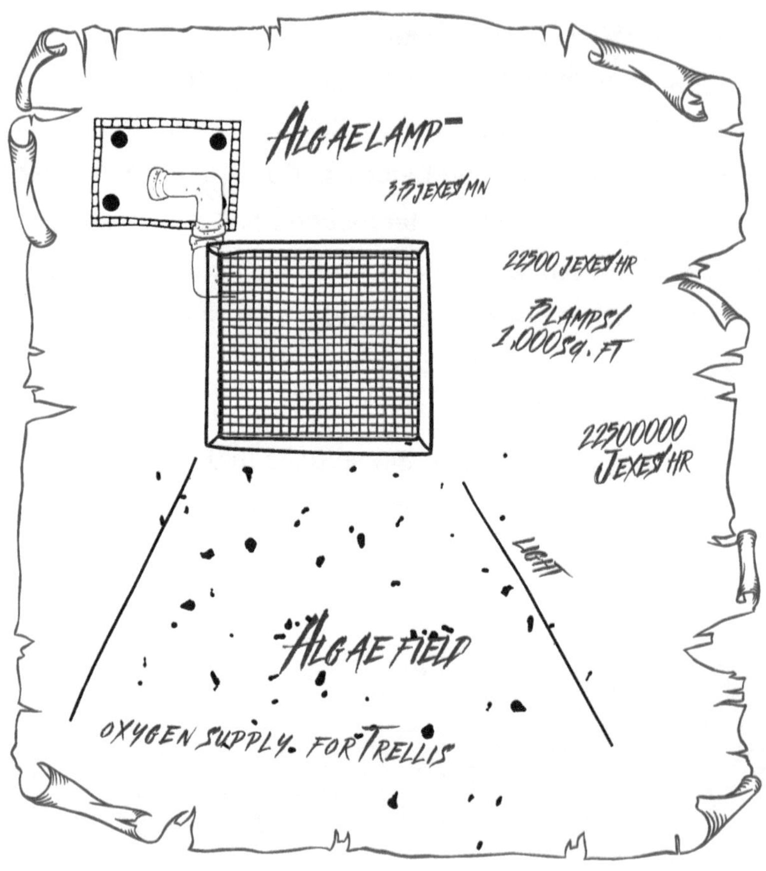

My stance is united with the ground as energy runs through my legs, up my spine, and into my fists. Power surges through my body as I let my fists fly to the padding on the wall in front of me. An electronic sign above the padding reads the amount of power from my punch: 127 jexes.

Like ghosts haunting my mind, I hear the voice of my father: *"your best is 192 jexes. How are you going to improve if you aren't even building from your best?"*

I thought my father might be the best. Head of Facilitators in the Trellis Facility, he could see patterns in community member movements and decipher uprising plans when they were still in a seedling phase. Or my great-great-grandma who was the lead scientist on the Trellis project. It was her work that built this facility and brought a community 6,000 meters under the sea.

Every generation seems to have the greats: the influencers, the inventors, the mountain movers, and the culture shifters. I used to think it was possible to arrive there— wherever that was.

I square my stance again. A dim, orange light reflects off a grey suit that covers my neck to my feet— everything except my hands. Sweat streams from my forehead. I give a quick right jab, a sharp left jab, then a kick with my right foot. 424 jexes in total. It should be closer to 500.

My workmate, Leal, swings his lanky figure at the punching pad to my left. The orange light bounces from his afro curls as he raises his skinny arms. With all the power he can muster, Leal throws a punch at the padding on the wall. The sign reads 73 jexes.

Leal is what changed my perspective of greatness. Honestly, I was frustrated when he and I were assigned to work as Facilitators in the security station together. I had trained all my life and worked myself to exhaustion with the hope of being assigned as a Facilitator. And there he was— a small-framed teenager with as much physical grit as a piece of seaweed.

Facilitators are not just the most intelligent, they must be the most intuitive. Quick reactions, but no errors — that's what's expected from us. As a kid, when the rest of the group would go from trainings to designated sleeping hours, my father would pull me from sleeping time for more training. Since I was six years old, I was pinned against the highest-ranking Facilitator.

Now, as I look to my left at the scrawny excuse for a Facilitator, I realize that he had a greatness no one could ever train. The sign above Leal mocks his weak, 73-jex-punch. But, in the quiet of our workstation, Leal has explained to me what that actually means.

A beeping sound rings throughout the room.

I move with a line of people in red and grey suits to the next training station. I step up to a cardio machine, putting my right foot into a boot holder, followed by my left. The boot holder suctions around my calves as I place my arms into holders that tighten like sleeves up to my elbows. Without hesitation, I move and the machine levitates me from the ground. I run in place in the air with the machine holding me up. An electronic screen in front of me shows the amount of energy I produce in a given amount of time: 620 jexes per 30 seconds. It dips to 590 jexes per 30 seconds. Run faster. 699 jexes per 30 seconds.

In my mind, the numbers have always been a sort of ranking system— almost as harsh as my father himself — ever urging that I can produce one more jex.

But to Leal, they mean something different. The amount that I run produces energy that can power my cardio machine or a screen. Together, as the row of people in red and grey suits run, we generate enough energy to power something larger, maybe the machines that process our food or heat the facility. Leal sees everything as a whole system. He understands how the moving parts work together, while I could only see myself— one moving part pushing to be the best.

Looking at the screen ahead, my heart jolts as I see I've dipped to 531 jexes per 30 seconds.

A beep sounds.

I stop moving and the machine lowers to the ground, hissing as it releases my arms and legs. The screen shows a total of 180,533 jexes for the total amount of time. I should have averaged about 20% more than that. I step from the machine and over to the area where people circle around a padded floor.

A young man in a red body suit, Desman Sphyrn, picks up a cross-shaped weapon and centers himself before a circle of onlookers. On assignment day, Desman was given the role of a Promotor— a person who preserves the history of humanity to inform our future.

Trellis

Another person, Jarret Carpio, steps to the center of the circle with a cross-stick in his hand. His grey suit reveals that he has the same role as me— a Facilitator, who ensures the physical safety of the residents in the Trellis. Jarret's stature compared to Desman's is the very reason why I wonder why Promotors and Facilitators train together at all. Desman is large and muscular for an average 19-year-old, but compared to Jarret, he looks like a single krill on its way to being swallowed whole by a whale.

With the dim, orange light shining to the center of our cluster, an electronic sounding bell beeps. Tension flashes in the stares between Jarret and Desman as they move slowly around the circle, looking for a chance to strike. Jarret makes the first lunge to knock Desman's knee with the cross-stick, but Desman rolls over Jarret's back and lands on his feet.

The heat from their sweat and the tense breath from the small circle of bodies warms the room. Desman leaps toward Jarret's back, maybe in an attempt at a headlock. But Jarret swings his cross-stick with enough force to send the helpless Promotor flying outside the circle.

All eyes look to the fallen Desman, then to a tall figure amidst our circle.

"That's enough," says the figure. It's Emmon S. Plangon, a Facilitator Head and our direct supervisor.

A girl pulls Desman from the ground, with her red hair spilling over his shoulders as she lifts him from behind. That's Arianelle.

"I'm fine," Desman says as he holds his side and straightens up. He doesn't turn to look at Arianelle as he makes the best attempt at walking back to the circle. Leal always says there's a spark in Desman's eye when he gazes upon the beautiful Arianelle. He actually used those words— a *"spark in the eye"* and *"he gazes."* Could someone be any more melodramatic?

"I'll remind you," Plangon says as he paces the circle of people, "our practice today is to stay physically adept and prepared for any sort of dissonance we may find in our community." He stops and turns to face Jarret. "We are not here, Mr. Carpio, to cause permanent damage." Plangon holds his stare with Jarret. The muscles around Plangon's mouth break the silence as a smile widens on his face and turns away from Jarret.

"However," he continues, "I like your enthusiasm. Gia Hamiltoni." Plangon looks at me. "Step up please."

Desman hands me his cross-stick. The metal weapon feels heavy in my left hand. I step from the circle and face Jarret in the center. Orange light illuminates his face.

The bell beeps.

Tension flickers in Jarret's eyes. His muscles become alert, ready to move. When we were in this circle ten days ago, I buckled him at the knees. Plangon pointed out Jarret's flaw— that he uses brute force and is unaware of his unprotected areas. Jarret has attacked other people at the knees ever since. However, Jarret's actual greatest weakness is that he is an idiot. It's not really a flaw I can help my team member develop, but I can use it to win a fight, every time.

Jarret is confused when he shifts to pace the circle and I don't move. I do this about 15% percent of the time. He can't get past the initial unpredictability and starts the match with a slight sense of uncertainty in his movement.

He has no idea which hand is actually my dominant because I start with weapons in a different hand every time. I'm naturally right-handed, but I've made my left almost equal.

I swing the cross-stick in my left hand while shifting weight to my right leg. His full attention is on blocking the blow. There's a cross-stick in his right hand which could be used as a shield, but he tries to be clever by reaching with this empty hand to yank the weapon from my grip.

This is my favorite part. When he's completely out of his wits for a moment as I let go of the cross-stick in my left hand and lunge to the right.

It's an elementary move. I almost wish I could come up with something more complicated as I tackle at his waist, using his own momentum to flip him over his head and out of the circle.

He's not badly hurt. He leaps to his feet and all eyes look to Plangon to hear the word on whether this match will continue.

"It's finished," says Plangon.

Jarret throws his hands in the air. "Sir, I can—"

Plangon puts his hand up. Jarret murmurs his way back to the circle and keeps his pouty face to the ground.

"Leal Fitzgerald," Plangon's voice fills the room. "Please step forward."

Leal's thin figure approaches the center. His green-blue eyes shift around the circle as he uncomfortably rubs his arm as if he hasn't walked into this circle four times a week for the past year.

His shoulders are shrugged up to his ears and his gaze moves from the small crowd to me. Standing two feet from me, he waves.

I shake my head and try not to laugh at how ridiculous he looks in a circle of intensively conditioned Facilitators and Promotors. I look over to Plangon. He makes no expression, but I feel that somewhere, deep down, he has a little smirk.

I met Leal the day before I began work as a Facilitator. We were assigned to be partners in the security footage station. He was even scrawnier back then, giving that goofy wave as he walked into the security room to see me standing before a wall of screens that played footage of the Trellis community.

I remember Plangon escorting Leal to the room. I had known Plangon for years since he was in the same rank as my dad. He walked with Leal into the workstation and rolled his eyes as the scrawny character waved at me.

"Thank you for helping me find my way," Leal said as Plangon exited the door.

That's how the first week went with Leal. People exiting rooms, impatiently explaining things, and sometimes violently handing him objects. He was my only company in the workstation, but I barely talked to him. Instead, he filled the room with talk about the earth's surface, the history of humanity, and music.

That's when everything changed.

He played a song. Not on an instrument (I can't imagine he'd be a very good musician) but from the security speakers. A jazz song replaced his yammering about the surface. I nearly jumped out of my seat. I had only heard music as part of cultural trainings when I was a kid.

"Turn it off!" I yelled at him. Some mix of surprise and loss of control created a panic that would only stop when the music was off. I had never heard jazz.

He frantically threw his hands in the air, then turned the volume down.

"I'm sorry! I'm sorry!" he panicked.

"Are you crazy?" I looked him dead in the eye. "How did you play this? We'll get marked down for sure."

"Have you been listening to anything I said?"

I hadn't.

He explained, "I said I can tap into the Promotor's files to pull up cultural information."

"What are we going to tell Plangon when there's footage of us tapping into files we don't have access to?"

"I told you already, I can override the surveillance of our room. The audio is off. No one can hear us."

I just looked at him. I was stunned. It wasn't because he liked a particular type of music or that he went out of his way to get it— although I had never met someone before who liked music. My father had created the tightest security codes known in history. There was a constant stream of people assigned to try and get past his security and no one had ever succeeded. But, there I was, looking at a twerpy 18-year-old who broke past not just one, but two different facets of the security system. And he thought he was only listening to jazz music.

Leal once played a song that went like this:

The star that shines next to the other

might be as bright as its brother.

But the only ones taught through generations

are the lines we draw in the constellations.

That's what history is like and what the greats are like. One star might have been just as bright as the one next to it, but humans only knew the names of the ones connected by imaginary lines they created.

Leal is great. It's a fact. But, as I look at him standing two feet away, he is also definitely a loser. I'm not trying to call him names, it's just that he would obviously lose in any physical fight. And it's hard to say what history will decide to remember. If history forgets him, it will be missing out on a great. But if it did remember his greatness, it might leave out that he is also a loser.

I hear a very faint sound of a door opening.

The electric bell beeps.

Everyone leans in as if to see what I will do. I had so arrogantly taken advantage of Jarret's greatest weakness. Plangon probably chose to put me against my own: Leal, my best friend. The crowd remains silent, waiting to see if I will take him down. I won't— or at least not badly.

From the corner of my eye, I see a figure behind the onlookers. It's my father.

Our facility rests on the seafloor thousands of meters underwater. No sunlight shines here. Temperatures are near freezing. Yet, this facility knows nothing colder than the silence of the Senior Facilitator, staring as his daughter remains motionless in a fight.

The electric bolt of his presence jumpstarts my limbs in motion. With more energy than I've ever given to a fight, I jolt toward my best friend.

I don't know what happens, except that I feel the energy draining from my arms as I lift them and look at my hands. It seems like there should be something physically flying off my fingers, like a light fading as my hands power down. I look past my palms and to the ground where Leal stretches across the padding. I hold back a gasp, my eyes widening. My teeth clench together as I hold back a string of "I'm sorry" and "are you okay?"

"Lea?" I whisper between my teeth as I bend down to him.

He lets out a grunted, "oooouch." His jaw moves to the side as he opens it.

Others from the circle rush in to see if he's okay.

"As I said to Mr. Carpio—" Plangon begins his speech to me, but my father breaks in before he can finish.

"Give me an analysis," my father walks forward with his posture straight like a cross-stick.

"Mr. Hamiltoni?" Plangon turns toward my father.

"Step back," my dad calmly walks toward me and the crowd surrounding Leal moves back.

I stand facing my father.

"Unlike the minimal training required for your cluster," my dad speaks to Plangon, "Miss Hamiltoni is extensively trained in all fields, including human anatomy and emergency medical procedures."

Miss Hamiltoni— he doesn't even call me by my name. He's hardly more of a father than Plangon. Maybe "father" is too familiar of a term to be calling him in my thought life. It doesn't sound like we're on a first-name basis, so I can't call him "Garridon" either. "Mr. Hamiltoni," that's what I'll have to call him; or "sir."

Mr. Hamiltoni's spine is still straight with arms linked behind his back as his head twists in my direction. The pace of his speech slows slightly and he enunciates: "Give me an analysis."

I want to mouth "I'm sorry" to Leal as I see the muscles in his face cringe with every short breath he takes. But, with the gaze of Garridon Hamiltoni weighing on me, I have no room for empathetic remarks or even emotions.

I need to stop looking Leal in the eyes. Put the sting of guilt to the side and look at the object of study.

I can tell by his breathing he has fractured ribs. With my strength and the surface area my fist can cover, it's probably two. Since I was acting on instinct, I would hit him with my right fist, injuring his left side. His right jaw is visibly dislocated which means that my second hit was to the jaw with my left hand. He might have crumbled to the ground in pain, but he obviously fell backward—implying some sort of force. I must have hit him somewhere to make him land on his back. Assuming muscle memory from training kicked in, I would have given a blow to the back of the knee.

"Two fractured ribs on his left side, dislocated jaw on his right, and a strained hamstring behind his left knee." I can almost taste the metallic cold on my tongue as the last words leave my mouth and I turn from being a machine back into a human.

Garridon looks at me for a moment. Maybe pleased? I don't really know. His facial expression doesn't change, but I feel the weight of his displeasure leave my shoulders.

"Miss Fisciatta," Plangon turns to Minji Fisciatta, a girl in the crowd who also works in surveillance. "Ask the medical cluster for a compression strap."

Minji runs off as I kneel to help Leal sit up.

"If it's no bother," Garridon's tone is condescending, "I will be at the next mental maintenance. I question if these trainees are being kept to the expected standard." He looks directly at Plangon and pauses. Then he turns, exiting the room.

Chapter 2: Beauty Looks Down on Me

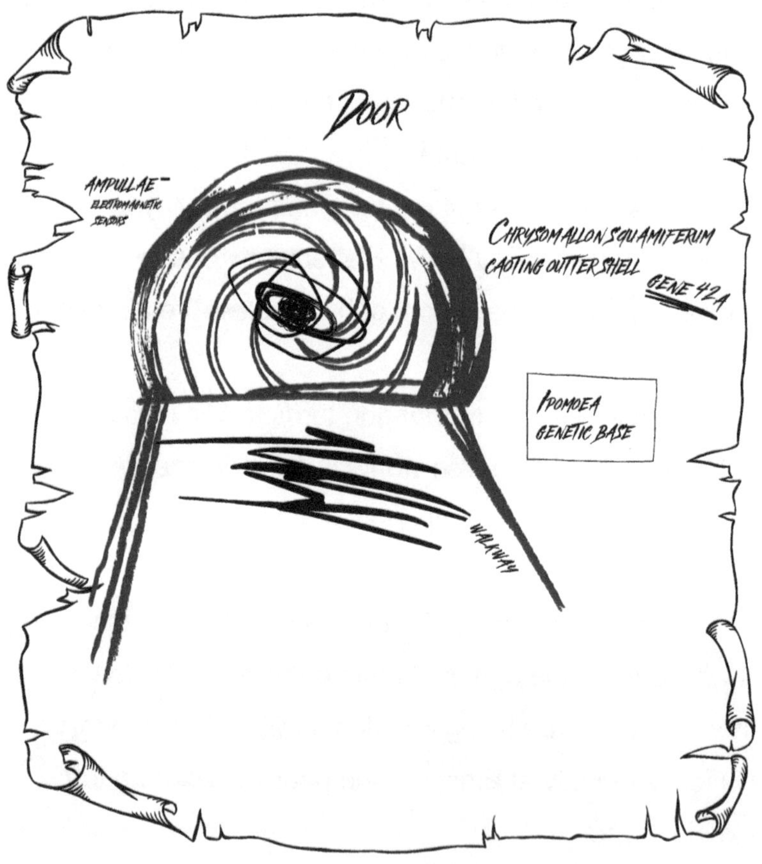

It's different in my sleeping quarters; slower maybe. There are no cameras in my head. There is no one to hear my thoughts, judge my moves, or attack my questions. I turn to my side as I lay on a platform in the middle of a dimly lit space.

The ocean might sound beautiful, but I can't hear it. I want the peace from swaying water to move across my ceiling as I lay in bed staring upward. Videos and journals from people who describe the ocean say waves are loud and roaring and, when someone's close to the ocean, it silences everything else. Waves are loud, full of thundering power. They're also silent and stilling.

I don't have any real understanding of these things but, when Leal and I watch footage of the earth's surface, I feel like there's beauty I was meant to experience. But it doesn't exist anymore— unless you're one of those Surfacer weirdos.

I roll onto my side and close my eyes. I listen for the quiet. There are no noises, but there is also no peace.

I've never really seen the outside. A few times, technically, I have. When I was a kid, we took field trips to the algae fields. Our facility is segmented into 30 different areas, called phrames, which operate as working, training, eating, or sleeping areas. There are small windows in Phrame 22 which look out to a patch of green organisms that give us oxygen. I wish I could go there— swim out in the green. What it must be like to be able to step outside whenever you want.

I roll to my other side and try to keep my eyes closed. This is usually how I spend my designated sleeping hours— wishing for stillness. I don't wish for darkness, I have enough of that, but there is something romantic and alluring about nighttime. Stars piercing through a sheet of black. I can barely imagine that. What holds burning orbs of light in place so far above the earth's problems? Even after earth's wars, the stars must still be there, shining beautiful and unbothered by our devastation. Whether there's anyone to watch them or not, they display their performance and stay wonderful in their own right.

I've read poems by people who've watched the stars for hours— all night, even. Why did people even have ceilings if they could see the stars? I would stay out all night. I would do that right now. Instead of staring at my wall.

I turn to my ceiling. No stars, but it's faintly lit green, the whole thing. The lights never turn off here, just different colors. And those colors have nothing to do with a time of day.

A buzzer sounds.

That's what tells me the time of day. It's morning for me, but nighttime for someone else who will leave the workstation for designated sleeping hours. What it must have been like when the sky told everyone around whether it was day or not. No human could program or synthesize time, but everyone went by its rules— like magic.

I roll from the bed and put my feet on the ground. I don't know what it's like to feel something beneath my bare feet. The cold ground, grass, concrete— it all would have felt different. Shoes were important on the earth's surface,

I've seen a lot of advertisements for them. I would wear shoes if I could. Instead, there's a layer of soft padding around my feet that's a part of my microbial suit. Laundry detergent— that's another thing I've seen in earth advertisements. But our suits are made from microbes that take care of a lot of things earth people needed— deodorant, body wash… I think Leal nearly passed out the time we found instructions for a tampon.

Standing from a raised table in the middle of my sleeping area, I walk to the circular doorway. The door seems almost like a dark, raveled flower petal that twists together in the center. When I stand in front of the door, it untwists and slinks open into the walls.

Corridors are lit in different colors as I go from walkway to walkway. The walls are usually blank, but I walk past an occasional screen. There's one to my right which displays the principles of maintaining the Trellis: Facilitate community through safe procedures, Promote harmony through proper emotional responses, and Cultivate symbiosis through mutual effort (FPC). The screen switches to a message from Head Facilitator, Gaines Cyro, about how to maintain a healthy Trellis by supporting each other.

A person turns from a connecting corridor and walks in front of me. Apart from the fact that I see her on surveillance sometimes, I can tell she is a Promotor because her suit is red. Mine is grey. Those are the colors of the two groups that hold the executive roles in Trellis. The other suit color is green, but I rarely see it. Cultivators wear green suits, and they hold the jobs which keep the physical systems running in the Trellis: mechanics, cooks, cleaners— those sorts of jobs.

A grey-suited person turns into the hallway and takes a formation walking behind me. His name is James and he's a Facilitator. The corridor fills with more and more faces that I recognize, though I've never talked to them. We're discouraged from talking to one another in transition times, but a murmur always rises in corridors as they fill with Trellis workers. People in security understand why we're discouraged from talking when in crowds. The audio can't pick up and parse apart what each person says.

Leaving the tunneling corridors, I enter a domed room. People stream into the room from different walkways and join a line that snakes around the circular space. Along one of the walls of the room, an old woman in a green suit stands behind a metal cart. As people line up in front of the woman, she holds a device to each face. The device scans facial features, then beeps. Once it beeps, the old woman reaches her hand into the metal cart, pulling out a green sphere and handing it to the person in line.

Six minutes and thirty-two seconds, that's the average time it takes a person to get through the food line and exit the room. The A.I. on our surveillance gives seven minutes and thirty seconds before alerting us that a single face has been in the room for longer than it should take.

This room means that, for a maximum of seven minutes and thirty seconds, the workers in Phrames 20-30 have a chance to speak at a normal talking level and say almost whatever they want. What might the inhabitants of an advanced underwater society do with such unadulterated freedom? Maybe this room should be a symbol like the Areopagus where the ancient Romans debated matters of truth and justice. Maybe it could be like the Old State Meeting House where Americans fanned the flames of revolutionary ideas.

Or, maybe it looks like this: Jarret stands slightly out of line, letting people go past him. He works in surveillance and knows he can't risk letting people in front of him for more than a few minutes. Luckily, he doesn't have to wait any longer because the object of his odd behavior has entered the room. Arianelle walks in with Desman at her side and Jarret steps in line like he has incidentally arrived just in time to be next to Arianelle. He turns to smile and say hi. To his demise, Desman steps in front to get in line before her. Not that Desman cares to reach the front of the line quickly, but he does care to win Arianelle's heart before Jarret.

Leal arrives in line next to me as I step behind Arianelle. His countenance is usually full of brightness, like he can radiate excitement about whatever stupid fact he learned that day. But not since that physical maintenance session. He hasn't talked much to anyone else in our cluster, especially not Arianelle. He usually weasels into conversations with her and bores her to death with something like metabolic activity in hydrothermal tube worms.

Arianelle stands with her back turned toward the front of the line. Desman and Jarret are both turned toward her. Her red-brown hair flows over her red suit and it's like red waves sway around her shoulders as she moves. She seems almost beautiful, but not beautiful like stars in the sky.

Arianelle is alluring, men are attracted to her. But attraction is often fleeting. I can think of different seasons when Jarret or Desman have doted on different females in our years of training, but they always moved to the next. Why? Because the females were attractive— not beautiful.

I read about an ancient mathematician who saw no logical reason to live, but, when he saw the beauty in the way the different pieces of the world fit together in patterns, he didn't want to die. Logicians throughout time periods and cultures would write about this kind of beauty. They started with problems or work that seemed tremendously boring, but they were devoted to it. And, in this devotion to an unattractive work, all the pieces of the puzzle would come together and create a revelation of beauty deeper and truer than anyone could have known without being devoted to the work. Something truly beautiful must take time. There is no beauty without commitment. That's what makes Arianelle only an attractive person.

"Ara, nice work in the mental maintenance," Jarret's figure stands above Desman in an attempt to block Arianelle's view of him. "Maybe sometime we can work together to train for different scenarios."

That's not very likely to ever happen. Facilitators and Promoters are only ever put in training simulations with their designated partners.

I only see the back of Arianelle's head as she looks in silence. Maybe she gives him a sympathetic smile for his attempt.

"Sure, Jarret," her voice inflections are annoyingly genuine sounding. "If you can find a way for us to train together, I'll be there."

It bothers me, how nonchalantly she responds to these attempts. It's not flirty in the least, like she honestly doesn't know that she's the first place prize to these young men. She acts like she has no clue that everyone stares at her when she enters a room.

She turns around and flashes me a quick smile. Maybe she could feel my eyes rolling at the back of her head.

"Hey, Gia," she leans past me. "Hey, Leal."

"Hi," I say.

Trellis

"Hey, Arianelle," Leal's eyes are glued to the floor as the words leave his mouth.

Arianelle leans forward and gives a little wave. "Hi, Minji!"

Minji Fisciatta stands in line behind Leal and gives a peppy sound "Hi!" Though Minji says hi to Arianelle, her eyes flash over toward Leal.

I feel my jaw clenching at this uncomfortable string of hellos and small talk. Why does six minutes and thirty-two seconds have to be so long?

We shuffle tiny steps forward to the place where the old woman hands out squishy green spheres to each worker, who then swallows the object and moves from the room.

"Hey Gia," Arianelle turns toward me, "this might be a weird thing to say, but I'm super impressed with your agility in all of your training."

What is she getting at?

"Thank you," I smile at her.

"Do you do extra training to increase agility?"

I hate this conversation.

"Yes," I say.

"Maybe sometime we can ask Plangon for a couple of extra minutes and you can show me some of the exercises."

Can this conversation be done now?

"Yeah!" my fake attempt at being genuine actually ends up sounding more enthusiastic than I mean to. "Let's ask next maintenance session."

"Let's do it," she smiles at me before glancing at Leal, who's still looking at the ground. "Well, I'll see you at the next maintenance." She turns as we reach the front of the line.

We move forward to the old woman, who hands out dark green sustenance packets. As Arianelle reaches for the packet, the old woman clasps her wrinkled hands around Arianelle's hand, then holds it for a moment, looking into Arianelle's eyes. Gazing at the old woman, Arianelle gives a faint smile before walking away.

Still looking at Arianelle, the woman waves the face-scanning machine in front of my face. It beeps and she hands me a dark green sphere without looking at me. I walk out of line, leaning toward Leal.

"Did you see that?" I ask.

"What?" he puts the sustenance packet in his mouth.

"That lady was being super nice to Arianelle," I pop the green sphere in my mouth and crunch. The green liquid inside moves down my throat and I'm left to chew the mushy shell.

"Arianelle's nice," he says. "People are nice back."

"No, it was different than that. It's like they know each other."

"Well, there are only 3,000 people in this place," Leal's voice carries a sarcastic tone. "Chances are good."

"Jeez," I say, "defensive much?"

"I'm not being defensive! You're making conclusions."

My jaw clenches as we walk toward the exit. I know what I saw. The old woman and Arianelle seem familiar with one another.

With Leal behind me, we exit the eating area into a tunnel-like corridor. Multiple tunnels join in domed connection points. From here, we can pick different walkways that lead to the phrames. Moving out of our walkway we enter the particular domed space that connects to Phrames 20, 22, and 21. However, instead of a walkway to Phrame 21, there's a sealed door. That's where the accident happened 15 years ago. It's a constant reminder of what many people lost that day— what I lost that day.

"It's always white here," Leal says after walking in silence for a while.

"You mean the lighting?" I look at the lights in the corridor which are bright white. It seems natural. Like the way the sun might have lit up the earth.

"Yeah, the lighting. Have you ever wondered why?" Leal asks.

"Not really," I say.

"What color are my eyes?" he asks, slowing down in the small, domed space.

I turn to him. "You already know. They're blue."

"I know. But like a blue, blue? Or like a brownish blue? Is there any green in them?"

"We're not supposed to be talking," I look away from him.

"It's fine," he says quietly, "the corridor has enough background noise with people walking. I think this light is the best place to see colors."

I keep my face straight ahead for a moment, then back at him.

"Yeah," I say, "greenish-blue. And they're bright."

"Green-blue," he says looking away from me. "Like coastal waters. Yours are also blue."

"I know."

"Deep blue," he keeps talking. "No green. No brown. Just dark blue, like the deep ocean."

"The deep ocean is black; there's no sunlight here."

"Not this far down. I mean open ocean, where things like whales, sharks, and jellyfish live." Leal's tan skin looks darker as we leave the bright lighting and into a purple-lit corridor.

Getting closer to the entrance to our workstation, Minji crosses a connecting corridor to pass by us. She gets rigid, looking down and giving a lightning-fast wave before gluing her hand to her side.

Trellis

"Hi Minji," I say.

Leal says hi after me.

"Hi guys," she smiles at me, then tries to smile at Leal, but ends up shooting her stare to the ground.

Leal doesn't notice but continues toward a dark doorway that unravels as we approach. The doors are a deep, grey color, but the ruffles in the flower-petal-like doors sometimes catch the light and flicker with a glimmer of gold. The doors seem delicate, like someone could tear right through by accidentally touching them. But, in fact, the doors might be strong enough to be bulletproof. I read that once in a journal entry from the lead scientist that made the Trellis, but I wouldn't know how much force that is because I've never seen the kind of gun that has bullets. We have some that sting or incapacitate, but none with bullets.

Walking through the threshold, every wall in the room brightens as screens turn on and surveillance videos display in individual squares from floor to ceiling. Toward the front of the room is a control panel with two chairs pulled to it. Leal grabs one of the chairs, sits in it, and puts his arms up to the panel in front of him. The control panel is like a long table that has different things embedded into it: keyboards, a few buttons, and a spherical ball. Leal runs his hand over the ball to scroll through different screens with coding on them— paragraphs of letters and symbols giving the commands for the software.

I pick up a holopen from the counter and point the small device at different videos on the screen. Generally, the security system algorithms will decide which footage to play on certain parts of the screen. Different boxes on the screens play real-time footage from surveillance cameras throughout Phrames 20-30. Each video on the screen is a different size depending on the probable importance of the footage.

If the system registers people doing something they shouldn't, they are moved to higher importance. More often than not, this happens when people are in the wrong place from forgetting which time of day it is. A Facilitator might walk to his sleeping quarters because he thinks it's his designated sleeping hours when really he should be walking to his training quarters. This footage would appear larger on my screen, and I would look through the footage and data to verify if something is amiss. If someone is in the wrong place, I send a message to another faction of Facilitators who sort it out.

This footage is automatically flagged for Plangon and my father to see since they are the Senior Facilitators. Occasionally, they will request that Leal and I leave our workstations to personally take care of the issue.

That's why some of us train in the same cluster and see one another often. It's also why I rarely see people in green suits. While other workers in surveillance observe footage of the Cultivators, Leal and I track the Promoters and other Facilitators.

I see Desman and Arianelle on my screen, still walking to their lecture quarters where they will teach younger generations our history and values. But I don't see people like Leal's parents— they live in the Cultivator's quarters.

A yellow dot appears on the screen of two females walking through a corridor. Yellow dots appear when the surveillance registers questionable audio signals. Usually, a keyword sets it off— something like resist, uprising, or scheme.

Seeing the yellow dot, I point the holopen toward the footage and push the button to play the audio over our speakers. The room fills with the conversation between two girls in red suits.

"*Gaines Cyro*"— one of the girls had said the name of our Trellis leader, which placed the yellow dot to notify me to listen in.

"I mean," says one of the girls. "It doesn't even seem like he's aged!"

"Yeah!" agrees the other, "I remember watching inspirational talks given by him for our trainings ten years ago. He looks the same now as he did then."

I turn down the volume, changing its status to "harmless," but I listen to the conversation in the background as I walk to the control panel by Leal to pull up the two females' profiles. Leal types with more power and speed than I've ever seen him use in a training session. He switches between five different screens filled only with code.

Pulling up the profiles of the two girls in the hallway— the names Ezri Smith and Liara Fernsby appear on the screen followed by personal information: job descriptions, family connections, emotional fitness scores, intellectual ability scores, physical capacity scores, and personal notes updated by supervisors.

I walk backward, facing the screen and pointing my holopen at the profile descriptions. Clicking on my pen, the profiles project from the screen in front of my face. With the information at my eye level, I stand crossing one arm over my body and the other using the holopen to scroll through the information.

"Done!" Leal says with excitement. "Three minutes, five seconds. Either I'm getting slower or there's more information to look through these days."

Before the start of each workday, Leal looks over the coding for our main information to make sure nothing has been tampered with and that all the coding looks fine. I'll be honest, I have almost no idea what he does. I've used codes before, I can type basic commands using the trowel—a device used inside an open wall to control the surrounding hardware— but I'm really not sure what Leal does. Apparently, he does it very well because, until Leal came along, no one had ever been accepted as a Facilitator with a physical fitness score less than 60.

He begins typing again as I stand before the projected holograms of the two profiles. Scrolling with my holopen, I select the place with a yellow flag and click options: Speaking in Corridors, No Threat, Notify Supervisor.

Clicking submit, their supervisors will be notified to remind them that conversations in the hallways are restricted to work-related conversations. The footage and marks will also be sent to Minji and Jarret to verify that I didn't mark anything out of place for personal reasons.

Certain markings that I put can bring someone's emotional fitness score down or, potentially, threat level up. That's why they need to be verified. It's also the reason why I have the job that I do. My scores in every area are high while my threat level is low. Leal's threat level would be lower if he'd stop talking about the earth's surface all the time.

I've known since childhood— the things I can and can't say. My dad made sure of it. He had a clicker, I remember that. When I was six, I went to the training room during designated sleeping hours. It was after some lecture that day when I pushed the lecturer to tell me more about the Alaster ship. I asked if the submarine was really attached to the Trellis somewhere in Phrame 21 as the Surfacers say.

After that lecture, my dad took me in for what I thought was a normal training day, but he just had me stand with my back to him. He clicked the button, then hit the back of my head. I fell to the floor the first time, then he told me to get up. So I got up, with tears in my eyes, and faced him. He clicked again, then hit me across the face. I fell again. He told me to get up. He did it once more.

I remember being dazed, but I couldn't feel anything— not pain, not anything. I felt dizzy but knew he'd tell me to get back up. I pushed myself up and faced him. No more tears, just six-year-old me swaying back and forth and trying not to fall over. I heard him swallow and it seemed like his eyes were red and glossy. He told me, "that's enough." He choked over his words though, then cleared his throat and walked away.

Something weird happened after that. My lecturer had a clicker. When I asked about Alaster, she would give a click. At first, I would flinch. It would make me want to cry — the sound of the click would. So I'd shut down and stop asking questions.

I found myself wondering why the lecturer all of the sudden had a clicker, but I can't play dumb. My dad must have given it to her. I don't know why that was his method of teaching what I can and can't say, but one thing is for sure— he was committed to ensuring I had the highest score in every category. Very committed to fixing an unruly child like a mathematician is committed to solving a difficult problem. Does that make him beautiful? I don't see how he could be anything close to beautiful. Maybe beauty only exists with commitment, but commitment sure exists without beauty.

"Gia Hamiltoni," a voice plays through the speaker and fills the room.

"Yes, sir," I say, recognizing the voice— it's Plangon.

"Did you verify the flagged footage in section 17 at the south end of Corridor A near Phrame 19?"

"No, sir. I was just filling some profiles and was about to get to the next task."

"Never mind that, Minji flagged the footage near Phrame 19 and I want you and Jarret over there."
"Yes, sir." I click the holopen and the projected profiles fade away. "Be right there."

There's yelling when Jarret and I turn the corner to Corridor A near Phrame 19. This is the closest I've been to the Cultivator's quarters.

"Don't stick your grimy, grey-suit hands on me if you want to keep this whole place from uprising!" yells a woman in a green suit. Four other green-suited people stand next to her and two grey-suited people face opposite.

It's the old woman from the sustenance room earlier today. She stands firm, yelling at the two Facilitators. She holds a trowel in her hand.

"Hello, ma'am," Jarret says as we arrive.

"Don't placate me, son," says the old woman. "I know you and your greasy-fish friends are—"

"I hear what you're saying," says Jarret smiling, "maybe we can talk about this."

When situations get heated, physical intervention is the last resort since we want to protect people rather than harm them. Unfortunately, not all Facilitators are trained in negotiations, which is why they send people like Jarret and me when a situation turns moderately hostile, but not physical.

"There's nothing to talk about you dirty—" the woman starts speaking before a green-suited man cuts her off.

"She's feeling a little upset," says a young man with short, brown hair, "because she came out here to do her work and was stopped by these two Facilitators. I think there's been a misunderstanding and, if it's alright, we'd all like to get back to work."

"With a trowel?" I ask. "Someone who works in food processing needs a coding device for work?" I look at the old woman.

"Yeah," says the old woman, "I need a device for good work since you sorry humans have a black hole for a heart and would starve hundreds of people."

"I can assure you," Jarret says to the woman, "we're in this together in the Trellis and we don't wish to starve any—"

"There's no time for your empty words," the woman throws her hands in the air and puts the trowel toward the wall.

The two other Facilitators standing by lunge for the old woman, pulling her to the ground.

I swear, it's like the training for other Facilitators teaches how to not use their brains. Just think, what could happen to community morale and support if two young Facilitators tackled a helpless old woman to the ground with four other Cultivators witnessing to spread the word?

The corridor fills with shouts from the four Cultivators. Standing to their feet, the two Facilitators pull the woman from the ground and keep each of her arms in a grip between them.

I pull out my incapacitor and point it at a Facilitator in a grey suit. Jarret does the same.

"Your help is no longer needed," Jarret says, "please release our community member and report back to your phrame."

The two look confused and don't release the old woman.

"Leave," I say. "Now."

One releases, but the other doesn't. I pull the trigger, a flash of blue electricity sparks from the end of my gun, and the Facilitator falls to the floor.

I put the gun back in my belt. "Take your friend back to your phrame, you'll both need to be debriefed. It was on a low setting, he should be able to walk if you support him."

The timid Facilitator puts one arm under his companion and they limp past Jarret and me to leave the area.

"Now," I say. "I understand we're greasy-fish humans with a black hole for a heart, but you can help us all get back to work by explaining what you're doing with a trowel away from your workstation."

"He told me what you and your heartless crew did to Phrame 21," the old woman spits.

"Phrame 21?" I try to hide my intrigue.

"Ma'am," says Jarret, "we aren't sure exactly—"

"He who?" I ask. Something inside me flinches, like a click will sound to stop me from asking questions about Phrame 21.

"Alaster," says the woman.

Trellis

"A submarine?" Jarret scoffs.

"Norma," says one of the Cultivators, "please don't do this."

I hear footsteps coming from a corridor connecting on the right.

"You'd shut it if you knew what was good for ya'," yells the woman, shaking the trowel in her hand. She turns to me. "Yes, the submarine."

Wait, it sounds like the footsteps are behind me. Where are the footsteps coming from?

A girl in a red suit turns around the corner from the corridor on the right.

"Ara?" exclaims Jarret.

"Wha—" Arianelle's gaze moves around the people gathered in the hallway.

"What are you doing here?" I demand.

"Why aren't you in your lecture room?" asks Jarret.

Her eyes shoot toward him. "Why do you know where I should be?"

In our joint trainings, it's clear that Facilitators occasionally observe the Cultivator quarters when there's a threat of uprising, but Promoters don't know that we keep track of anyone else. People in my position aren't allowed to discuss the nature of our work.

"You're a lecturer," I say. "Where else would you be? It was a logical guess."

Arianelle's glare doesn't lift from him. It seems like Jarret confirmed a suspicion that was already haunting Arianelle's mind.

"Listen," the Cultivator who had previously interrupted takes a step forward. "We'd all like to get this settled and head our way. Norma, why don't you hand over the trowel and we can get back to work."

"No," I say, "explain what you were going to say about Phrame 21."

"Gia," a deep voice sends chills to the bottom of my stomach.

My eyes widen and my jaw clenches as I turn. I face the last person who should ever have heard that question leave my mouth: my father.

I stand tall and firm, but my insides crumple to the floor. I look him in the eye, but my soul shrinks back and wants to hide.

"I'll take this from here," he says.

That's a command to walk away, back to my workstation, but I'm frozen. I feel like a six-year-old afraid of a monster.

Jarret's shoulder brushes past mine and wakes me from my nightmare. I walk past my father in the direction of my workstation.

"If you don't know," the old woman yells down the corridor, "you'd better find out."

Trellis

I turn and make eye contact with the woman. My father's back is to me so he can't see as I draw closer to hear to woman.

"Alaster is alive," she says, "and he's taking people to the surface."

I turn and walk away.

My hands tremble slightly as I enter the workstation where Leal sits before the control panel. It's just him and me in the room. I feel safe. My heart slows.

"It's still going on," Leal says.

"What is?"

"The old woman," he stares at the security screen like he's watching a movie.

"We don't need to watch this," I say, seeing that my dad is still in the corridor. It feels like he somehow knows I'm there and will look directly into the camera at any second to tell me to get to work.

"This is literally our job," he throws his hand toward the screen. "I'm watching suspicious footage."

Three more Facilitators are in the area since Jarret and I left. The audio from the surveillance plays through the speakers. I let out a sigh and take a seat. It feels like I don't have anything in me to fight with Leal.

"She's been siphoning resources somewhere," says Leal. "She says that Alaster and her family communicate to her through the lights and they told her that the siphon was closed."

"Why wouldn't her family talk to her in person?" There are a lot of things that I could ask about Leal's weird explanation, but that's what I ask.

"Her family is dead."

"Oh," I don't know what to say.

"They died in the accident in Phrame 21."

I'm silent.

"I know what you've done!" the old woman's voice sounds through the speaker in our workstation as she yells at my dad and lifts the trowel above her head.

"What's she accusing him of?" I ask.

"Closing off her siphon of sustenance," Leal responds without looking away from the screen.

"Grandma, no!" Arianelle puts her arm around the woman and holds her back, but is too late as the woman throws the trowel at my dad.

"Grandma?" Leal sits back in surprise. "This is like a soap opera. Your father, her grandma, everyone mixed up in a riveting drama."

"This isn't funny."

"I didn't say it was—"

"You're making jokes. It's not funny."

"Sorry," he rubs his arm. "I was trying to make light of a dark situation."

I don't say anything back.

Trellis

"You want to know what I think is strange, though?" asks Leal.

I keep my face to the screen. A Facilitator grabs the old woman and another grabs Arianelle, pulling them apart.

Leal turns toward me. "Your dad hasn't denied there was a siphon that they closed off."

I turn to look at Leal. Where would a siphon even go?

The old woman's voice screams from the speaker. "I'm not wrong!"

I turn back to the screen.

It seems like the old woman is trying to reason with the other Cultivators even more than the people dragging her away. "Ara will tell you! She's seen things too! Don't leave them there! They need sustenance!"

My father turns toward Arianelle and the others as the old woman's voice fades.

"Arianelle will go in for reviewing after this?" Leal questions.

"Yeah," I say.

"What happens to the old woman?"

I hesitate. "I'm not sure."

Arianelle's small frame stands between the four Cultivators and my father when the Facilitator releases her arm and she steps forward. There's an air of defiance about her.

"I don't wish for any more trouble," says my dad. He sounds almost caring. "You'll be taken in for review, and I hope things will run smoothly so we can all get back to our respective positions."

Arianelle turns her back to my father to face the others. "It's true," she says. "There is something going on here." She turns, facing my father, then walks past him with the Facilitators at her sides to escort her to the reviewing rooms.

Leal leans with his arms crossed. "Her emotional score will be marked down for that."

"Yeah," I keep my eyes on the screen.

Arianelle steps through the hallway like shocks of blue electricity trail behind her.

"She could even lose her position for that," says Leal.

"Yeah," I say again.

Where no one else would blame her— even when her grandmother would never know the difference— Arianelle defends her grandmother's word at the risk of her own position. She strides through the corridor with a sense of freedom, though she is escorted by doom. Like a star staring down billions of miles to meet eyes with the cowardice I showed today, Arianelle is something truly Beautiful.

Chapter 3: Facts Drift Like the Sea

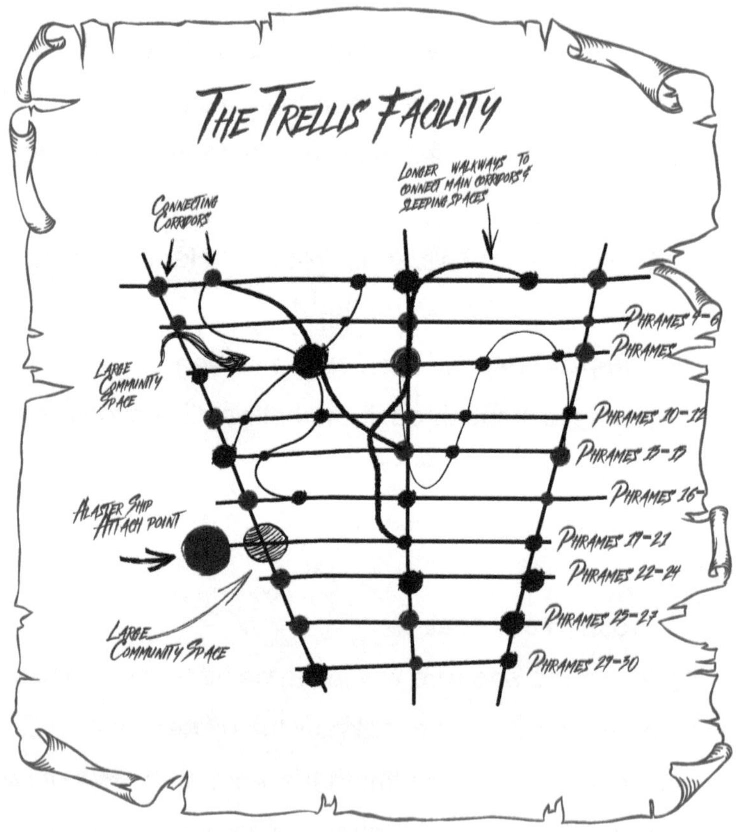

Leal leans in his chair, rolling his fingers lazily over the sphere on the control panel. A picture of a musician appears on the screen where he should be watching a video of a training session where one of the participants is over a minute late. A minute and a half, two minutes— the participant finally arrives, unbeknownst to Leal as he stares at pictures of Louis Armstrong.

That's the only reason Leal and I know anything of the surface world. The first time Leal hacked into the Promoter educational resources, he opened a portal from my section of screens into a beautiful universe of forests, music, and fresh air. No one else in the Trellis sees this footage. An average person might know what a tree is or what music is from our cultural trainings in school, but no one else knows how we turn off surveillance in our room each day to open a world outside our own.

I stand, staring at the screens in front of me and biting at the end of the hologram pen. In a place where I have access to magic, wonder, science, and nature, I can't stop thinking about doom. What will happen to Arianelle? The reviewing rooms aren't in our surveillance clearance, so I can't tell what happens to her or the old woman. Even if I did know where they were, there's nothing I can do for them. I try to think about something else.

"Why does the hologram pen do things when I tap it but not when I bite it?" I ask.

Leal turns his chair to face me. "Because it senses electromagnetic changes at a certain point of contact."

"Meaning?"

"Your finger gives off tiny electromagnetic energy when it meets the pen, your teeth don't really."

Trellis

A voice sounds over the speaker in our room: "The text in front of you is different than the other material in our books." Footage in front of me shows Desman stepping toward the front of a crowd of students. He doesn't typically lecture by himself. Arianelle would normally be in the lecture room at this time. "It's a first-hand account, directly from the journal of the lead scientist on the Trellis project. Here, the scientist describes her ideas on the physical properties for the Alaster submersible, which—"

I double-tap the holopen to turn off the audio.

"Leal?"

"Yeah?"

"How do you know all this stuff? I mean, we all went through the same training, and you and I hear the same information from the surveillance every day. Why do you know—" I struggle for words to finish the sentence "—other things?"

Leal swings his chair toward me as I sit down in mine.

"My dad is a mechanic," he says. "He would take projects to our sleeping quarters and explain things to me. He was the head mechanic, actually, he knows every inch of this whole ship and how it all works."

"Did your dad do poorly in training?"

"What do you mean?"

"I don't know," I look at the ground. This seems like an uncomfortable assumption to be making about

48

someone's dad. "I guess, if he's so smart, how did he end up being a Cultivator?"

"Oh," Leal looks off to the distance, somewhere past me. "Well, is there something wrong with being a Cultivator?"

"No," I nearly jolt forward to save my words. "No, sorry, no. There's nothing wrong with Cultivators. It's just that people with higher scores in training end up being in one of the other two roles."

"You know," Leal leans back and looks toward the ceiling. The blue light shines on his curls. "I wondered my whole life what it was like to live up here."

"Where?"

"I mean, to be something other than a Cultivator. In trainings, the Promoters seemed like they had important roles. It was like they kept the secrets of humanity in their informational tablets. And Facilitators, they seemed so mysterious, and maybe like they secretly ran the place. And both of those roles got one more ration a day because they needed more sustenance for their physical training. It seemed like the life."

I had grown up in the Facilitator area with my dad. Other than our instructional classes, I had never known what it was like outside of this life. That is, before Leal opened the universe on our screens.

"Well," I say, "what do you think of this life now?"

"I think it's a trap."

Trellis

"A trap?"

"Yup, we're trapped," he swings around his chair nonchalantly.

"What do you mean?"

He swivels his chair back toward me. "For every 144 hours in the Cultivator quarters, we got two hours of free time. Not work time, not designated sleeping time, but actual free time. There are more screens there, you know, and more things to tell us how to work together. The screen would tell us that we accumulated an extra hour of free time over the last 50 years."

"How did you do that?" that's exciting— the idea that free time can be earned.

"They told us it was because we worked harder and made more efficient systems. But the truth is, I think it was a trick to make us work harder. We always had the hope that we could become more efficient and earn more free time. Now, as a Facilitator, they get us to work hard because we fear losing what we have— the status, living quarters, or extra ration. But there, we didn't have much else to lose. We'd always be one mishap from a riot if there wasn't hope that we were working toward something better."

"I— " I have a hard time knowing how to respond. "That sounds like a terrible way to live."

"Well," says Leal. "I felt closer to people back then, less suffocated or something. And that two hours with my family, I wouldn't trade it for ten extra rations." He pauses for a moment. "I think my dad knew that. He is a smart guy, like you say. He fell in love with my mom during training. I think he chose to be a Cultivator."

"Chose?" it never occurred to me that anyone could choose to be anything.

"Yeah, I'd be willing to bet he failed his mental trainings on purpose. There's no way a guy like that could end up being something other than a security Facilitator. Who knows, maybe he'd have been maintaining the security system instead of your dad."

This last comment is stinging somehow. Not that I ever felt the need to defend my dad or anything, but the statement seems a little presumptive.

"Sorry," Leal must have read some distaste in my facial expression. "I didn't mean anything against your dad."

"I don't care," I say, "except that you should watch what you say about Trellis leaders." I look back to the screen as if I'm working on something important.

Leal leans back in his chair. He hums a quiet tune. Soon, his voice covers the otherwise silent room with a song he must have learned long ago because I've never heard it:

The sunset lingers a little longer.

The starlight clings a little stronger.

The moon, she sings a little softer

all to be close to you, my dear.

His voice melts away the grip of the Facilitator life. Maybe this is what free time is like. Maybe it's what spending time with family is like. It feels like how we're supposed to live. I can see why Cultivators would work for the hope of more of it.

I think of Arianelle's pure, green eyes, searching for answers that are more important than her own safety— what her grandmother was talking about must have been important. Maybe the hope of something else is worth the risk it takes to find it.

I don't remember the first time I met Arianelle, but I remember a sort of feeling I had toward her when we were kids in training together. She was curious about everything… to a fault.

My memories of her are blurry. We had taken a trip one day on our education training. It was to the physical training space— a place I now know too well.

"When you are 18," a red-suited guide explained as a group of us kids had entered the training room, "each of you will be assigned as either a Facilitator, Promotor, or Cultivator."

Arianelle raised her hand above her head.

The guide ignored her. "This space is for Facilitators and Promotors. Some of you may end up training—"

"Will we be there forever?" Arianelle interrupted.

"Eh, um, be where?" the guide was flustered.

"Be in the role we're assigned?"

"Em," the guide must not have known what to do when she was interrupted. "You will always stay as a Facilitator, Promotor, or Cultivator."

"What if someone wants to change?" Arianelle asked before the guide even finished explaining.

"Change?" the guide seemed surprised. "A person can be demoted, but never change groups."

"So we'll do the same thing forever?" Arianelle's eyes seemed innocent.

"Well, you can change work functions within that group, but you will remain in your assigned group for your life, I suppose."

"What abou—"

"No more questions," the guide put her hand up.

"But how many people are assigned to each role every year?" Arianelle didn't listen to the guide.

"That's enough," said the guide.

"Where will most of us end up?" Arianelle was asking questions, but she looked out into space as if asking no one in particular— just wondering about what these facts meant for our futures.

I wondered the same thing. But I didn't say anything. How many people would be Facilitators? Could I be one? Would Arianelle be one?

Trellis

I don't remember exactly what happened next, except that I did something risky when the buzzer rang and we had to leave the training area. Us kids began to crowd toward the door as Facilitators and Promotors trickled in. I looked around, seeing where the guide was among the group. I grabbed Arianelle's wrist and pulled her to the edge of the group, behind the guide and next to a man in a red suit.

"How many people get selected to be Facilitators each year?" I whispered up to the man.

"Um," he looked around, seeming confused. "Two pairs of youths are introduced each year. So, I guess four people are selected."

"And how many Promotors?" I asked.

"Six," the man responded.

"And the rest are Cultivators?" Arianelle asked.

"Hey!" the guide shouted when she noticed that Arianelle and I lagged behind.

I don't remember anything else from that moment, except being scared. I was scared when the guide spoke with other people in red suits. My heart sank as I looked over to Arianelle. Why did I grab her wrist at that moment? I could have found out those answers without her. I felt bad that I had dragged us both into trouble. At the same time, it was somehow comforting to look at her and feel like another human was in the same situation as me. We were in trouble, but we were in trouble together.

At least, we were until my father came into the room. Like a cold wave rushing away all sense of comfort, Arianelle was taken from the room. As a Trellis head, my father ensured that I was controlled the way he thought best. I was confused when he said my punishment was to miss designated sleeping hours and go back to the physical training room. According to him, if I was ready to start asking those questions, I was ready to begin training. Designated sleeping hours lasted 7 hours for kids— that's how long I trained.

My head jerks up in surprise as a buzzer interrupts my thoughts.

"That's our cue to get sustenance," Leal says, typing on the control panel. "Then we come back here. Then we sleep. Then we train. Then we eat. Then we come back here." He finishes typing and the screen turns dark. "We're trapped."

The yellow lighting in the eating area seems almost sinister as it fills with Facilitators and Promoters who line up for sustenance packets. Leal and I remained silent the entire walk. Jarret walks in with Minji, but he stays beside the line, looking around with a hopeful gleam in his eye. Minji takes her spot in line— also with some sort of longing in her stare as she steps next to Leal. The lighting in the room reflects off her jet-black hair, and the yellow seems less sinister, maybe more like sunshine.

Her frail arms glued to her side, Minji's head is turned slightly downward as she gives an awkward smile. "Hey," she says.

"Hi, Minji," I say, leaning past Leal— who is looking off toward the entryway as if thinking about something else. I nudge him in the stomach and give a nod toward Minji.

"Oh," Leal shakes his head, coming out of his brain universe. "Hi, Minj."

The muscles in Minji's face tense as she seems to hold in a smile, keeping her face downward, maybe trying to hide the excitement that Leal just called her by a nickname.

As Desman walks into the room, Jarret's brows furrow at the entryway in search of Arianelle. Desman steps in line. Jarret drags his feet behind him.

"Where's Ara?" Jarret turns to Desman, not hiding the obvious competition between them over Arianelle's heart.

A green-suited man waves the face scanner in front of my face, it beeps, and he hands me a sustenance packet. I put it to my lips, open my mouth, and the green pod turns to mush in my mouth.

"Yeah, I did notice the glitch in the camera in that phrame about 10 hours ago." Behind me, Leal talks to Minji as the young man in the green suit hands Leal a sustenance packet.

"So strange when stuff like that happens," says Minji, receiving her sustenance packet. "Do you think people tamper with the cameras or something to make that happen?"

"Actually," Leal steps out of line, still holding his sustenance packet, "I think we'd see it if someone physically messed with a camera. More often than not, there are issues with our systems because they're biotechnology. The same happens with the doors. Some things, like the lights, are just biological, so they take care of themselves. And the screens are just electrical, so we can have a constant supply of electricity to them. But some things are both and are harder to know exactly how or why they glitch."

Leal clearly enjoys his undivided audience as Minji refrains from eating her sustenance packet and hangs on every word of Leal's lecture on the machines in the Trellis.

"Sorry to interrupt," I cut into Leal's speech, "but we're standing here too long."

"Oh," says Leal, "right. We've probably been in here close to five minutes."

Leal turns toward the exit, slamming into Desman's body like a child running into a wall.

"Get off me!" Desman shoves Leal, crashing his flimsy body into mine.

Trellis

A fishy, oily smell fills the room as I catch Leal's arms, saving him from crashing to the floor, and a green liquid runs down Desman's red suit.

"Agh," Desman looks down at his suit, where Leal's clumsy move had smashed their sustenance packets, leaving them both without food and covered in a dark, green goop. "Now this?" Desman yells, towering over Leal.

I pull Leal to his feet, then move in front of him. "It was an accident." My fists clench as my chest puffs toward Desman.

"Yeah?" Desman's jaw clenches as his nose gets close to mine, "and I'm sure Ara going in for reviewing was also an accident."

I stand my ground, without saying a word. How would he know we had something to do with Arianelle's situation?

"It seems you and your pet," Desman points to Leal, "are taking a lot from people these days. Maybe it's time you start making reparations."

"People," Jarret's voice cuts in, "we can't fight outside training. This will go against everyone's emotional fitness score."

Desman and I don't break our stare.

Minji's thin arm shoots in front of me. "Here," she holds a sustenance packet between Desman and I. "You can have mine. It was an accident."

Desman's muscles seem to relax a little. "I don't want your food, Minji." His anger flares back as he faces Leal. "I think this twerp better explain what's going on," he leans toward Leal, but Minji steps between them, her arm extended toward Desman with the sustenance packet in hand.

"Take it," she says, with her arm straight out, but head faced toward the floor.

Desman looks directly into Minji's eyes. He says nothing, turns for a moment toward me, then walks to the exit, slamming shoulders with Jarret on his way out.

"Minj," Jarret says, voice wavering, "we need to get out of here."

The four of us walk in silence through the exit and toward our workstations. My anger begins to settle and my limbs relax as we pass the white light around Phrame 21. I glance behind my shoulder at Leal, his blue-green eyes looking ahead at Minji. I've never walked these corridors with anyone other than Leal. I turn my face toward Minji. Her eyes are dark brown, maybe even black. She looks back at me and gives a little smile. It seems like a nervous smile, like she was embarrassed or worried about what I'd think for stepping between Desman and me.

A deep breath leaves my lungs as we get back to the workstation. Back to normal, Leal sits in his seat, typing in his clearance password to pull up the security footage all over the room. I relax in the seat beside Leal.

"Gia?" Leal turns toward me. "I've never asked you this."

Leal turns down the volume. I feel my heart racing. What could he possibly have to ask me that needs that sort of introduction?

He stays silent and doesn't ask the question.

"What?" I ask.

"Do you?" he pauses for a moment. "What do you think of the Alaster ship?"

I let out a breath. Relief washes over my face. He did not need to preface that question with that much tension.

"I don't know," I say to him. "It doesn't seem likely to me that it still exists." He looks a bit disappointed at the answer. "Why? What do you think?"

"It could be real," he looks a bit embarrassed for saying it.

"What makes you say that?" I try to not be demeaning, it's just that the only people who believe in Alaster are typically Cultivators who seem to believe in anything that will make them feel better.

"I don't know," he turns away from me.

"No," I move closer to him, "you can tell me."

"No, let's drop it."

"Leal," I say, "you literally tell me everything. You rant about byproducts of microbes when you should be paying attention to the screens. Don't stop talking now."

Looking around the room, he leans to the control panel and starts typing in codes to override security in our room. Once the security is blocked, he pulls up images of blueprints to the Trellis Facility. Bird's-eye view of the metal facility is crisscrossed over the ocean floor. I can see the domed rooms where the corridors are connected, and larger domes where the living, working, and eating phrames would be.

"This is the place where the Alaster ship should have attached," he points to one of the large domes. "And that's Phrame 21. When you look at these blueprints, it's clear that there was access in and out of the Alaster submersible, and there aren't any records of it being detached."

"Okay, but someone would have seen it before Phrame 21 was blocked," I say to him.

"Right," he says, "I originally looked into this to prove Norma wrong. That's what I would have said to her too."

"Wait, you want to prove Norma wrong?"

"Well, no," he stutters, "not actually. I was just reasoning in my mind why she was crazy."

"Whatever, keep talking."

"Then I looked at old surveillance, just to check the space where the Alaster ship would be, and I found this." He pulled up old footage of the area, which was the old meeting hall— the largest dome room where past generations could gather in a large crowd for events.

My heart sinks a little. I hadn't seen the room since I was four. I had barely remembered it, but the image on the screen made it feel like the space, and everything in it, should still be there, exactly how I remember it. I fight a wave of grief that crashes over me.

"What about it?" I ask, trying not to think too deeply about what I was seeing.

"This back here," he points to an entryway at the edge of the room, "it's sealed off."

"What do you mean? There isn't a door there to seal."

"I know, but the blueprints show that this is the corridor that should lead to the Alaster."

"Okay, so they sealed the door a long time ago to block the way to the submarine."

"But why would they do that?" Leal says this almost in a whisper.

"So that people don't get hurt trying to get in it or something."

He leans back in his chair, not seeming convinced by my answer.

"Okay, let's just say, hypothetically, this submarine exists. What would that change? We're still down here. We can't go up there. It's still not safe."

He doesn't answer.

"What?"

Still no answer.

"Leal! What?"

"There isn't enough oxygen down here!"

"What are you talking about?"

"The algae fields," he says. "My dad is a Cultivator, a mechanic— he worked on everything in this facility. He would talk to me about the algae fields. The oxygen we get from them isn't enough to support all the people we have here breathing. He believed that Alaster was somehow out there, providing oxygen for us."

I swallow, trying to think of what to say. Leal looks at the ceiling.

"So," I say, "this isn't about proving Norma wrong, but about proving your dad right?"

"It's about finding the truth." Leal sits up in his chair and looks at me. "I try not to cause problems around here by making wild assertions, but some things don't seem to fit together."

I look ahead at the screens which show different angles of the walkways around the sealed entry to Phrame 21. There's a girl in the corridor. At first, I think she's

Arianelle, but a closer look shows that she has darker hair and I don't recognize her face.

"6,000 people came down to the Trellis 300 years ago, and now we have half that," Leal starts ranting about things that don't make sense to him.

"There have been accidents," I say.

"Yeah, the first one took out 3,000 people. I know we have accidents."

"Can we stop talking about this?" I keep my eyes on the screens.

"3,000 people," he says, "our community has had 3,000 people for 300 years."

"Leal, stop," I say.

"Why? Why hasn't the population grown more than that?"

"Leal, stop talking."

"No, I'm not—"

"No," I say. "Stop talking and come look at this."

I tap on the screen in front of me and rewind the video to the girl in the corridor.

"What?" Leal asks. "She's just walking."

"Watch," my eyes remain toward the screen as the girl in the surveillance video walks out of the camera's view.

"Okay?" Leal doesn't get it.

"Look," I point to the neighboring screen which shows an empty corridor.

"I still don't see the problem."

"The girl should have shown up in the next screen."

"What do you mean?"

"I mean," I shift my chair toward Leal, "the girl walked through this camera view and doesn't show up in that one."

"She disappeared?"

"No," I look away for a second, "there's nowhere to go. People can't disappear."

Leal rewinds the footage and we watch it another time.

"She's gone," I whisper.

Chapter 4: Monsters and Brine

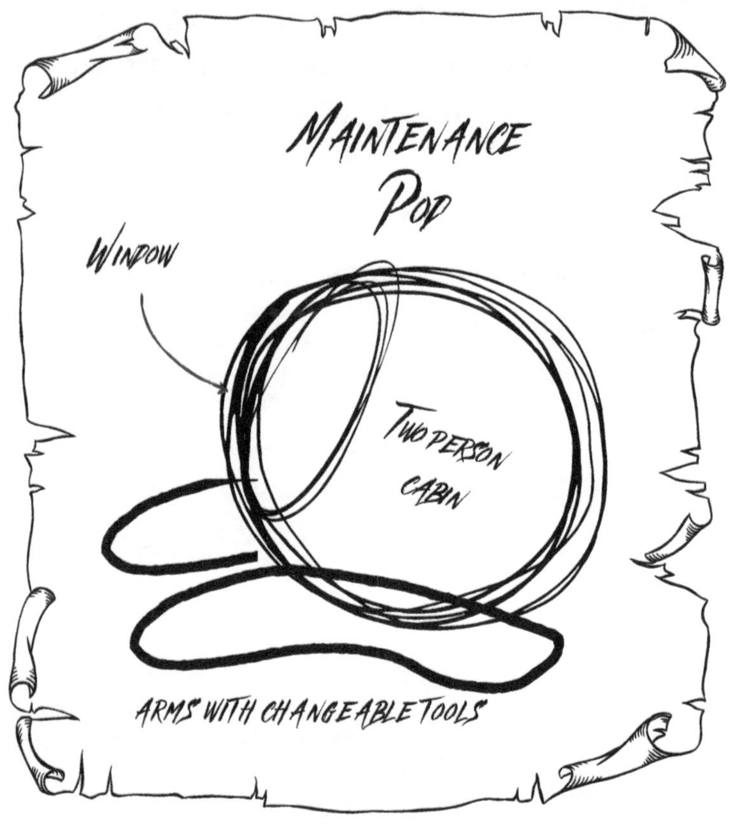

I walk through the blue-lit corridors in complete silence. No one walks beside me or arrives from another walkway. It's not protocol for a Surveillance Facilitator to review flagged footage with a Trellis Head, but Plangon sent a message to immediately come to his workstation. What's going on that I would be called out of my workstation?

Arriving at Plangon's office, the dark door is twisted in the middle— it's shut and it doesn't open at my presence. The Head Facilitator workstations are locked with a different system than others so they can't be broken into.

"Gia Hamiltoni," I speak toward the door.

"Come in," Plangon's voice says over an intercom as the door slowly creeps open.

The lighting is yellow-green as I stand in Plangon's office. It's strange— security footage plays on the walls around him. I've been in Plangon's office once before and my father's plenty of times. Every time an outsider is present, the security footage should be off.

My father's workstation is connected to Gaines Cyro's quarters— the Trellis Head has his own personal phrame. In fact, my dad's workstation is the only way out of Cyro's personal phrame. The only one who can open the door to my father's workstation is Cyro or my father, meaning those are the only two who would ever have access to Cyro. I don't know why my father was given that workstation instead of Plangon.

The footage behind Plangon shows the Cultivators' living areas. I try not to seem distracted, but I haven't really seen those. It looks like a labyrinth of walls that people weave through to enter cramped sleeping quarters.

Wait... the biggest video at eye level shows a sea of people in green suits with one grey one. The person wearing grey is my father. He's speaking to a Cultivator in a crowded, domed room. Why would Plangon have this footage up when I come in?

"Gia," Plangon motions for me to sit in a chair that's in the center of the room with videos playing on every wall. "Thank you for coming. We need to have a discussion about Arianelle."

My posture perks up.

"Wait," I say, "what about the footage I just sent you?"

"The footage?" Plangon seems surprised. "That's obviously some glitch with the cameras."

"But—" I interject.

"Gia," he puts his hand up. "I understand what this area means to you."

"It doesn't have to do with that," I know better than to interrupt a superior. But it's Plangon; he's quicker to listen than others. "I checked the codes on the footage, and the footage hasn't been corrupted or replaced with old footage."

Plangon raises an eyebrow. Maybe I shouldn't have said that. We were never actually trained to check for those things. Those are techniques Leal and I came up with to deflect security on our own workstation.

"So there's a wiring issue with the cameras," Plangon doesn't dwell on the eyebrow-raising statement I just made.

"If it was a physical problem, the camera wouldn't show footage of the corridor at all."

"Gia—" he doesn't want to hear what I say.

"These are real-time recordings of the walkway."

"Gia—"

"There were time-stamps and everything."

"Gia, stop," he squeezes his eyebrows between his thumb and index finger. "I don't want to see you take this turn."

"What turn?" I ask.

"Listen," he says, "I would not typically say this..." He hesitates. "I care about you."

I don't have words. I'm not sure anyone has ever said that to me.

"Your emotional stability scores are fine right now," he says.

I roll my eyes, "this isn't necessa—"

"No," he interrupts, "you need to hear this. Your scores are good, but you know as well as I do that marks against your score put you on a high-surveillance list, and then more marks come when you're in a state like this, and eventually, you get demoted."

"That won't happen."

"I know it doesn't seem like it, but this is exactly how it started with your mom too."

"With my— what?" I've never heard of marks against my mom's mental stability.

"No one told you?"

"No."

"Oh," he looks beyond me, bites his bottom lip, then looks back at me. "Maybe it isn't my place. I just assumed Mr. Hamiltoni would have told you."

"Told me what?"

He sighs. "Your mom's emotional stability was visibly compromised before the end of her life."

"Why?"

"Because of stuff like this, Gia." He points his hand toward me and motions up and down. "Stuff like chasing after crazy theories."

"What crazy theory?"

His eyes widen as if he just witnessed someone talking to non-existent voices in her head.

"That's enough," he says.

I look down. This was never going to lead anywhere, I probably shouldn't have pushed it.

"Here's what I'll do," he sighs. "I'll have some people double-check the footage and I'll send someone to see if the camera was physically compromised. And," he pauses for a moment, "I'll let you know whatever they find."

I look up. He smiles at me.

"Thanks," I give a grin back.

"But that's not why you're here." He fixes his posture.

"Right," I said, more excited than I mean to, "what is it about Arianelle that you wanted to talk to me about?"

"As you may know, she's in the reviewing rooms."

"Yes," I confirm.

"We believe she has some intel on schemes to sabotage the facility. Here's the thing," Plangon leans in toward me as if to tell me a secret. "I think she's convinced that she's on the right side of a fight that doesn't even exist. Her grandmother's conspiracies didn't spread very far with the Cultivators— probably because they are so outlandish— but I think Arianelle believes they're real. She isn't withholding information because she's a defector or wants to cause trouble; I think she's been led astray."

I also lean in. "I agree with you, but what do I have to do with it?"

"She won't give anyone answers," says Plangon. "Now, normally we would mark down emotional stability and go through a demotion process, but I want to stop that if I can."

"Okay…?" I still don't see what I can do to help Arianelle.

"She asked for you."

I sit up straight. I thought she hated me.

"That's right," Plangon says, "she wants to talk to you. Again, normally something like this wouldn't be allowed. But, considering the circumstances, I'd like to smooth this over without too severe of consequences. If you can get answers about how she got involved and if there's anyone else in on this siphoning conspiracy, I think we can settle this. Besides, you're our best Facilitator trained in negotiation."

"Yeah," I say, looking past Plangon and to the footage of my father. He had moved to a different corridor and now speaks to another Cultivator. Something seems out of place. I am trained in negotiations— trained enough to see that Plangon is using tactics on me. Trained enough to know that he's communicating multiple messages by having security footage on the screens.

"So will you have a conversation with Arianelle and see what you can find out?"

"You're asking me?" I turn my gaze to him.

"Well, no. I'm telling you, but it sounds nicer if it comes out in a question."

I smile. "Yes, of course, I'll talk to her."

"Perfect," he says. "You don't have much longer for designated work time before getting a sustenance packet and going to sleeping hours. I wouldn't like you to miss a sustenance time, so I'll send you to reviewing rooms just after eating. I hope you don't mind this cutting into sleeping hours. I know you're used to it."

"No problem," I respond. If my father was giving these orders, I would be sent directly to the reviewing rooms, missing both the sustenance time and sleeping hours. Plangon knows I'm used to missing sleeping hours because he saw the way my father trained me. It feels nice to have Plangon look out for me.

"Plangon…" I say.

He looks at me, waiting for what I'm about to say.

"Thanks," I smile.

"Of course," he smiles back, and motions with his hand for me to leave.

I stand to exit.

"Gia," Plangon says, stopping me before I exit, "be careful with yourself." He quickly glances toward the screen which shows my father, as if to ensure that I took notice of the footage.

The corridors are teal-blue as I leave Plangon's workstation and make the journey back to mine and Leal's. If someone as trusted as my father is being watched by surveillance, what does that mean for me? Maybe Plangon is showing me something I haven't realized before. It's the job of Leal and me to watch the Facilitators and Promoters, and we are trained more rigorously than those who watch only Cultivators. If even my father is on high-up surveillance, maybe Plangon is trying to show me that those who have higher roles are also more heavily watched on surveillance. Maybe my father's up to something and he's warning me not to get involved. What could it be?

I hear voices in the otherwise silent corridor. In this walkway, I know there's a connecting point between

Trellis

Phrames 20, 22, and the closed door to Phrame 21 where the accident happened. Trying not to seem too suspicious I slow my pace as I walk by the corridor. Peering down the walkway, there are workers in green suits in front of Phrame 21. There's an open panel in the wall next to the door. Maybe they're trying to fix a wiring issue.

One of the workers picks up a thick piece of metal and jams it in the center of the closed door.

"Now try it," says a worker who stands in front of the open paneling.

The worker with the metal bar forces his weight onto it.

It looks like he's trying to pry open the door.

Why would someone open a flooded corridor? Maybe I can check the maintenance records in my workstation and see what they are trying to fix.

Leal's attention locks to something on the screen as I enter the workstation. He types on the control panel and the screen fills with writing. It's too hard to see what he's looking at from where I stand, but it doesn't look like the numbers and symbols in coding; it looks like words. I step closer to him.

"Weird," Leal says, looking at the screen.

"What is it?" I ask.

"They're dispatching a maintenance pod— outside," he says.

"That's not that weird," I say. "What's broken?"

Occasionally, something outside the Trellis needs work. It could be a light that grows the algae fields or one of the outdoor turbines that generate electricity. No matter what needs fixed, we usually have to send a crew of people inside a maintenance pod to go fix it. When something outside breaks, maintenance Cultivators climb into a small submersible pod with a window that lets them control the arms of the pod and fix whatever is broken.

That's the closest thing to outside I ever get. In fact, I get a bit excited when something breaks outside the Trellis because we get to watch their security footage. Even though I don't leave my workstation, I can see the outside just as if I were in the maintenance pod.

"Well," says Leal, "it's a methane tank that's having issues, but that's not what's weird."

"What's weird?"

"They didn't send my dad," Leal answers.

"I don't see why that's weird. They don't always send your dad every time something breaks."

"Yeah, but the methane equipment is very particular and dangerous."

"So," I say, "what does that have to do with anything?" I lean toward the screen, with my arm on the control panel, as the footage shows a group of Cultivators piled into a cramped submarine. The maintenance pods are meant to hold two people, but three squeeze into the pod on the screen.

"This isn't right," Leal says, holding his stomach.

My eyebrows shoot up. Leal looks like he might be sick. What could make him get concerned like this? All my attention hones in on what he has to say.

"In order to access the methane tanks, the Cultivators' pod needs to travel over the brine," he says.

"What's the brine?"

"It's like a saline pool that shoots out methane," Leal doesn't remove his stare from the screen.

"That explanation doesn't help," I say.

"It's like water with a lot of salt that makes it more dense than the surrounding water," Leal grunts a bit in frustration. "Never mind. Just assume it's like a pond at the bottom of the ocean and it releases dangerous chemicals."

"The pod will be fine, right?" I ask. "It goes by those sorts of chemicals all the time."

"My dad showed me videos of it when I was younger," Leal seems almost in a trance. "I think he's the only one who knows how to work on the equipment out there."

"Maybe they trained someone else," I say.

"Look," Leal points to the screen. A fourth Cultivator steps into the pod— It's Norma, Arianelle's grandmother.

A chill goes down my spine. Why would they send a cook to work on specified equipment in a dangerous area? I begin typing on the control panel, telling the facial recognition systems to identify the other three Cultivators in the pod. Their profiles appear on the screen: Julie Porter — cleans the cooking equipment. Harl Prince— cleans waste facilities. Jennifer Brown— maintains screens and trowels.

"None of them are mechanics," I say.

"All of them have low emotional fitness scores," Leal responds.

The security footage from the submarine's camera turns on. It's pitch black, then a light turns on, shining through an expanse of limitless ocean. It's like the Cultivators are vulnerable from all sides as the light shines only enough to show a short distance in front of the pod.

"Not just that," I say, "they all have a recent record of dissonance." My attention moves between the maintenance pod's footage and the profiles which describe each Cultivator.

Julie Porter— physical altercation with a Facilitator.

The pod moves over hills of white sediment.

Harl Prince— sabotaging the facility equipment. The pod's light shines over a lone sea cucumber, worming its way through the dirt.

Jennifer Brown— spearheading plans for an uprising in Phrame 2.

Trellis

The footage shows something that looks like a mist that stays in one spot.

Norma Delphino— spreading propaganda about Trellis heads.

Bubbles release from the mist. An eel swims over and dives in.

"That's the brine," Leal says.

The eel swims back out of the brine, but can't seem to get very far. Convulsing, it twists itself into a knot, floating back into the brine. It tries to swim back out, then twitches and floats back down.

"What's happening?" my heart races as the eel's struggle seems to foreshadow fears I have for the Cultivators.

"It's going into toxic shock," says Leal. "The brine is like a poison to the eel."

"Why did it go in there in the first place?"

"I don't know," says Leal, "to find food maybe."

"Food?" I say. "Then other things can live in there without going into toxic shock?"

"I don't know, Gia," Leal says, his gaze fixated on the screen. He types on the control panel.

"What are you doing?"

"I just want to see if it seems like any of them know what's going on."

Audio from the maintenance pod fills our workspace. I take a seat in the chair next to Leal.

"I'm suffocating," says a voice from the screen.

"Everyone is, Harl," says another voice.

"Look," says one of the voices, "another eel is swimming over the pool."

"Careful not to drive over the brine," says a man's voice. "It looks dangerous."

"I'm doing my best!" snaps another voice. "You, keep on the lookout. We should be coming to the place where there's damage."

"Can't they send a remote-controlled camera to look for this sort of thing?" someone in the pod asks.

I look to Leal. "Can they?"

He swallows. "Yes."

"What is that?" a voice exclaims over the speaker.

Panicked, my eyes search over the screen to find what the voice yells about.

"Shut up, Jules," says the man's voice. "It was just another eel coming out of the brine."

"No! It was thicker, and it flashed red!"

"There's nothing there."

"Look, there it is again!"

From the brine, a tentacle rolls like a wave from the mist then settles under the surface and out of sight.

There's silence. All eyes fixate on the pool of mist.

Flashing red, a peak rises from the brine. It's big enough to fill the entire sustenance room.

"Leal," my voice trembles, "what is that?"

Trellis

An eyeball centers over the screen, eclipsing anything else in the camera's view.

"I think," Leal's voice is weak, "it's a squid."

Voices scream over the audio feed: "Go, go, go!"

A shrill cry: "I'm trying!"

Leal types in the control panel; flagging the footage for superiors to see it.

The camera view turns, shifting away from the creature, but revealing a tentacle as thick as a fully grown human. Something shoots out toward the pod, yanking it to the creature and entangling it in a mess of tentacles. Screams flood over the audio.

I type on the control panel, scrambling to do something to get them out.

"Leal!" I give a desperate plea, as if Leal can do something that I can't.

"I flagged it!" says Leal. He pushes every alert available on the panel. "I don't know what else to do!"

At once, the screams stop. The screen goes blank.

Silence creeps over the room. Sweat drips from my forehead.

I type in the call code for Plangon's office.

"Plangon!" I yell to the control panel.

"I see it," a voice sounds through the audio feed. "Minji and Jarret flagged it a minute ago. Don't worry, a team was already on the way. We'll get those Cultivators out of there."

80

The audio turns off. I lean back in the chair, looking down at my trembling hands. Hot breath leaves my lungs as I look over at Leal, who stares at the screen as if in shock.

A buzzer sounds. I jolt in surprise. It's time to get sustenance.

"There is no team coming," Leal whispers. He looks at a screen that shows the dispatched pods. "Only the one maintenance pod ever left the facility."

"Lea," I say, panic flooding my mind.

He turns toward me.

I nod my head toward the camera in our surveillance room. We never deflected the surveillance in our workstation. They can hear everything we say.

Chapter 5: A Promise

A screen with Gaines Cyro's face is against the wall as we leave the workspace. A wide smile is plastered across his broad face. His facial structure is strong and his hair is dark. No sound comes from the screen, but Gaines Cyro has the voice to match his masculine face. I remember it from promotional videos during trainings. Words float across the screen:

Many people.

One Community.

One Trellis.

Support one another.

A murmur rises as the corridors fill with workers from our phrame. The white light looms around the closed entrance to Phrame 21 as we walk toward the eating area.

"I wonder if it was the squid," Leal says quietly.

"What was?" I mumble.

"The accident," he responds.

Questions swish around my mind like distant creatures that I can't fully perceive. There's so much I don't understand, but I don't even know what to ask to figure it out. The accident from 15 years ago— it was said that a sea creature crashed into the Trellis, cracking the side. The pressure from the ocean sent floods of water through the corridor which would have flooded the Trellis if they didn't close off Phrame 21.

The monster outside, Arianelle's request to talk to me, the siphon, the disappearing girl. How is this all happening? Are they connected?

I don't make eye contact with anyone as we step into line, though I feel Desman's stare on my back. Leal hunches and wraps his arms around himself, rigid as he crosses his arms and steps closer to me than usual.

My jaw clenches. I sense each step he takes behind me as the line moves toward the sustenance packets. While I seek to uncover questions and answers much bigger than myself, Desman's annoying presence pulls me from my thoughts.

"Hey, Gia."

My eyes shoot up at the person in front of me— it's Jarret. So engrossed by Desman in my vicinity, I didn't even notice Minji and Jarret in front of me.

"Do you know when Ara will be joining our training again?" Jarret asks.

"Yeah," Desman's broad shoulder cuts between Leal and me as he positions himself in front of me. "When will she be joining us? Where exactly is she?"

With Desman in front of me, I exaggerate my movement as I turn toward Jarret.

"I don't know the answers," I say with a calm tone. "It's not actually up to me."

"Excuse me—" the old man giving out sustenance packets cuts in to get Jarret's attention.

Jarret turns, as if his mind was summoned back from another world, and accepts the sustenance packet from the man.

In my mind, there's a wall between Desman and me as I step toward the old man and act like I can't feel the tension from the imagined weapons Desman fires my way.

The sustenance packet feels harder to chew as I put it in my mouth. It slithers down my throat and I force myself to swallow. My stomach is full of spite and mushed fish pieces as I exit the eating area.

Leal's footsteps flutter to my side as I march down the corridor, having left the area without noticing if he was next to me.

"Are—are you okay?" Leal asks.

"Fine," I say, with my jaw still clenched. Then I look over at him, seeing my friend— someone with care in his eyes and a lightness in his footstep which shows his anxiety about saying the wrong thing. My limbs relax slightly. "I'm fine," I exhale like a sigh of relief.

"It's ok," Leal says almost in a whisper.

"What is?"

He wrings his hands together and hesitates. "It's okay that you're not fine."

Emotions flash in my mind like lightning— vulnerability, defense, letting go because Leal is safe, defense again because the Trellis is not safe and it's watching. I can't find words to respond. His shoulders creep up toward his ears as my silence goes on— like insecurity is creeping inside him for saying the wrong thing.

"Thank you," I say, looking straight ahead.

"You're welcome," he says, putting his hand awkwardly on my shoulder.

Everything inside me tenses. I even hold my breath as I try to decide how to react.

"Anyway," Leal says uncomfortably, releasing his hand, "it's time for sleeping hours and you have somewhere to be."

"Yup," I say, still walking forward.

"This is my turn," he points toward the corridor to the sleeping quarters.

"It is," I say, pausing for a second and looking down the walkway. "And this is my—uhh— straight," I motion to the corridor in front of me.

"Sure is," he says.

"Okay, then," I say. "Ummm— bye."

"Bye," he gives a stiff wave and turns down the corridor.

Arianelle sits at a table in the center of a blank room. The air is tense as I walk in like I could take a knife and physically cut right through it. I sit across from her, putting down the electronic tablet in my hand. She glances at the tablet, which is lit with her profile on the screen. This tablet is more of a prop. If there was information that she didn't need to know, the tablet screen would be off and in my lap, or not there at all. But I place it on the table and turned toward me so it looks like I'm reviewing her information. On one hand, it communicates that I'm the one in the room who ultimately holds power since I bring in her profile and the potential to change her emotional fitness score. On the other hand, it communicates a sense of companionship— the screen is lit, on the table where she can see it, meaning I am transparent about the information I hold and she can be secure. Not that she is consciously aware of any messages I send. If psychology serves me right, this should all create an emotion of fear of potential consequences, but a trust she can avoid them by confiding in me. I'm both the bad person and the good person.

"Hello, Arianelle," I feel uncertain of what emotion to bring to the conversation since I'm not sure how she feels about me.

"People call me Ara," she says, her red hair cascading over her red-suited shoulders. Her beauty isn't diminished from the hours in holding cells. And, potentially, neither is her defiance as she stares straight back at me with her chest forward and no hint of a smile.

I was 13 when my father began making me watch recorded footage of negotiations when others my age were in designated sleeping hours. Wait, I remember watching one of Vega Delphino— Ara's mother. Plangon had sat down with her, and she gave that same, defiant stare. Plangon's biggest mistake was his voice inflections. He was placating her, and she knew it. She wouldn't bargain with someone who wouldn't talk straight with her.

Trellis

"Ara, then," I say. I sit back slightly in my chair. "You asked me to come," I say directly. "Tell me what I'm here for."

"Tell me what's going on," she says.

"We're sitting across from each other in an empty room when we should both be in designated sleeping hours. That's what's going on."

"What's going on in the Trellis?" she asks.

"You'll have to be more specific."

"Okay," she folds her arms, "why would my grandma make a siphon if there weren't people being hidden somewhere in the facility?"

"I'm wondering that same thing," I respond. Ara's question indicates that she wasn't physically a part of her grandmother's schemes and may not have insight into the entire situation. On the bright side, Plangon may be correct that Ara isn't actually part of an uprising.

"Where is she now?"

"Who?"

"My grandma."

I pause. I try not to picture the giant eye covering the camera view or the screams pouring into my workspace.

"I don't know," I say.

"You don't know or you won't say?

"I—" I feel exposed. I know someone is required to observe the footage of the negotiation between Ara and me. I hope the person doesn't consider me compromised. I hope it's not my dad. "I think she was sent back to work."

"I don't believe you."

"Well, then don't," I respond. "Tell me why it is you asked for me."

I feel the stare of my father creep down my spine. He isn't in the room, but I remember the feeling of his figure behind me as I watched the footage of Plangon and Vega. He made me point out every mistake so I wouldn't make the same ones. I found all the mistakes, except one. It's that Plangon used a "cooperation method" to draw out what Vega wanted— he dangled what she wanted as an incentive to cooperate. Strong-willed people, my dad had told me, would find it despicable and insulting that a negotiator would expect them to trade in their own values.

I don't remember what Plangon was negotiating with Vega, but I remember the sliver of emotion that slipped from my father as he explained that mistake. As if that conclusion came from some deep reservoir of pain. But the emotion fleeted like a shadow, and my father continued to explain what Plangon should have done. He should have convinced Vega that the answers to her problems were synonymous with what Plangon wanted.

"I want the truth," demands Ara.

Well, it looks like what we want might actually be the same.

Trellis

"Just tell me what you want to know and I'll do my best to answer completely," I sound genuine… I think I am genuine.

"Is there actually a siphon that my grandmother was maintaining?"

I'm required to say no. If I say yes, or even *maybe*, it shows that I doubt the credibility of the Trellis leaders.

There's tension between our stares. If I say no, she'll think I'm lying and be finished talking with me. If I say nothing, it looks like I'm withholding information.

My hand creeps to the tablet on the table. I pick it up and begin tapping on the screen as if I'm taking notes.

"I'll have Leal look into it," I say. I don't actually type anything on the screen or make a note, I'm not going to forget what I just promised and neither is the person observing this negotiation. "Is there anything else we can look into for you?"

"Do you think I'm crazy?"

"Excuse me?"

"Do you think I'm wrong?"

"Can you say more?" that's the classic question to get someone to explain their thoughts and give you more information without offering your own thoughts.

"I was looking through old content once," Ara's voice gets softer and her green eyes look to the ground. "I don't know why; just trying to see ineffective lecturing material so I don't make mistakes I guess. I found a video from the old Trellis Head, Victoria Menhit. She seemed really nice, but the video was cunning somehow."

"Ara," I lean over and try to meet her eyes. "where is this going?"

"You should watch it sometime."

"Okay?"

"I think it will explain things— Video CZ204 in the 'ineffective' file." Ara looks back up at me. She rubs her arm.

"Ara," I say gently, "tell me what's going on, maybe I can help."

"Maybe you can't," she sighs.

"Then why did you ask me to come here?"

Ara's body becomes completely still. Her deep, green eyes don't waver as she locks directly onto mine. "I trust you."

It feels like gravity increases ten times as I search for words to say back to her. Why would she trust me? The only person in this world I trust is Leal, and even with his harmless demeanor, I still can't completely let go around him. What reason have I ever given her to trust me? I feel a sense of responsibility. Like I've been handed her beautiful, pure soul and sent on a quest to answer all its questions.

The muffled sound of a door unravels behind me. I turn. Like a dream shattered into a nightmare, my father's figure looms in the entryway.

Trellis

"I'll take it from here," he says to me, motioning toward the doorway.

I look back at Ara, almost in a trance as I meet eyes with someone who would give me something as valuable as her trust.

I promise. I can't say it out loud, but it's etched in my mind. I promise to find the answers for Ara.

Chapter 6: Mental Training

I barely remember the journey when I arrive in my sleeping quarters and collapse on the raised platform in the middle of the empty room. My bed is like a block of metal covered in something that looks like pictures of moss I've seen on a tree. I don't really know what it's made of, it might be alive like our microbial suits. Regardless of what it's made of, I'm grateful for the cushion. I close my eyes, releasing a breath; releasing the tension in my body. My mind winds like the tunnels of the Trellis Facility. It's like someone released sleep gas in the tunnels of my mind and I see nothing but misty corridors. Ara's figure appears out of the mist— standing, with the same glare she gave me from across the table. My clouded mind moves past Ara. More figures appear through the mist— a disappearing girl, a crazy grandmother. My mind keeps going. Then, as if cutting straight through the haze, a sheet of metal, higher and wider than my eyes can see— Alaster. The submarine captivates my attention and my mind zooms like I'm walking up to it. As if the submarine takes my thoughts down with it, I drift off to sleep under a wave of unanswered questions, churning with a sense of wonder at the magnitude and mystery of the machine.

It feels like only seconds later that I wake to the sound of a buzzer. I put my feet on the floor and open my eyes.

Orange light fills the room. As the door unravels and slinks open, the hallway is deep red. It reflects off the grey suits as people join me in the walkway; marching like machines to the demand of the Trellis Facility. Gaines Cyro smiles wide across a screen. The red light from the ceiling reflects from his teeth like blood pouring from his grin. The image fades and a slogan replaces the smirk of our Trellis leader: Facilitate community through safe procedures, Promote harmony through proper emotional responses, and Cultivate symbiosis through mutual effort (FPC).

Facilitate community… to keep people safe—that's my main role in this system. I swore by it when I was assigned as a Facilitator. It seems distorted as the words reflect the red light. Every step toward my workstation is more uncertain. Keep people safe from what? One step. Safe from uprisings? Two steps. From accidents? Three steps. The lighting is almost dangerous, like it's warning me of some imminent danger. I stand before the door to my workstation. Staring at it, the black door slinks its way into the wall.

Leal hunches in his seat over the control panel. His focus is unbroken as I take the holopen from the podium in the center of the room. How do I get the answers I need? Do I tell him? There's no way to get the security bypass without him noticing. Wait a second— a small image in the left corner shows footage of Leal and me, both sitting before the control panel. It's old footage. Leal already has the security bypass up.

"Leal?" I lean from the podium.

"Ah!" Leal leaps, spinning in his chair and landing to face me. His mouth is wide open as his chest rapidly expands and contracts. "I didn't hear you come in!" He wipes his forehead.

"What are you—" I step towards him with my head tilted, trying to see over his shoulders to the screen behind him. "What are you looking at?"

"It's uhhh—" he puts his hand out like he's trying to block me from coming over.

I stop, putting my hand on my hip. Does he actually think he can stop me from figuring it out by putting his hand out? He looks like a frantic idiot.

"Okay, okay," he waves his hand back and forth, apparently reading the attitude on my face. "Just—" he pauses, putting his hand on his forehead "—I know we shouldn't be doing this. I don't want you to get in trouble too. Just don't let anyone find out about this, okay?"

I move forward and take the seat next to him, meeting his gaze as I sit.

"You can trust me with anything," I say.

The edges of his mouth lift to a faint smile. He turns toward the screens and rolls his hand over the sphere in the control panel. Video footage scrolls across the screen. First, a tentacle rolls from the brine pool then falls back in. My stomach tightens; the video is muted so we can't hear the screams that should come from the maintenance pod. The video angle switches to a camera attached to the outside of the Trellis. It shows the maintenance pod from the outside as it wavers toward the brine pool.

I feel all the life drain from my face. Breathing becomes forced as screams flood my mind.

"I can't watch this again," I plead.

"You don't have to," Leal says, typing on the control panel and scrolling more. "Look at this."

Another video appears on the screen. It's the same camera angle outside the Trellis, but the time stamp is 15 years ago. White particles float in the water before the camera. Eels slither around the brine pool.

"What is this?" I ask.

"Nothing," replies Leal.

"What do you mean nothing?"

"Keep watching."

Will this video show a monster destroying the side of the Trellis 15 years ago? I breathe in. Does this show the moment that a third of the Trellis population was drowned in Phrame 21? I breathe out. Is this the moment that caused my mother's death?

The screen goes black.

"What—" I stare for a moment. "What happened?"

"Nothing," Leal motions at the screen. "The footage ends here. The camera doesn't turn back on for another week."

"I don't understand," breath escapes with my words as I try to keep control of my mind. "Why— it stops — why would it—"

"Gia," Leal puts his hand on my shoulders and meets my eyes with his. "It's going to be okay. I don't know what happened, but I'll figure it out. I promise."

His eyes seem strong. The weakest I've ever felt, Leal seems more secure than I've ever seen him.

"I promised," I mumble, turning my gaze to the floor.

"Promised what?"

"Promised Ara."

"What did you promise Ara?"

"I would find the answers."

"To what?"

"Everything," I look up at him.

The room is cold. It's like the air settles the mist around my mind with a frozen silence. I fill my lungs with air that's as cold as the bottom of the ocean. I know what I need to do.

Warmth flares up my arms as I turn to the control panel and my fingers run wild over the buttons. Where do I start? I need to know what happened to the disappearing girl. Who was she? Where did she come from? How did she leave the camera's view?

On the screen, the girl appears near Phrame 21 in the video recording. She doesn't appear where the next camera picks up.

"I don't understand," Leal says, trying to be patient. "What does this footage have to do with the squid?"

"I'm looking for something."

"What?"

"I'm not sure," I stand up, pointing the holopen at the screen, then hold my thumb over the back of the pen for three seconds. "Run facial identification," I say into the holopen.

The girl on the screen is projected in front of me as the system runs through data to find a facial match. A red X appears on the screen, saying it found no matches.

"She can't not exist," I say.

"Maybe we can run a more advanced search," Leal suggests.

"What would that do?"

"It searches for each component of the body rather than the body as a whole," he starts typing on the control panel. "Each facial feature— eyes, nose, mouth, whatever — as well as each gesture the body makes."

The tapping sounds from Leal's fingers stop. "Huh," he says, crossing his arms and leaning back.

"What is it?" The print on the screen is too far away for me to read from where I stand.

"Her eyes match with the eyes of an infant who was killed 15 years ago in the accident in Phrame 21."

"So, somehow someone from the accident is… alive?"

The weight of implications hangs in the air. Before Leal has a chance to respond, a buzzer sounds over the speaker system.

Like a programmed machine, my body moves toward the exit. Leal's eyes are glossed over as we enter the orange-lit corridor and walk toward our mental training. The lighting turns to a sickening yellow through the walkway and people shift around me like shadows moving in and out of my line of sight.

If someone from Phrame 21 is alive, could there be others? After all this time, could my mom be waiting behind an inch-thick doorway? I want to go there now. I need to find out now. But how do I get in? Did that corridor open for the girl in that video? Maybe that's how she disappeared. But, then, who controls the door?

Maybe Plangon knows. But why wouldn't he have said something in that meeting about the disappearing girl? He probably doesn't know anything, he didn't even know that people could deflect the security surveillance.

Oh no.

"Leal," I whisper, pulling us both out of some deep spiral of thought. "Did you set the surveillance back to normal?"

There's no response. I look up at Leal. His face looks pale and sick under the yellow lights. Heat flushes to my face. We forgot to change our deflected security, so the video footage currently shows us in the corridor and in the workstation.

A girl next to Leal squints her eyes and tilts her head, as if asking what we're doing. We're acting too panicked, drawing attention to ourselves.

I straighten my posture and look straight ahead.

"What do we do?" Leal does his best to whisper.

People stare at us.

"You're drawing attention," I try to remain in a whisper. The regular mumble in the corridors picks up.

"How much more conspicuous can you be than being in two places at once?" Leal tries to keep his composure.

"Well," I say quietly, "we can't turn back now, that's sure to be noticed."

"Let's just say we forgot something in the workspace. My dad did it all the time."

"Forgot something?" I somehow yell-whisper with tension in my body and voice. "Leal, we don't own anything!"

"We can't just walk to the mental maintenance and hope no one notices for an hour."

"What other option do we have? This way, at least we have the safety of a crowd. We'll be with people the entire time. Unless you're looking for a specific person, how often do you notice an individual in a crowd? If we turn back now, we'll be the only two in the corridor."

"I rarely notice individuals, unless I'm looking for something specific," says Leal.

No one in the crowd of grey and red suits looks at Leal or me as we walk through the corridor, but I feel like every camera peers down on my movements and every microphone leans toward my conversation.

"Unless I'm looking for *someone* specific," Leal leans toward me as he whispers words that amplify my rapid heartbeat.

"This is our best bet," I say, looking at the entrance to our training area.

Mental training exercises vary, which means our clusters rotate between stations. At this training, we're assigned to the simulator. A one-way glass separates a group of Promotors and Facilitators from the person in the simulator. The simulator gives different scenarios depending on the role of the person in the simulation, but, apparently, it's important for both roles to understand the protocols of the other.

I usually feel annoyed that I have to sit through Promotor simulations even though it has nothing to do with my job. But right now, that issue seems far away. My mind is focused on every person in surveillance rooms, hoping that, by some miracle, they don't notice Leal or me sitting in our office while also in training.

"Gia Hamiltoni," Plangon's firm voice says my name. I jump, snapping out of my hopeful reach toward the surveillance system to blot out my mistake. My mind is filled with panic. Did Plangon call on me because the mistake has been discovered? The buzzing anxiety settles as I realize Plangon is calling me to enter the simulator.

I stand without a word and enter the blank room behind the one-way glass. The simulator often chooses scenarios with either physical combat— like an uprising— or a quick fix—like the need to rewire a piece of the Trellis that has been tampered with.

The simulator begins to create a room around me — dim, blue lighting, a podium in the middle of the room— I begin to recognize it. A control panel appears at the edge of the simulator room in front of a wall of video footage. A typical Facilitator workstation appears around me. It's like the simulator knows what I left in my station; like it's mocking me.

Looking around the room, I see no signs of incorrect wiring or dangerous defectives in the room. There's some sort of uprising on the screen. A man in a green suit stands on his workbench with his fist in the air. A second person, this one a woman in a grey suit, tries to pull the man down, but he swings his arm around and knocks the woman to the ground. Another person in a grey suit approaches the man with an incapacitor and shocks the man.

This looks just like my workspace. I'm tempted to type codes and reactivate surveillance in the room. But I know better, it's only a simulation. I run through the options in my mind as people in green suits dog-pile on the one Facilitator in the area. Do I dispatch more Facilitators? No, there aren't enough of us and they wouldn't reach the area in time to stop the violence from spreading.

A Cultivator on the screen gets close to the entryway and I hit the control panel to seal off the area. No one in the simulation can leave. There's no chance of squelching the violence and two Facilitators are in the room. There's a covered button on the control panel. I have no other option. I flip open the cover, push the button, and type in my access code, which sends gas to the closed area. Simulated bodies fall to the ground. A buzzer sounds as the consequences of my decision are clear. Projected images in the simulation fade— the podium disappears and the wall of surveillance video turns back into a sheet of metal. I stand in the center of a blank room, looking at my reflection in the one-way mirror, knowing that a panel of critiques awaits on the other side.

A slow clap fills an otherwise empty-sounding room as I exit the simulator. My father, standing before my cluster, faces me and claps. Does he know? He knows. He probably saw my mistake on the surveillance screen and is here to escort me to the holding cells.

"Well done, Miss Hamiltoni," he says. "That was nearly perfect." He turns to face the group of Facilitators and Promotors. Maybe he doesn't actually know about my mistake. "Can anyone tell me what mistake Miss Hamiltoni made?"

Wait, what's going on? As my father's figure moves to the side to ask the room of trainees about my mistake, I see a red-suited young woman with long, red hair. It's Ara. What is she doing back with the cluster?

Desman sits next to her, raising his hand.

"She chose to gas the room instead of just seal off the corridors," Desman says, "which was a waste of sleep gas. Everyone knows we have limited storage capacity for gases, which means we need to use gas as a last resort." Desman can't hide the proud smirk on his face.

"Thank you for your input Mr. Sphyrn," my dad responds. "However, that is not correct. "This simulation had two Facilitators in comparison to eighty people of the community. Just sealing them off could have led to severe injuries to the Facilitators. Not to mention, we never would have been able to stop damage to the Trellis infrastructure or further violence without calming the people somehow.

Who knows, maybe they could have damaged the Trellis enough to cause another flooding accident. Gia was correct in gassing the area. Can anyone else point out the mistake?"

There is silence.

"Clearly," my dad looks over to Plangon, then back at the cluster, "your training has been failing you. If someone can't point out the mistake, I'll need to add more stringent trainings for all of you."

It seems like no one knows the answer.

My dad stands firm, his hands clasped behind his back as if he was a kind, patient man waiting for an honest answer.

Leal fidgets.

"Mr. Fitzgerald," my dad puts Leal on the spot. "If you please."

"Well," Leal's voice cracks. He clears his throat before speaking in a quiet and high-pitched voice. "She took 48.2 seconds after the uprising broke out to make a decision. This was almost enough time for the riot to move into another phrame."

"That is correct," my dad looks over to Plangon, "maybe you're not so poorly trained after all." He looks at the cluster as I take my place in the group. "Thank you, Mr. Fitzgerald. If it's all the same to you," he turns toward Plangon, "I'll be watching the rest of the simulations."

"By all means," Plangon says. "Thank you for joining us Mr. Hamiltoni."

I feel a release of pressure as I realize my dad did not come to drag me to the holding cells. But a discomfort rises in my chest as I become aware of my dad taking his place in the group. He doesn't look at me, he probably won't talk to me again today, but I can't get the feeling of his presence out of my mind.

Garridon Hamiltoni has a comment about most simulations. Desman's simulation includes an unruly student who asks hard questions about the earth's history.

"I heard the Alaster ship is connected to a blocked off phrame in the Trellis," says the simulated student.

"Well," Desman replies to the holographic student in the simulator, "this is a common myth started by Cultivators early in Trellis history. More recently, we've been strategic in understanding our systems and how things work, and we can say with certainty that the Alaster ship doesn't exist, but is an embellishment of the facts."

"How did we all get down here?" asks the student.

"We got down here…" Desman hesitates and fidgets with the tablet in his hand, "because… We got down here as a result of our own hard work." He regains some amount of arrogance as his posture straightens and he seems to think he's come up with a clever answer. "As people created a united system, the early Trellis community came from the earth's surface by their own ability to collaborate. This is why we value individuals and the ability to work as a community."

A buzzer sounds to end the simulation. Desman hardly exits the simulator and pauses before us as if ready to be praised. The facial expression on my father remains unchanged, but I can't help but sense that there's a small smile beneath the surface of his face. Desman walks slowly to take his seat, as if he is searching for some sort of reaction from his judge.

"I don't find it helpful to point out the mistakes in this simulation," my father says from his seat. "Instead, as a thought exercise, can anyone come up with a better response to the student's question?"

Silence, again, hangs in the room.

"Perhaps my question is too broad," my father says this with a hint of cynicism toward our inability to answer the question. "What did the student want to know?"

"He wanted to know how people got to the bottom of the ocean, sir." Desman responds.

"Right," says my father. "On the surface, yes, that was his question. But people can be smarter than what you give them credit for. This student wanted to know something deeper. What do you suppose he was trying to figure out?"

Silence.

"Gia?" my father turns toward me. "How would you categorize this question?"

"Origins," I reply mechanically. My mind flashes through mental exercises when I would read questions and statements of people from the Trellis and connect them with deeper implications.

"Explain, please," says my father, "so others can understand."

"It's a concept from psychology," I say. "There are categories of information that people want to understand. Some are more informational-level— like, *what are the food pods made of?*"

I hear a few chuckles.

"With information-level questions," I continue, "people are just curious to know the simple answers. If someone asked what food pods are made of, a satisfactory answer might be a list of ingredients. Some questions, however, are more implicit."

I look around the room. Everyone still seems to be following. "These questions answer things like— *who am I? why am I here?* These are in a 'self-actualization' category. Sometimes, people ask information-level questions to work out a deeper question they might have. For example, someone might want to know where they came from to get assurance of why they are here and what their purpose is."

"In this case," asks my father, "what should the response be for this kind of question?"

"Responses depend on context," I say. "In the case of this simulation, I would start with 'probing' or asking more questions to understand what the student actually wants to know. If, for example, Alaster exists somewhere, does the student want to know if people can find it and get up to the earth's surface? If that's his deeper question, the response should address the longing to get to the surface. It has nothing to do with the original question— how did people get down here— but it may be the sort of answer that stops the student from wondering things that lead to defective tendencies."

I feel uncomfortable as I look around the room, seeing some blank stares of people who don't understand, but making eye contact with Ara, who understands perfectly. She's hearing how I was trained to hear people's questions and give answers to fit what the person wants to hear. It's as if I manipulate truth to make a person think they've been understood. I look into her eyes, almost begging her not to think I tricked her into trusting me.

Did I trick her into trusting me?

"Thank you," my father says, "I'd like to dig deeper into this. But, for time's sake, I think we should move on."

I don't break eye contact with Ara. Less forgivable even than the time I beat Leal in the physical training— it's like I look at Ara's trust in me, as I've beaten it to the ground, and I beg for it not to be broken beyond repair.

It's Minji's turn as the simulator creates a corridor around her and she's confronted with a closed door. It has been manually shut by a Cultivator. Minji attaches the trowel to the wall beside the door and types in override codes. It doesn't work; the door stays shut. Using a special tool on the trowel, she pries open the metal paneling on the wall. With accuracy, her delicate fingers choose a single thin wire from the option of about thirty that are plugged into the door's side. She simply unplugs the wire, and the door shoots open.

When the buzzer sounds, Minji's shoulders are hunched and her head is toward the ground as she scurries toward her seat. We wait in silence, but my father makes no sound of criticism or questions to the group.

My mind goes to the blocked entrance to Phrame 21. If we can recode and rewire doors to command them to open, why couldn't the Facilitators get that door open? If it really did open for the disappearing girl, does she control the door?

Leal stands for his simulation as my father continues in silence after Minji's performance. Something inside me feels protective, like I need to defend Leal against my dad's stare as the simulation creates a world around Leal. The scenario created for Leal looks like the Cultivator section of the Trellis. I've never been there, but maybe Leal feels more comfortable there since that's where he was raised.

The simulator is equipped with a moving floor, so it isn't a problem when Leal starts running through a labyrinth of walls. Virtual water rises at his ankles. Leal runs for the exit and sees a trowel against the door. Normally, there shouldn't be a trowel laying around in the Cultivator quarters, but, if we need something to complete the training exercise, the object would need to show up somehow in the simulation.

Leal opens the paneling against the wall, pulling a cord from the code box and inserting it into the wall. As he types on the small device, alarms sound throughout the facility to identify the flooded area and command all to evacuate immediately. As the water rises, Leal keeps typing. He hits one last button and the doors seal shut.

Leal did everything to protocol. The buzzer sounds. My stomach churns. I know it's only a simulation. But I feel nauseous at the simulated picture of Leal sealing himself in a flooding room. If Leal is gone, is there anyone else left in the world to protect? And protect from what? I find myself at the other end of self-actualization questions. Ara's trust broken; I might not be able to protect Leal— what am I here for?

My dad's only comment as Leal leaves the simulation is that Leal is slow and should work harder in physical maintenance.

When the simulations end, I try to file out of the room with the rest of the cluster.

"Leal," I hear my dad say behind me. I turn around. Even though he's not talking to me, I'm sure he's trying to get my attention. "I'm glad to see the slight swelling beneath your right eye has gone dow—"

"Well, yeah it's been long enough since Gia beat me and—" Leal stops his rambling as he notices my dad's irritation from being cut off.

"—since an hour ago," my dad's voice is stern as he leans toward Leal.

My dad switches his glance and stares dead into my eyes. It feels like a bright interrogation light shines out everything around me except the glaring realization that

Trellis

Leal must have deflected security into our workstation by playing old footage from when his face was still slightly swollen.

My dad steps toward me. This is the moment. I'm ready for it. We'll be taken to the holding cells. But maybe I can say something that will save Leal.

I open my mouth to speak. My father puts his hand up, silencing me. He leans toward me, his face is inches from mine.

"Be careful," he says between clenched teeth, then walks out the door.

I release the breath I had been holding and notice Leal's puckered mouth, wide eyes, and raised eyebrows, unable to snap back to reality.

"Lea," I say. His head shoots in my direction, but the expression on his face doesn't change. "Come on." I take his arm and pull him toward the door.

Leaving as quickly as possible, I stride through the corridors which link our workspaces in Phrame 29 to the training facilities in Phrame 20. When we get back to the workspace, both of us slam down into our chairs. Leal gets to the control panel before I do and starts typing.

"Wait," he says, "this can't be right."

"What?"

"Are you sure we had forgotten to switch back to normal security?"

"Yes," I lean toward the screen to figure out what he's getting at. The coding all looks normal, like surveillance had never been deflected.

"Well," he flops all his weight in the chair and lets out a deep breath, "whatever happened, it's back to normal now."

Chapter 7: In League with an Enemy

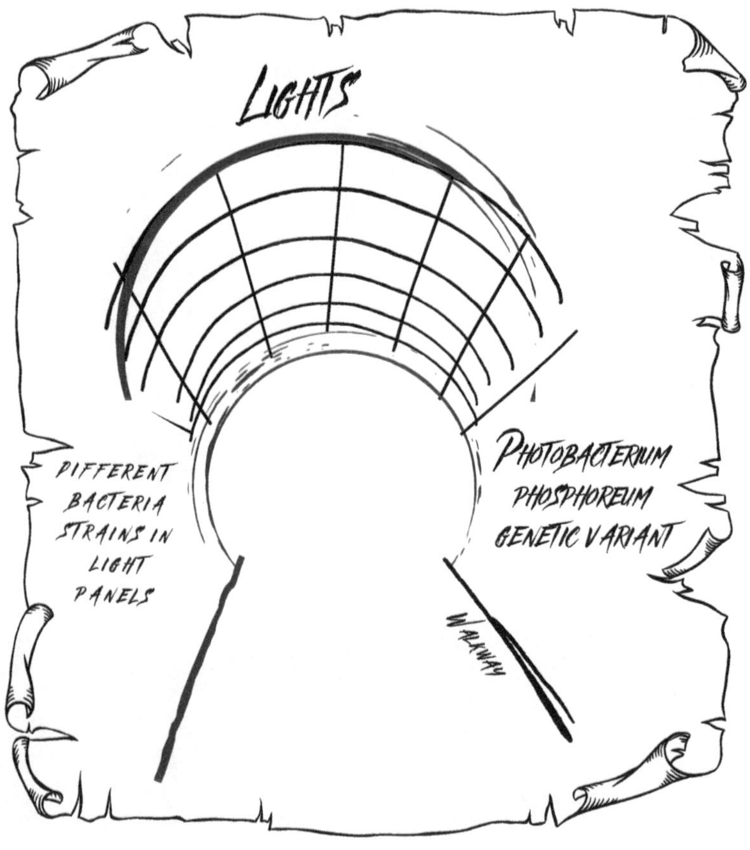

Deep under the ocean— I always know that's where I am, but right now it's how I feel. Like an air bubble trapped underwater, there's a safety net around me that keeps me from drowning, but it feels fragile. We can't deflect the surveillance, not now. We're sure to have a flag from the algorithm from all that's happened over the past few days. But I have so many questions. I look over to Leal sitting in his chair, so close to me, but if I reach out to him, it's like I'll break the protective forcefield and all will cave in.

Like shadows of sea monsters lurking around me, questions swim around my mind— big enough to feel threatening, but not close enough to make out the truth of what they are. Lights from the screens reflect off Leal's face. I can tell he feels the same as me as his body remains frozen, but his mind is in a different realm, running like an overworked machine.

Looking over the screens, searching for something — I don't know what. I feel hollow as I see Ara lecturing before a group of students. Do I sit in my underwater room, afraid of breaking my invisible wall of safety and succumbing to the pressure of the Trellis system? Ara moves across the room, her red hair swaying with each step. A beautiful person— one who sacrificed for someone else. Am I spectating in a comfortable room while I watch her drown?

My eyes remain on the screen as a buzzer sounds. Corridors in the security footage fill with red and grey suits. I shake my head, looking over to Leal, who stares at the screens, undisturbed by the buzzer.

"Lea," I say.

He doesn't move.

"Leal," I say louder, putting my hand on his shoulder.

His head rotates toward me.

Trellis

"It's time for sustenance," I say.

It seems quieter as the room lines with people who want their sustenance packets. Or maybe I'm just hearing less as my attention falls under a sea of thoughts, occasionally surfacing to notice what's around me. Jarret and Minji enter the room. I brace myself for the moment Ara and Desman appear. Is there a way I can explain myself to them? How can I tell Ara that I will still fight to find the answers for her?

Scanning the room, I want to get the moment over with; to see them and know if I can somehow fix the situation or if she will forever feel betrayed. But I don't see her or Desman. Red and grey-suited people flood through different arched entryways like streams flowing into a river, but Ara doesn't come through any of them. Leal and I move through the line. She still doesn't show. I almost drop the green sphere in my hand as I look around the room rather than pay attention to the sustenance that's handed to me. I put the sphere in my mouth. Wait— I didn't notice who handed me the sustenance packet. Was Norma back or was it someone else? I glance back as a man puts a sustenance packet in Leal's hand.

The raveled door to my workspace untwists as Leal and I approach. A figure stands before the wall of screens. Is it my father? I force my muscles to stay relaxed as my body prepares for the worst. The figure is a man, but the posture isn't stiff enough to be my father. Is it Plangon here to take us into questioning? No— the frame is still too small. I step into the workstation.

The figure whips around and I see his face— it's Desman. His chest moves rapidly as he grips the control panel behind him.

"Gia!" he releases his grip on the control panel and moves toward me.

Reflexively, my feet ground to the floor and I put my right arm up as a shield with my left arm ready for a blow.

"No, Gia, listen," there's panic in Desman's voice as he shakes his hand to signal that he's not there to fight. "I need help."

He looks me straight in the eye with no hint of arrogance in his tone. He must be desperate. I loosen my stance, putting my arms to the side. A small noise sounds behind me, like a flutter. Leal walks through the door and stands next to me, eyes wide at Desman.

"What are you—" Leal's voice gets high-pitched at the end of that sentence. Is it out of surprise? Or maybe fear? Either way, he can't seem to find the words to finish the sentence.

"Listen," Desman's words are quick as he tries to explain himself. "Ara was in here."

"What do you mean?" I question.

"There was something she needed to know— days ago—" Desman sounds panicked as he forces the words out. "She had been looking through old Promotor material during sleeping hours and came in when she wasn't supposed to. She told me later— I never would— I never would have let her come if she had told me what she was doing— you know that—I need help."

"Slow down, Desman," I say. "What exactly are you looking for?"

"I don't know!" Desman sounds desperate.

"Then why did you come here?" I raise my voice. "Do you have any clue what trouble you'll get us all in for being here?"

"I—" Desman's shoulders drop. It's like he could collapse to the floor at any moment "Gia," he looks at me. It seems like tears well in his eyes. "I don't— I'm not used to not knowing what to do. I have backup plans for my backup plans. I do what's needed to survive in the Trellis system and work overtime to make sure neither Ara nor I end up on the wrong side of the history books. There's nothing else I care about. Please— I— I don't know what to do."

I look at Leal, who stands stiff and silent, seeming unsure of what to do. I walk to the control panel, take a seat, and begin to type. I disable the video and audio in the room. I don't know who is looking or what they'll see, but it's the best I can do to avoid getting in deeper with the algorithm. How are we going to explain our way out of this?

"Do you know her access code?" I ask.

"No," he says.

"What's yours?" I request.

"A2014," he says.

I open Desman's profile, scrolling through the text until I find the information on his work partner— Arianelle Delphino; 19 years old; Promotor; Access code A1020.

"You have the ability to see our access codes?" Desman asks.

I don't answer, but take her access code and look for previous times she signed into a device.

"Why would you have access to our codes?" Desman demands.

I still don't answer.

"You could log in as any of us," Desman speaks as he processes.

"But I don't," I say.

"Leal could log in as anyone," Desman seems in a daze.

"He doesn't either," I respond, still looking at the screen.

"You watch us all the time?"

"It's part of our job," I say.

"Do you watch us in our sleep?"

"We watch the Trellis community to ensure safety and lower the potential for uprisings."

"In case someone accidentally starts an uprising in their sleep?"

"As if you're so much better," I turn toward him. "You infiltrate people's minds about the accidents and Alaster ship, but you don't even know if any of it's true."

"It's protocol," Desman fights back, "it's not up to me what we say, I trust whoever provides the information."

"So it's okay for you to follow protocol, but not me?"

"You people!" he leans back, as if coming to a realization. "You see what we search. You see what we write. You can see messages to one another. Nothing—nothing is private."

"Consider yourself lucky," I shift violently in my seat to face him. "You're only watched by us. You have no idea how suffocating it is to be watched by Trellis heads. Always be aware that any wrong move will be marked by a computer and added to a score that determines whether you're suited for this role. And—" I find that I'm lifting out of my chair, raising my voice. I've never felt so out of control. "And I have no idea what happens to me if I'm not suited for this role. People disappear, Desman! I don't know what happens to them! I don't know what will happen to Leal and me! You're not the only one who's protecting what you care about. "

He puts his hands on his head. "We're not just being watched for our safety. We're being stalked." He looks to the ground and breathes rapidly. "Every move—watched. Coming here, I was being watched. Ara breaking in here, they saw it. What will happen to us? What will happen to her?" He sinks to the ground.

Anger fades, but my heart still races. The only thing worse than Desman's arrogant demeanor is seeing him writhe in the uncertainty of what to do— to see him losing the battle of protecting someone he loves.

"We'll figure this out," I try to reassure him.

He stays near the ground with his hands over his head.

I shove his shoulder. "Get up," I say. My mind flashes with images of Garridon Hamiltoni hovering over me, demanding that I get to my feet. I am my father. I'm trying to protect and to fix, but I am him. "We're going to fix this." Maybe my father had been trying to protect me. It doesn't matter— the only one he needed to protect me from was himself.

Leal places his hand on Desman's shoulder. Leal stays there, not pushing, not helping Desman up, just holding his hand there. Desman's breathing slows and he looks up at Leal.

"Unlike you," Leal says, "I often don't know what to do. I can tell you this, we're going to do something, and we will get out of this together." Leal grabs Desman's hand and helps him to his feet.

"Gia," Leal turns to me, "pull up what Ara was looking at." I feel anchored by Leal's words, but humbled. He extinguished a fire of emotions when neither Desman nor I could see past our own panic. I've always known Leal was great, but maybe he has some strength that we could never see.

"She tried to log into my workstation screens," I say, quieter. "I don't think she realized the same access information is required for any screen."

"What do you mean?" Desman asks, getting up from the ground.

"I mean, no matter where she is in the Trellis, Ara will only be able to get information that she has access to. So coming to our screens didn't give her the information we have."

"So," Desman looks up at the screen like some opportunity lies before him, "all information is accessible from anywhere in the Trellis if you have the right access code?" Desman asks.

"Almost," Leal speaks up. "There is certain information that is only accessible from the offices of the Trellis heads. There are no access codes for higher security information because codes can be hacked. The security system is partly biological."

"Biological?" Desman sounds surprised.

"She was looking at old Promotor footage," I say, reading Ara's search history. I see it— the video she had told me to look at: CZ204. I open the file and an image of the old Trellis leader, Victoria Menhit, plays across the screen. Leal taps the screen to play the audio from the recording.

The video shows Victoria Menhit, sitting upright in a room with plain, white lighting, which highlights the shine of her light-brown hair.

"Hello Trellis community," her smile seems kind as her head tilts slightly, touching her perfectly straight hair to one of her shoulders. "Today, we are going to talk about the lights as an example of how we work together."

She stands as the camera view pans out, showing more of her body. "As you can see, I'm wearing a white suit today. That's because I want to actively show you the distinct colors in our home. Are you ready?" She smiles as she stands before a doorway that flashes open. She walks to a corridor where the lighting turns blue.

"Have you noticed how the colors change all around in here?" her suit looks blue under the light. "This area is blue, but if I walk over here, it turns purple." She turns down a connecting corridor where the lighting turns purple. "Now, look upward at the ceiling." The camera moves to the ceiling, showing translucent panels that each radiate purple.

"Each tile of lighting contains a colony of bioluminescent bacteria which thrives off the byproduct of the colony next door." The camera moves back to Victoria as she smiles wide. "That's just technical jargon," she chuckles a little. "Simply, it means that, when one color of bacteria dims, another color colony can get brighter. When some blue colony dies, the red bacteria might eat the byproduct. That means that the colors will change from blue to red as the blue bacteria die and the red grow. Next, the yellow bacteria will grow as the red die, and this whole corridor will start to turn orange."

Through all the explaining, Victoria doesn't lose her smile or pleasant annunciation.

"I know what you're thinking," she says, starting her way back to the first room with the white light. "What does this have to do with how we operate as a community?" She leans with her shoulders back and head high. "This physical structure is an example of our social structure. You see, we all work together, just as the bacteria work together. But, through the seasons of life, one colony dims, or dies, so the other colony can get brighter."

"Excuse me, Mrs. Menhit?" a small voice sounds off-camera. The video zooms out to show a little boy in a green suit, tugging at the former Trellis leader's arm.

"Well, little Zed," she says smiling at him. "I was just explaining about our wonderful lights and how we operate as a community in the Trellis system."

"Oh," the boy says in a high-pitch, baby voice. "It is, like, how sometimes it may seem like some Trellis members seem to fade while others burn brighter?"

"Why," she says, smiling big, "you took the words right out of my mouth." She puts her arm around the boy and looks at the camera. "You know, Zed, the generation before yours had an entire hour less of free time, but they worked hard, then faded so that your generation could spend more time with one another."

"Is my daddy working hard to give me more free time in the future?" the boy asks.

"That's exactly right," Menhit smiles directly at the camera. "Remember, we work hard now so our children will have a better future."

The two figures fade from the video, then words appear over the screen: Cultivate symbiosis through mutual effort. Give your community a better future by working today!

The video goes blank.

"What is this?" I ask.

"It's the kind of stuff they play in the Cultivator phrames," Leal explains instead of Desman. "My parents would have to watch this kind of thing as part of continued training."

"Why would they play different footage in different phrames?" I ask.

"I don't know," Leal rubs his arm. "Because we have different roles, I guess. They wanted us to work hard or something. There are more screens on the walls in those phrames. And the screens play videos like this."

"Well," Desman butts in, "maybe not this one." He points to the file label for the video. The label says: Ineffective.

"What does that mean?" I ask.

"We show different footage to trainees in order to educate them about the Trellis or raise community support. Material is labeled as ineffective if the trainees don't seem to understand after watching the footage." Desman sighs and looks down, seeming to switch from the conversation entirely. "I guess everything makes more sense now."

"What does?" I ask.

"Ara," he crosses his arms and looks at me. "She left again… Hey, if people were watching her, why was she able to get around?"

"Either no one noticed she was in the wrong place, or…" I trail off.

"Or what?"

"Or the Trellis heads released her just so they could follow her. It would be to see if she'd go to conspirators in an uprising."

Desman shakes his head. "I can't believe I'm hearing this."

"Where did Ara go?" I demand, a little annoyed at his attitude— as if his role is more innocent than mine.

"I'm not sure," Desman says, "but she came back different. Ara— she's always got her head in the clouds, you know? She wonders about everything, including the dark and depressing stuff. It seemed like she'd been wondering something for a long time and she finally got a decisive answer. Whatever the answer was, it took some light or hope out of her eyes."

"How poetic," I cross my arms. "Can you just tell me what she said?"

"Whatever," Desman rolls his eyes. "Ara always says I don't understand her, I thought maybe you might since you're a—" he motioned up and down at me.

"Yes?" I straighten my posture.

Leal fidgets like he's uncomfortable.

"Forget it," Desman says. "You probably wouldn't understand her either."

"Try me," I lash back.

Desman lets out a deep breath. "*'We kill fish to eat'*— she used to say. *'Billions of bacteria in our lights die every day. Us humans are miles under the sea and the earth wouldn't know the difference if we all died today. What makes us care what lives and dies?'* That's the kind of thing she was saying a few days ago. Like I said, she wondered about the dark stuff too."

"What would you tell her?" I ask.

"I don't know," Desman seems annoyed. "That she's important. I'm important. Life is important. She kept asking me *'why— why isn't a bacteria's life important '* and *'do I decide which life is important?'* I mean, what do you say to that kind of thing?"

I just stay quiet. I don't know. I don't know what to say to that because I wonder the same thing.

"She's asked these kinds of things since I can remember," Desman says. "But it seemed like the past few hours tipped the scales in her reasoning."

"What happened?" I ask.

"Her grandma is gone," says Desman. "But you probably already knew that."

I swallow.

"She's lost a lot, Gia," Desman rubs the back of his neck. "And the Trellis seems like a system to her— like a colony of organisms where things live and die, and the life and death hardly matter. When she found out about her grandma, the hope was gone from her eyes. It's like she's made herself face a dark reality that everything lives and dies and it doesn't matter what we do."

"Well," I exhale, "it sounds like you were wrong about one thing."

"What?" he gets defensive.

"It sounds like you do understand her."

Desman brightens a little. Like he could smile, but won't.

"But, do you think she's wrong?" I ask.

"About what?"

"Is there meaning to our lives?"

"Yes," he says, "of course there is."

"Why?"

"Because— why are you even asking this?"

I was hoping Desman's optimism was backed by some resounding logic. Can it be that he thinks our existence is significant just because he feels it is?

"Can we just keep looking for what Ara found?" Desman changes the subject completely.

"Her search just ends here," I say.

"Where?" asks Desman.

"This video was connected to Victoria Menhit's name after Ara had found her on the names of people who died in the accident, 15 years ago," explains Leal as he reads the information on the screen. "Ara was trying to find more information about the accident and the casualties, but her access was denied. Then she searched for footage from 74 hours prior, and her access was denied again."

"What was 74 hours prior?" Desman asks.

I look at Leal. That could have been the time that the girl disappeared around Phrame 21. Had she seen something? I type on the control panel to pull up the footage.

The system locates footage from the correct time but in a different phrame. I type in the information again, specifying that I only want footage from the camera where the girl disappeared.

Words appear before my face: FOOTAGE NOT AVAILABLE.

I try again. The same sentence appears on the screen.

"What's going on?" Desman keeps his eyes on the screen, searching for answers.

"The footage is gone," I say.

"Disappeared?" asks Desman.

"Deleted," says Leal.

"Wait," Desman turns Leal's entire chair toward himself and hovers over Leal. "You can delete footage?"

"Not me," Leal says. "Only the Head Facilitators can delete footage. So, it had to be Emon Plangon or Garridon Hamiltoni."

"So, we can delete footage," Desman wanders away from Leal and looks at the footage on the screens.

"No, I said—" Leal tries to explain himself.

"Sign in as them," Desman says.

"What?" Leal seems confused.

"Gia, you just typed in a code to override security in this room, you must know some magic codes to make the system think you're a Facilitator Head." I've never seen Desman have such sound reasoning. Unfortunately, he's still wrong about how security works.

"It's not that easy," says Leal.

"You were just pushing buttons before!" Desman says back. "Just push more buttons."

"What footage do you even need to delete anyway?" Leal asks.

"Do I have to spell it out for you?" he says back. "Ever since our fight in the dining area, everything has been downhill. Maybe we can erase all of this— marks, algorithms, Ara wandering around, everything."

"We can't delete any footage," Leal says.

"Why not?" Desman asks in a softer tone this time.

"This problem doesn't have to do with code, it has to do with location. Access to Senior Facilitator information is only available in their workspaces," explains Leal.

"So, we've already been running around this much," says Desman. "Why not just go there now and delete suspicious footage of all of us? It'll be like nothing ever happened."

"The door's locked," I say, with my arms crossed, looking at the floor.

"We can open the electric panels beside them and send a command for the doors to open," Desman uses all his knowledge from training to form a plan.

"Not these doors," Leal says. "They made sure there's no way for them to be hacked."

"Why are these doors so different?" asks Desman.

"They only open to DNA," says Leal. "My dad said he worked for ages to switch security when Gia's dad became Senior Facilitator. He said he had to modify the genes into an entirely new microbe species to get it to work."

"What are you even talking about?" Desman presses.

"I'm trying to tell you," says Leal. "There's a thumb scanner in front of the door. But it's not a thumb-*print* scanner. There's a colony of microbes inside the scanner that eat skin cells on the thumb. The byproduct of the bacteria changes depending on the genetic make-up of the skin cells they eat. The door responds to the byproduct. But, the door will only open to the byproduct produced from Garridon's DNA."

"So, it's a thumbprint scanner that's not a thumbprint scanner," Desman says, trying to work out what Leal had explained.

"That's what I said," Leal states.

"It opens the door based on DNA," Desman continues.

"Y-yes," Leal hesitates, "that's what I just said."

"Well," Desman says, "doesn't Gia have half his DNA?"

"What are you implying?" Leal sounds worried.

"Maybe Gia's DNA could open it," Desman suggests.

"No, no," Leal waves his hand back and forth, "it's not worth the risk. Garridon Hamiltoni's DNA will open the door, but anyone else's will sound an alarm."

"But," I say, still with my arms crossed and eyes on the floor, "it's biological, not mechanical." I look up at Leal.

"Gia, there's no way that would work," Leal gestures dramatically with his arms.

"In a virtual system, you have to input an exact code for a result," I say, trying to defend the idea. "But, a biological system adapts without our saying so. We don't know all the possibilities— maybe it would work."

"No, no, and no," Leal doesn't relent.

"What choice do we have?" Desman asks. "Ara has disappeared just for being in the wrong place when she was supposed to be working and for speaking out a few theories. Next case, we're all sure to get taken in for questioning. What more can happen if we go to the office and the alarm sounds? They'll just find us standing in the wrong place getting information that's none of our business like we are right now."

"How are you going to explain why we're walking in the corridors in the first place?" Leal still doesn't budge.

"Minji can mess with the surveillance," Desman says.

"What?" my eyes widen at Desman. Is it possible that another person can get past my dad's security? If someone can change security cameras, why hasn't Leal figured that out?

"Ara told me. Minji can disrupt surveillance inside corridors and make it seem like they're glitching. I don't know how she knows that, but Ara was certain. She can also shut down an alarm if it happens to go off when Gia tries to open the door."

"Why would Minji risk herself like that?" Leal asks.

"Trust me," Desman says with a smirk, "she'd help if *you* asked her."

"Me?" Leal asks. "Or Gia?"

"*You*, you idiot," Desman cackles.

"What about Jarret?" I ask, remembering that he would be in the workstation with Minji.

"But, why *me*?" Leal mumbles.

"Leal can just get in there and say you have some executive orders or something," Desman ignores Leal's mumbled question. "Make something up. Jarret won't know the difference, and Minji will probably play along."

"That's way too many maybes," I stand with my arms crossed.

"Fine," Desman throws his arms in the air. "I'm open to better suggestions."

Neither Leal nor I say anything in response. Desman has a point. We're definitely in trouble already anyway. If there is a chance for us to clear everything, why not take it?

I turn to the security screens and open a search for my dad. He's in his quarters, asleep. We have time.

"So," Desman says, after neither of us responds, "Gia and I will go to Garridon's workspace, and Leal can go to Minji to temporarily stop the surveillance."

Staring at the ground, Leal bites his lip. Slowly, I turn from the screen and look at Desman. Silence hangs in the room.

Chapter 8: Garridon's Workstation

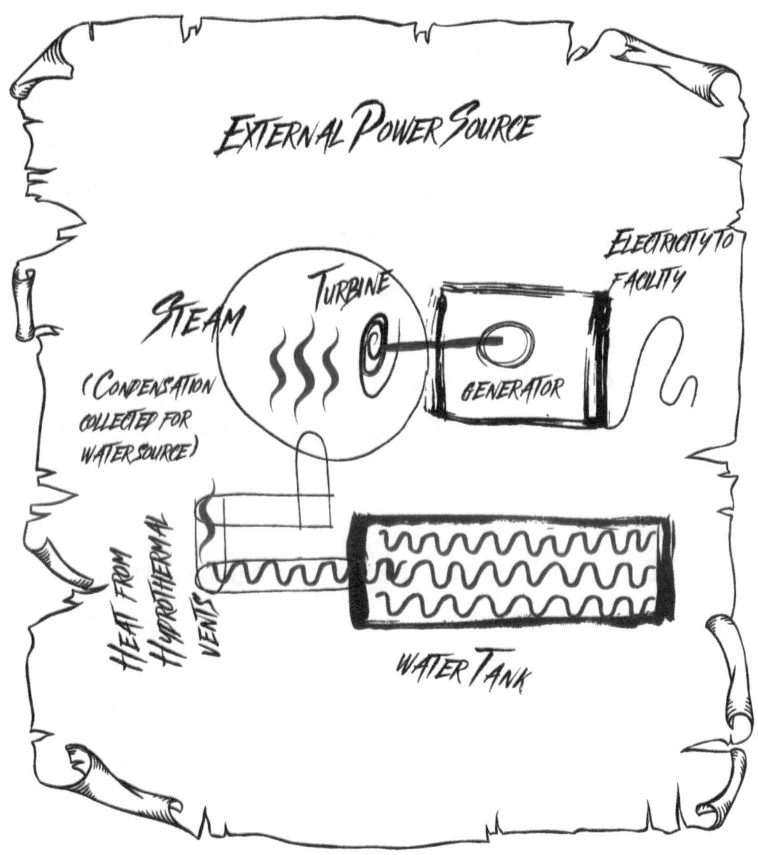

The walkway is lit a toxic green as Desman and I speed through the tunnel system toward my dad's office. No one else is around. There are no people flooding in or murmurs rising from the quiet, just the sound of soft thuds as our feet hit the ground. I hope that Minji was able to make the security cameras glitch. Leal left a few minutes before Desman and me so he could reach her. With any luck, we'll be able to walk through the corridors without being seen.

The heartbeat in my throat grows more rapid as we approach. The doorway to my father's workstation comes into view. I remember standing in front of that door before when I was a kid, though I don't remember why I had been there. I remember what the inside looked like. The room was filled from floor to ceiling with screens. Every wall in the domed room was covered with a screen except for an arched entry to a hallway and a round door on the opposite wall. The door— why would there be a door?

Desman steps to the side of the thumb scanner and motions for me to try it. I freeze. I remember what the door is for.

"Desman," my heartbeat might have come to a halt at the shock of my realization, "there's a doorway inside the workstation."

"Geez, Gia," he puts his fist on the door. "Don't do that! I thought someone was behind me or something. There's a door in every room."

"No," I say, "I mean, there's a door other than this one that leads into the office."

"So, what?"

"It's the only way to get in or out of Gaines Cyro's private living quarters."

Desman raises his eyebrows, like he's asking me why I'm bringing this up.

"That's the only place where none of us have surveillance access to," I explain. "He could be doing anything. He might just walk right in while we're there."

"Even if that did happen, I'm sure we could come up with an explanation about why we're there. We could just tell him we were asked to repair something."

"Only Cultivators repair things!"

"Then we're there for some sort of training exercise."

"Without our training leader?"

"Gia, I'll think of something!" Desman tries to whisper. "You're wasting time. Every second we spend out here is another second that someone might come in. Just open the door."

I take a deep breath and face the thumb scanner. I lift my arm and put my hand out. My hand trembles. I shake it around to get it to stop trembling. That doesn't work.

"What are you doing?" Desman asks.

"Why won't my hand stop shaking?" I whisper.

Desman grabs my hand with both of his, makes my hand into a fist, and then pulls out my thumb. He forces my thumb onto the round notch next to the door. He releases my hand and it falls limp at my side. The door doesn't open, but the alarm doesn't sound either.

"Maybe you need to hold it there longer," Desman says. "If there are microbes in there, or whatever, maybe they need more DNA to work." He reaches for my hand again.

Trellis

"Don't touch me," I yank my arm away. My senses seem to have returned at the relief that the alarm didn't go off. I put my hand out again and hold my thumb to the notch by the door.

A crack in the door opens as the door slowly unravels. Desman pushes part of the door slightly to make it go faster. Then a loud alarm sounds over the speaker system. I jump back. Desman and I both look around at the ceiling and down the walkways. The noise ceases.

"Minji," Desman says quietly, as if he has to force his voice to be brave enough to speak. "She probably stopped the alarm. It sounded like it only rang in this walkway. Maybe no one heard it."

There isn't anyone around. If we're lucky, he's right. If we're unlucky, we've been free to walk through the corridors because we're being followed.

"Let's just go," I say.

The door creeps shut as we enter a small walkway into the workstation.

"Want to know something weird?" Desman whispers as we walk through the hallway.

"What?"

"The door was hard."

"What are you talking about?"

"I've never touched a door until a second ago. They look so soft, but that one was as hard as metal."

Why are we talking about the doors? Does he have no concept of what we're getting ourselves into? I have nothing to say back.

"Woah," Desman turns in a slow circle as he gazes at the domed room. The screens are all off, making the walls nearly black except for the reflection of a small grey light from the center of the ceiling. A podium stands in the middle of the room. It has a few buttons, a glass sphere in the center, and the holopen resting on the side.

I roll my hand over the sphere in the center, with a memory of my mom doing the same when I was small. Her brown ponytail rested over her shoulder as her eyes kept straight at the screen in front of her. Why had she been in this room?

The screens turn on. Videos light up across the room as different squares pop across screens. From the ceiling to the floor, the domed place reveals glimpses into the daily lives of the Trellis members as they sit in their stations, sleep in their quarters, listen in the lecture halls, and—

"Wait," I'm surprised that I say this out loud. "What's that?" I point to the screen where kids in green suits pass a spherical object back and forth.

"I don't know," Desman says. "A game, probably. Those kids look like they're on free time."

"A… game?"

"Yeah," Desman says back curtly, "a game."

"Are they trying to hurt each other?"

"What? No, they're playing."

"Do they get anything out of it?"

"I guess someone can win."

"Win what?"

"I don't know, Gia! Can we focus on what we're looking for?"

It seems difficult to look away from the game. I scan the scene in the Cultivator quarters. Leal was right, there are more screens there, and more people too. There are a lot of people in the hallways all at once. It seems so full of life.

The doorway to my left is almost demanding me to rip my gaze from the screen and remember that the Trellis Head could come out at any time. I look at the Facilitator phrames on the screens. Plangon sits in his office, clicking a holopen, but I don't see Gaines Cyro. Maybe, even here, there isn't access to surveillance in his quarters. I feel a wave of relief as I see footage of Leal and me sitting in our workspace.

"Look!" Desman exclaims, pointing to a video of corridors. The video flashes off and on with static in between. "Minji did it! It looks like the cameras are glitching!"

I think I hear him chuckle a little as I let out a deep breath and pick up the holopen. Pulling my hand from the sphere on the podium, holographic files follow my hand and orbit the sphere. With the holopen, I swipe through them until I find the files I need to see.

"Wait," Desman says, "what are you doing? I thought we were deleting footage, not looking for it."

"I am deleting footage," I say. "As soon as I find what Ara was looking for."

"What?" Desman raises his voice and turns toward me. "We came here for one thing!"

"We are here to delete footage," I reiterate. "But I promised I'd look into some footage for Ara."

"This wasn't the deal," Desman wraps his fist around my entire hand and the holopen. I pull my hand back. He doesn't release.

"Let go," I demand.

"Let me delete footage of Ara, I'll get out of here, and you can search until Gaines Cyro gets up from his nap and catches you here."

"I said," I stare him in the eyes, "let go." He still doesn't release his grip. I go to punch him in the stomach, but he shifts his body to dodge the blow— providing the perfect momentum for me to flip him over my shoulder. He still doesn't let go, but the holopen squeezed between our fists opens holographic files that fly in and out of my vision as we each struggle for control. Then, I see it— a file I've needed since I saw the girl disappear before Phrame 21. A glowing blue file titled "accidents" flies over Desman's head.

I shift my body to face Desman, pull back my free hand, and punch him in the throat. His hands release their grip as he clenches his neck and falls to his knees. With the sound of Desman gasping in the background, I open the file.

There's the one I want— a short overview of the accident 15 years ago:

Trellis

Year 23 51

A large, unidentified marine creature punctured a minor crack in the exterior wall of the Trellis infrastructure outside of Phrame 21. Unable to maintain the outside pressure, the vacuum between the exterior and interior walls caved in as the interior wall let in water. The Senior Facilitator on duty, Garridon Hamiltoni, had no choice but to seal off Phrame 21 entirely…

Desman remains on his knees, breathing a little better, but still on the floor. Now, it feels like someone has punched me in the stomach. My dad… his own hands sealed the corridor. He had my mom's life— his wife's life — in his hands, and he shut the door. I try to look back at the files and finish reading, but I can't remember what information I was looking for. A disappearing girl, or something? How is this search going to help me find out what happened to her?

I look back to the file to find something— anything. There is a list of casualties. Skimming, I see Victoria Menhit's name. I skim across my mother: Britannica Hamiltoni. It looks so beautiful in writing. But the beauty seems so distant, like the quiet of the forest or the light of the stars that I will never see.

There's another name under Head Facilitator: Emon S. Plangon. I skim over the words again and make sure I hadn't misread. Wait, it's an overview of a different accident, one I've never heard of.

"Desman," I say quietly. With one hand on the podium, he pulls himself up and looks at the file.

"What?" he coughs, with one hand still gripping his throat.

"Was there another accident recently other than the one in Phrame 21?"

He shakes his head.

"Maybe there could have been an insignificant one that we never learned about."

"I'm a Promoter," he says, "I'd know if that sort of thing happened."

"Wait a second," I say, reading further the overview. "Year 23 66. Hydrothermal vent erupts, disrupting the movement of electrical turbines. A turbine, located outside the algae fields, breaks off its track and crashes into the side of the facility— flooding surrounding areas. The Head Facilitator, Emon S. Plangon, had no choice but to seal off Phrame 22..."

I stop.

"Phrame 22 isn't sealed off," Desman says with a tremor in his voice.

"They're killing us," I whisper.

"Ara!" Desman points to the list of casualties.

I look to a spot where Desman points: Delphino, Arianelle. Next name: Endermire, Joanna. My head swells as I read the next name on the list: Fitzgerald, Leal.

I take a step backward, putting my hands to my head and squeezing my eyes closed. Pressure builds around my mind. I can't stop it from growing more intense.

Trellis

I take deep breaths, forcing air in and out of my lungs. What do we do? What *can* we do?

"Stop," Desman whispers quickly, "Listen."

It's like the pressure in my head keeps noises from entering. I don't hear anything.

"We need to do something," I can barely hear Desman. His voice sounds far away. His body looks like a panicked blur shifting one direction and then the next, searching for somewhere to hide.

As I turn away from Desman, it's like a sharp knife slices through the dim image and, through the blur is the clearest figure I've seen— my father.

Stationed before me, my father doesn't move as reality falls back into place and I see and hear everything around me. Alert energy fills my body. I could almost hear the rustle of his perfectly groomed, black hair or feel the wind from any movement he makes.

"You're not supposed to be here," my father puts one hand to his head and waves the other in front of him — almost how Leal waves his hand when he explains something he's worried about. My dad's brows stitch together. He looks... well, he looks distressed. Is this some sort of trick?

I straighten my posture, realizing I had taken a defensive stance, ready to attack.

"Gia, I—" he takes a step toward me with his hand in front.

I shift back into my defensive stance.

"No," his voice hushes and he puts both hands out like he's surrendering. "Please, don't fight. Don't run."

"Don't," I say between clenched teeth as he takes a step closer.

Instead of walking toward me, he circles slowly past me, moving in the direction of the podium. "You—you have to trust me."

"I would never trust you," my teeth are clenched as the words leave my mouth. Never have words felt more powerful, like a single phrase created a crack in the universe. I've never been so sure of anything I wanted to say.

"I know how this seems," my dad's voice quivers.

Desman remains toward the back wall as my dad and I step slowly, facing one another. We circle like two people pacing around in a training match. As my dad reaches the center of the room, he puts his hand below the podium. Seeing the opportunity, Desman jumps on my father's back and tries to put my dad in a shoulder lock. But my dad flips the Promotor to the ground before pounding his heel on Desman's chest— possible fractured sternum with a ten-week recovery time; likely a minimally displaced rib fracture with a shorter healing time.

With Desman on the ground, my dad lunges toward me, cradling something in his left hand. I jump to the side. Instead of tripping over his own momentum like so many Facilitators, my dad lets his weight roll to the floor as he stretches a leg out straight and knocks my feet out from under me. Falling backward, I tumble over my head to land on my feet.

I try to jab him with my right fist followed by my left, but he dodges my blows and grabs my left fist. Then, the most unexpected of all, he wipes his left hand on my face, then lets go of me. I take a step back, stunned, trying to figure out what just happened.

With Desman on the floor, struggling between short breaths, my dad wipes his hand over Desman's face. A translucent, but shiny film covers Desman's face.

My father bends over with his hands on his knees. He even gives a small grin. "It's been a while since I've had to do anything like that." This is the first time my dad has seemed kind of human. "I told you to prepare for the unexpected." He walks to the podium one last time, reaching his hand beneath and then wiping the shiny film over his own face.

I can't seem to find the words, or even questions, to get any sort of answer.

"It's a reflective," my father says, interpreting the look on my face. "The light reflected back means that cameras can't distinguish facial features so you won't show up in a facial recognition search."

I look at the man standing before me. This must be some trick, but there's no reason for traps; he has the entire Trellis system under the will of his holopen. Why wouldn't he just take us to the holding cells?

"Why would a facial search matter?" It's such a stupid question, but it's the only one I could get out.

"Cameras can still see you, but they can't tell it's your face," he says, "but that won't matter where we're going."

We? The man whose hand closed the door on my mother thinks that *we* are going somewhere together?

"Gia," my dad says calmly, "I haven't given you very many reasons to trust me, I know. But, right now," he motions around the room as if showing off the scenario I find myself in, "you don't have a better option."

I'd rather find out what it's like to go into a holding cell than go with him. But if I sit around while another accident is being planned, he'd win. How could I live with myself if people die— if Leal dies— and I could have done something about it?

Chapter 9: Cultivator Quarters

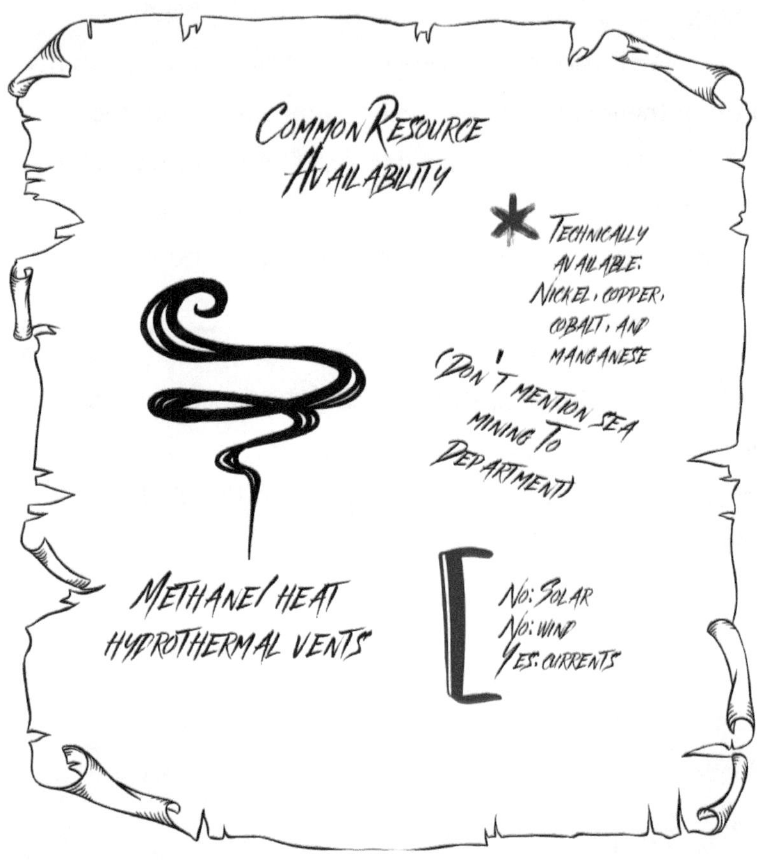

As walkways fill with people in dark green suits, the path seems less straight. The path twists, wavers, and connects in weird places. Soon, so many people fill the corridors that we have to squeeze to get past them. What if I lose sight of my father? What if we get separated from Desman?

I reach my hand behind me and find Desman's to pull him through the crowd. Our hands lock as I look behind and see him forcing his way forward. This is what it feels like to touch other people without fighting them. For a moment, my mind floats to some distant feeling of being cared for— of being held. A time when the movements around me were safe and I never needed to take a defensive position when someone came too close.

We enter a large room with people moving past one another shoulder to shoulder. My father stops near the edge of the room and taps a man on the back three times. The man doesn't turn around but puts something out behind him.

"Change into these," my dad says, handing out two green suits.

"Change?" Desman says, looking over the suit.

"Where?" I ask.

"Here," my dad says.

"Here?" I think my voice sounds less surprised than I actually am.

"Well," says my dad, "there, behind that sheet of metal." He points to the edge of the room where metal is peeled away from the wall.

I force my way through the crowd toward the wall. A thin, copper sheet of metal is pulled about two feet from the wall. I shimmy my way behind it, curling the end of the metal toward the wall to cover up the outside. Wires tangle through the wall like questions tangle through my mind.

Trellis

If my father knew about all of this, why has he let it happen? If Gaines Cyro and Plangon keep tabs on my dad, wouldn't they have noticed if he let these things slip? Where did the suits come from? Why is this metal peeled away from this wall?

I push my way out from the metal dressing room and through the crowd like I'm pushing through raging rapids toward safety. Desman changes behind the metal sheet after me. I really hope he's mindful of his movements so he doesn't injure himself more.

As soon as Desman pushes his way back through the crowd, my dad pulls the suits from our hands. Then someone moves past him and takes the suits, swiftly taking something before anyone notices it's gone. The only difference is that this swift movement seems orchestrated, like they often make trades in this fashion to avoid being seen.

"Time to go," my dad says when the suits are gone from his hands.

I flinch as he reaches his hands above my head.

"Duck," he says, placing his hand on my and Desman's heads. "Follow me and don't get lost."

Hunched down, I put my head below the shoulders of the surrounding people. My dad squats and moves his way through the tangle of green suits. I feel suffocated. The people create a canopy above us as we shove to exit the room. We must be ducking to lose the sight of the cameras. Desman grunts as he squeezes between people. It's hot. I put my hands in front of me and shove bodies to push myself forward and keep up. Sweat drips into my mouth as I gasp for air. Narrow, copper walls surround us when my father finally stands upright. Desman and I follow suit— standing to see a labyrinth of walkways and tight openings.

Official numbers are stamped near eye level on various walls; that must be how we tell where we're going. Where are we going? We take a right turn and walk single file past rows and rows of openings. I follow my father through a left turn. It's still not our destination, but another walkway. Another sharp left turns down a walkway. I lose sense of direction. I don't know my way out. We take another turn and I try to focus on something other than the fact that I don't know how to get out.

There are scratched-in etchings on the wall. Some sketches are low to the ground like children have made them, and some are just lines gashed into the copper wall near eye level.

My father slips through a small opening on the right, I turn behind and nearly run into him as he stops in a cubicle with only enough space to fit about six people standing shoulder to shoulder. Desman crashes into me as I stop abruptly behind my father. He tries to hold in a grunt of pain by breathing in slowly through his clenched teeth.

"You two," my father turns toward Desman and me, "wait here."

"What do you mean—" Desman squawks back.

"Wait," my father speaks slow, clear, and with power, "here." He slips past Desman and me and disappears through the small entryway.

Desman mumbles something under his breath while he holds his side with his back hunched. There are divots cut neatly in a row in the metal. Desman places his hand in one of the divots.

"What are you doing?" I yell as a piece of the wall slams toward the floor. It stops before hitting the ground and levitates like a platform.

"Relax," Desman scoffs. "It's just a bed. Are you sure you passed the Facilitator intelligence test?"

My jaw tightens as I fight to respond. In fact, I did pass the intelligence test with the highest marks— second only to Leal. I try to brush off his comment.

"How do you know it's a bed?" I ask.

"That's a blanket," he points at a piece of fabric that drapes across the piece of metal hanging from the wall. "These are rows of beds." Desman sticks his hand in another of the divots and pulls. Another piece of the wall becomes a bed that hovers above the first one.

I pick up the blanket. It feels scratchy as I rub it between my fingers. What is it made of? I touch the fabric of my microbial suit, which feels almost like a gel-like fabric in comparison to the actual fabric in my hands. I had almost forgotten that I was wearing a green suit. Rows of beds in a small space fixed in a labyrinth of metal walls.

The air feels warm in my lungs and all around my body. Trapped. I feel trapped, and I don't know the way out. Trapped in a green suit, trapped in copper walls, trapped in a small room. I take a step backward. Desman's hand shoots forward, grabbing my arm and yanking me forward.

"Watch out!" he shouts. "Look where you're stepping!"

I turn around and see a hole in the corner of the room.

"A hole!" I exclaim. Is there no end to the jungle of outlandish contraptions? "Why is there a hole?"

A smooth laugh sounds from the entryway. A large woman leans in the entrance, looking at me and smiling.

"It's a toilet," laughs the woman.

My eyes widen. A toilet? In the wide open right next to beds?

The woman laughs more, probably at the sight of the dismay on my face. "A great feat of human ingenuity—as my husband would say," the woman's voice sounds sweet. "He yaps on about bacteria that turns waste into methane and then the methane is used for the e-grid that gets turned into somethin' else important. Cyclical ecosystem— he calls it— says the Trellis is alive. I think that's why he and your father got along."

I look up at the woman. Her eyes flicker with warmth. She seems kind, but also powerful. She makes me feel the way I do when I've seen images of people huddled around a campfire. She's like low-burning embers keeping people warm, or she could be the dangerous, raging fire that burns everything down.

"Gia Hamiltoni," her mouth smiles wide as she looks me up and down. She picks up my wrist with one hand and squeezes my biceps with the other. Then she puts her arm on my shoulder. "Aren't you just the strength of your father and the heart of your mother?"

My hand clenches the blanket. I live in a place where I'm constantly sure that someone is watching everything I do. But, for the first time in my life, I feel seen. Some emotion bubbles in my stomach and I fight the tears coming to my eyes. I'm exposed and feel like I need to cover up. I melt down and sit on the bed.

The woman sits next to me, puts her arms around me, and pulls me close to her. The blanket in my hand is squeezed between my body and hers. A part of me wants to release and rest in her embrace, but I can't. Memories flash in my mind— every match in the ring, every training, every critique from my father. All I do is get watched and critiqued. My body goes stiff in the woman's hug. I don't even know who she is. And why should I feel known by someone who says I'm anything like my father?

The woman releases me and looks again into my eyes.

"I'm sorry," she says, standing back up. "It's just that I haven't seen you for a long time." She takes the blanket from my hands and wraps it around my shoulders. I stare at the ground, wondering what Desman thinks as he watches this whole drama.

"My name is Mabel," she says, "and I was friends with your parents. But you'd know me better as Leal's mom."

My eyes shoot back toward her. She's Leal's mother! Excitement flushes over me as I think of all the things I've learned about her over the years, but a sense of doom rushes in, and I'm reminded of the thing that brought me to Mabel Fitzgerald's sleeping quarters in the first place. Does she know? How could I tell her that her son is in trouble?

"What's the matter, Gia?" the woman must be able to read my face.

As I search for a response, I hear a voice shout over the metal cubicle wall.

"Mabel?" says the voice, "That you? I'll tell you, I've had the strangest—" the man stops his sentence as he reaches the entrance and stands in surprise at the number of people in the cubicle.

"Gia?" the man says in almost a whisper. He's dressed in a dark green suit and he looks around the room, searching over me and Desman before his gaze lands on Mabel.

"Mabel," he says, "what's going on?"

"Oh, Eddi," says Mabel, "I didn't think you'd be back. We can't talk about it here."

"Well," says the man, "we obviously can't leave either." He motions around the room at me and Desman.

"Why are you back?" Mabel asks.

"Am I not allowed to be back in my own home?" asks Eddi.

"You know what I mean," Mabel fights back. I'm starting to get a sense of the forest fire she could turn into. "You're still supposed to be at work."

"They told me to leave."

"Leave?" Mabel looks surprised.

"That's what I was going to tell you. Never in all of my days has anyone been told to stop work outside of designated hours."

"Why'd they ask you to leave?" Mabel sounds impatient.

"All I can tell you is what happened," Eddi says. "I went to work, like any normal day, and started my first project. Then I noticed some electrical readings were way off the charts. It wasn't on my list of things to do, so I ignored it at first—"

Desman shifts like he's impatient to hear the end of the story. Eddi pauses and Mabel shoots her gaze toward him.

"Please," Desman situates himself and motions quickly with his hand, "go on."

"Anyway," Eddi turns to Mabel and starts again, "I ignored it, but someone came from Electrical Charting and said his reading showed some issues with the hydrothermal vents."

My sense of urgency rises as I think of the accident. I sense Desman fidgeting next to me. His foot taps on the floor.

"First," says Eddi, "a vent was expelling more than the usual amount of sulfide, but, more importantly, it was even hotter than normal and releasing gasses faster— the result of which is that our turbine spins faster."

"Sorry," Desman tries to be polite, "can you, maybe, speed this up?"

Mabel looks at Desman from the corner of her eye. "Maybe it would be sped up if you'd stop interrupting."

Desman leans back and folds his hands over his lap as if to assure her that he's finished talking.

"What's the issue with that?" Mabel asks.

"Nothing, really," says Eddi. "There's a chance the heat or speed could damage the turbine, so it's never a bad idea to double-check that the physical mechanism isn't undergoing too much stress which may lead to severe damage. There are windows in Phrame 22 which look out to the algae fields. Follow a corridor near the fields and there's a lookout to the turbines. I was on my way out to see the turbines when I saw others there. I might not have left, except Emon Plangon was there with my colleagues and told me they had it all figured out so I should go home."

"Plangon?" Desman shot up from his seat.

"You know something, son?" Eddi asks.

"No," Desman looks down and rubs his hands together. "Not really. I guess, I just wondered why he'd be in the Cultivator quarters."

"A good thing to wonder," Eddi says. He looks back to Mabel. "I've never been told to go home outside designated hours. The whole thing seems off. Then, I stopped by the workstation to put my trowel back before heading to the sleeping quarters."

"And?" Mabel presses.

"And my name was on the log," Eddi says.

"What log?" for the first time, I hear my voice break in the conversation instead of just my thoughts.

"The job chart," Eddi looks at me. He doesn't seem irritated that I interrupted, but more inquisitive, as if I'm a mysterious creature holding a million unanswered questions. "There's a log of all the repairs and projects to be made throughout the Trellis. I typically run routine checks and supervise projects. But my name was on the list to personally fix the turbines. I nearly walked back to the phrame, but decided against it since that Plangon has quite a short fuse when it comes to Cultivators. I was so thrown off by the whole thing that I walked back here with the trowel still in my hand."

"What name was on the list?" the question seemed stupid and out of context as it left my lips.

"Wha—?" Eddi sounds confused. "My own name— Fitzgerald."

It's Leal. They've assigned Leal to fix the turbines. I'm sure of it. The accident is happening— now.

My feet shoot to the floor and I stand next to Desman.

"Thank you very much for your hospitality," I say quickly. "We'll be going now." I don't know what else to say to excuse myself. I grab Desman's wrist and pull him toward the exit.

Mabel steps in front of the small opening, crossing her arms.

"You'll be explaining yourself now," she says.

"There's no time," I plead.

She doesn't move.

It's so etched into my mind— the words I can't say. But what difference does it make now? We're on every watchlist and I'm about to lose the only thing in this world that's important to me. Why can't I make myself talk?

Desman shifts on his front foot, shooting his arm forward in a take-down move to bring Mabel Fitzgerald to the ground. As if by instinct, I throw my arm straight out, blocking Desman. I kick the back of his legs as I send a forceful blow to his chest, forcing him straight to his back.

Trellis

Leaning over Desman, I feel a sting of guilt as he struggles to breathe and I remember that he was already injured.

"Leal's in danger!" I finally find words as I hover over Desman and turn toward Mabel. "There's going to be an accident." I don't think my voice has ever sounded so desperate.

Mabel's eyes widen and her arms unfold.

"My boy!" Eddi's voice trembles. "Of course," he mutters, as if disappointed that he hadn't guessed that. "We need to go. Now!"

Chapter 10: To Save the Ones We Love

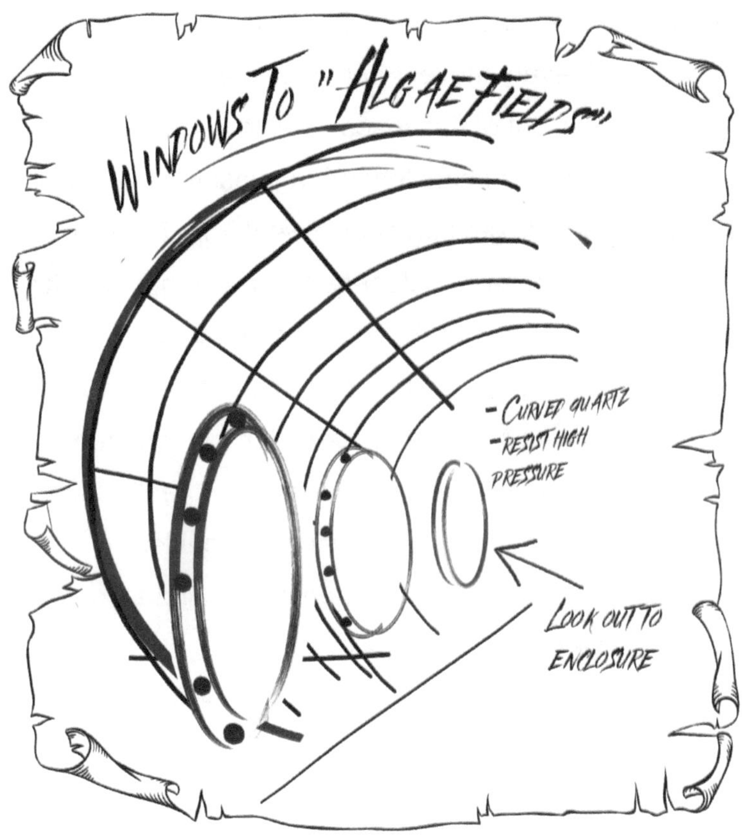

Eddi rushes past Mabel and out the entrance. Mabel runs behind and I pull Desman up, supporting his weight over my shoulder as we hobble out of the opening.

I turn left; the Fitzgeralds are already out of sight. I hobble in a narrow maze of copper walls with Desman's weight leaning over my shoulder.

Trellis

"Wait!" I yell, turning into a walkway, trying to listen for footsteps. Trying to remember the way.

The footsteps fade. I turn left into another narrow hallway. Desman gasps for air because my shoulder hits his chest with every move. I turn, hitting an enclosed cubicle. I swing out of the space, yanking Desman's weight with me as both our shoulders rub against the metal walls. The path seems to get narrower. Sweat from Desman's forehead drips on my shoulder as I take another turn. It's another cubicle. I look at the etchings on the wall. Two lines are sketched near numbers printed at the end of the row: 124. Did we turn there? I take a left turn and run into a dead end. I can almost feel the heat of my breath. I turn myself around with the weight over my shoulder.

Eddi leans through an opening, looking at me.

"Come on!" he motions to hurry.

Relief washes over me. Yanking Desman through a small entryway, he gets caught on the wall edge as I try to fit us both through a sharp left turn. He pushes my shoulder away.

"I can walk," he pants.

Something in me feels irked by his aggressive push away from me— as if he's not at all grateful that I just carried his dense body through a 3-foot-wide walkway. But the heat from his body is no longer on my shoulder and I can follow Eddi freely through the maze of walls.

Between a walk and a run, we shift as quickly as possible around each corner. Eddi zooms through the last opening and doesn't stop to talk to Mabel who waits for us at the entrance.

"Mabel," Eddi turns to his wife who jogs to catch up, "us three can go to Phrame 22 and find Leal. You find the others to make sure they're safe and I'll find you when we're done."

Mabel nods and runs down a corridor to the left.

People scattered through the walkways give confused looks as Eddi and I sprint past, with Desman hobbling behind. I jerk to the left to avoid a woman in the walkway. Then I run directly into a man. My sprint turns to a jog which turns to impatient shoving as I wade through a crowd of people in the corridors, tangling like the wires in the Trellis walls. I push forward to keep Eddi in view but look back to make sure Desman is still behind.

Desman clutches his side with one arm and shoves through the crowd with the other. Eddi twists between people, slipping through the crowd with more ease than Desman.

I don't look at the screens hanging above the crowd, but the brightness of the lights is overwhelming. A familiar feeling wells in my stomach— trapped. Bodies swarm around me and I squeeze through a mess of green suits to keep up with Eddi. Sweat drips from my forehead and I squint my eyes to keep the light from blinding me entirely.

In every training scenario, adrenaline coursing through my body signals that it's time to fight. It's time to take down an opponent— whether it's a Cultivator or a virtual system— it's time to take down an adversary. Like a staged drama, I wear a green suit and find that the enemy I need to take down is my own instincts. My inner urge is to grab the arm of the person next to me, yank him down, and trample toward the exit. The need to grab the trowel from Eddi's grip, run to the wall, and type commands to seal the corridors.

I stumble over a kid whose shoulder hits my waist. Someone to the right hits my shoulder and I get shoved back and I'm forced to look at the screen. The light overcomes my mind and I can't see anything but the words hanging above my head: Cultivate Symbiosis. My feet tumble over someone else's and I trip to my knees. Hitting the ground with my palms, I feel hands reach around me.

"Come on," Desman grunts as he lifts me to my feet and shoves me forward. I lose sight of Eddi twisting in the tangle of bodies, but, instead, feel Desman's full arm around my waist to navigate me.

I breathe a little deeper as the crowd thins and there's space on either side of me. Desman releases his grip as Eddi comes in sight and transitions to a jog. As fewer Cultivators line the corridors, screens become more scattered along the walls and nonexistent across the ceiling. We turn to an empty corridor and I instantly recognize where I am. We've arrived in Phrame 20. Only a few more walkways before we reach the meeting point between Phrames 20, 22, and the closed door to 21.

With the corridors empty, I can't help but feel the pressing eyes of every camera bending down on us— three green-suited figures running through the walkways. At the same time, my panic and adrenaline subside as I'm comforted by the dim, blue lighting and embrace of the spacious walkway. Under any other circumstances, I'd want to throw my arms out and smile at the freedom of running through an open area. Maybe this is what it's like to run through a meadow.

But I can't wonder about that now. Not with an accident underway and Leal in Phrame 22. We turn at a corridor on the left. I finally see it at the end of the tunnel— the sealed door to Phrame 21. At the end of this walkway is the domed area which connects Phrames 20 and 22. Just one more turn.

At the end of the tunnel, I see someone in a red suit pass between the corridors. Then someone in a grey suit. That's strange— it's not a transition time— not many people should be crossing the area. Moving closer, more people cross my line of sight at the end of the tunnel. Reaching the end of Phrame 20, people slow their walk and stare as we enter the connection point.

Trellis

"Hey," a young man in a grey suit puts his hand out to stop us. "What's your business in this connection point?"

I recognize him. I can't remember his name, but he lives in the Facilitator's Phrames and surveys Phrames 10-13, where Cultivators work. He's never technically been flagged or put on a watchlist, but he did trip one time in the line to get sustenance packets, landing on the counter and smashing some of the packets. I had to interview witnesses from the incident in order to determine ill intent on his part or not.

"We need—" Desman starts speaking, but Eddi interrupts.

"Here to make some repairs," Eddi cuts in.

People stare at us and I am more aware than ever of what it means to wear a different colored suit.

"You're going the wrong way," says the young man. "Cultivators were instructed to meet at the other end of Phrame 22."

"Our apologies, we just forgot this," Eddi holds up the trowel in his hand. "We just needed to take the quickest way back to the corridor to make the repairs."

The young man shakes his head and walks away.

"Desman?" a girl slows her walk past us and furrows her brows at Desman.

"Evelyn!" Desman exclaims. "Have you seen Ara?"

I wouldn't have known that girl's name if Desman didn't say it. But I've noticed her flirt with Desman when

Promotors fill the corridors after switching between lectures.

"What are you wearing?" Evelyn looks Desman up and down.

"Doesn't matter," Desman asserts. "Where's Ara?"

"I'm not sure," Evelyn cocks her head to the side and drags out the sentence. "She could be walking toward here from the sleeping quarters. Do you know what's going on here? I was dragged out of a lecture and—"

"Thanks," Desman cuts her short. He turns toward the corridor to Phrame 22 and leaves the girl standing in the hallway, gazing after him.

Eddi and I follow after him and march through the corridor with heads turning toward us as they walk by.

"Where might we find Leal?" I say, turning toward Eddi.

"Maybe near the North end of Phrame 22, but it shouldn't matter," Eddi's voice remains unwavering and matter-of-fact.

"Doesn't matter?"

I nearly stop in shock. Of course, it matters. What else would we be doing here?

Desman takes a sharp right turn down a corridor.

"Wait!" I say.

He doesn't stop walking.

"Where are you going?" I yell after him.

"To find Ara," he says, not turning back.

"We need to stop the accident," says Eddi, still not changing his tone.

Desman marches forward.

"Desman!" I try one last time to stop him. I have the urge to go along with him. If Leal was coming from our workstation or from the sleeping quarters, he'd come from that direction. I could find him and stop him from coming into the accident area.

I take a step down the walkway toward Desman.

"Gia," Eddi's voice says behind me, "I can't stop this without your security clearance."

I stop but keep my stare toward Desman as he advances down the corridor. What if we don't make it in time? What if the entire phrame floods while we're all in it? I could go find Leal now and make sure none of us are in the corridor. But all the others would be lost.

I turn to face Eddi.

"What if we don't make it in time?" I try to hold back the shake in my voice.

"If we keep standing here, we won't," Eddi doesn't quite answer my question.

"We could find him now," I plead.

"Or we might miss him," Eddi argues, "and let everyone else perish as well."

"He's my only family," I can't hold tears forming in my eyes. "I can't lose him."

Eddi crosses his arms and looks away from me, as if fighting off tears himself.

"Promise me," I plead. Tears roll down my cheek. "Promise me we won't lose him."

Eddi finally looks at me with glassy eyes. "I promise."

I sniff and wipe tears beneath my eyes as I follow Eddi in the direction of the algae fields.

Eddi and I run past small, round windows in a line down the corridor. I had taken field trips to these windows; they seemed more magical then.

As a kid, I'd stand on tiptoes to see out the window to a lit-up area. That was the closest thing to outside I would ever know. It was technically inside because it was an enclosed space with a ceiling, but it was filled with water. Along the bottom of the space was a long field of seaweed, and in the middle were floating pieces of algae. Looking out the window toward the ceiling, there was a sheet of green. The Promotor on duty would explain that there were lights above the plankton which kept it all alive, and the algae kept us alive because it gave us oxygen. In turn, the Cultivators kept it all alive by working on the systems which gave electricity to the light, regulating the temperature in the water and maintaining the ecosystem of the entire area. We all kept each other alive, like the Trellis was one organism. And, someday, many of us could be Cultivators too.

Wonder had filled my mind as I stared out the window and considered how magical it must feel to be a Cultivator. To be a part of the whole system and see it all every day. As kids, we weren't allowed to go to the service rooms that looked out to the electric turbines. That meant there were even more 'outdoor' sections that I would never see.

"Strange," Eddi says as we jog toward the entrance of a room.

"What?" I ask

"This door is always closed," he answers. "There's very restricted access."

The room is lit with the faintest lighting I've ever seen. As my eyes adjust to the light, I can't tell the color of the suits which are speckled throughout the room as people move around different pieces of machinery. Some people read information from their tablets while others type on screens attached to machines. None of the people look like Leal.

"Can I help you?" a woman in grey looks from her tablet at Eddi.

"I'm here for repairs," says Eddi.

"Great, another Cultivator," the woman rolls her eyes. "We've been told to wait for a tech supervisor before beginning repairs."

"Yes, I'm the supervisor," Eddi says.

"You?" the woman puts her hand on her hip. "I believe the supervisor we're waiting for is a top-level Facilitator."

"I'm Mr. Fitzgerald," says Eddi. "I'm the expert on this system and unless your tablet is telling you to wait for someone else, I'm here to fix this turbine."

The woman looks at her tablet, then back at Eddi. "Okay, Leal, have at it then."

Eddi walks to a machine with a screen attached to it. He opens the paneling below the screen and inserts the trowel.

"Gia," he says, standing back, "type in your clearance. I can access the deeper level communication between the systems and override the command to the turbine."

I type my access code into the trowel and step aside. The woman, hovering next to Eddi, looks at the screen, then looks me up and down when she sees the access level of my clearance. She doesn't say anything, but purses her lips and squints her eyes, like she's trying to make sure that her eyes are perceiving the correct color of suit.

Eddi's fingers type at a frantic speed as endless numbers and text scroll across the screen. I look out to the front of the room, where actual windows line the wall. It's what I'd wanted to see my whole life, but it was just black out there— there was nothing to see. I take slow steps to the row of small, black windows. Leal hates the idea of the outdoors; I wonder what he thought of windows. I never asked him. I'll have to ask him what he thought of trips to the algae fields when he was younger.

"There's a button to your left," Eddi says in my direction, but he doesn't look up from the screen.

I look to the left and barely make out a black button along the wall. I press it. Bright lights outside the windows illuminate the darkness. The open ocean lies just in front of my view, followed by rows of giant, metal spheres, reaching further than I can see.

Between the metal spheres, it just looks like white sand. But, there's something growing in the sand. They look like grotesque plants— like a skeleton version of a flower. And there's a giant white thing moving next to the skeleton flowers. I lean in further. It's moving. A slug-like blob wriggling on its own through ghostly pale sand. It's disgusting. Maybe Leal was right about the outside.

"Those metal pods house the turbines," Eddi says, still not looking from his typing. "If one of the turbines breaks, it shouldn't be catastrophic, but one could theoretically get out of control enough to damage the side of the Trellis. But I can fix that. I can— wait."

Eddi stops typing. He stares at the screen.

"What?" I ask, stepping to the screen where Eddi gapes.

"No," he says. He shakes his head and frantically types. "No, no, no, no."

"What is it?" there's urgency in my voice.

Eddi's eyes shoot straight into mine.

"Eddi," I panic, "what is it?"

"Wait," says the woman, still standing beside Eddi. "You're not Leal?"

Eddi turns to the woman, but is still speechless.

"What's going on?" the woman demands.

"I've made a mistake," Eddi turns to the screen again and starts typing. "There must be a mistake."

"A mistake is right," says the woman grabbing Eddi's shoulder and pulling him from the machine. "You have three seconds to explain yourself."

"Everyone out!" Eddi yells.

"By what authority do you—" the woman asserts.

"Get out of Phrame 22!" As Eddi yells to the room, the woman grabs Eddi's forearm, swinging him around and slamming his chest to the control panel.

"Who are you?" she demands, keeping him pinned to the control panel.

I sense someone step close behind me. I swing my arm behind, grabbing the person behind me and flipping him over my shoulder to slam him to the ground. I look at the person lying on the floor in front of me— it's Jarret.

"Gia?" Jarret stares at me from the ground. "What's going on?" He stands up. "What are you wearing?"

"Someone explain what's going on," the woman holding Eddi commands.

"This is a top-level Facilitator," Jarret says, motioning to me. "And, I don't know who that is." He motions to Eddi.

"Let him explain," I say to the woman, pointing to Eddi.

"I can explain," Eddi says, gasping for air as he's released from being pressed against the control panel, "but we need to get out of Phrame 22."

"No chance," says the woman.

"You don't have an option," I assert. I like having the power of my title back. "Everyone, out."

Chapter 11: Life and Death; Fight and Surrender

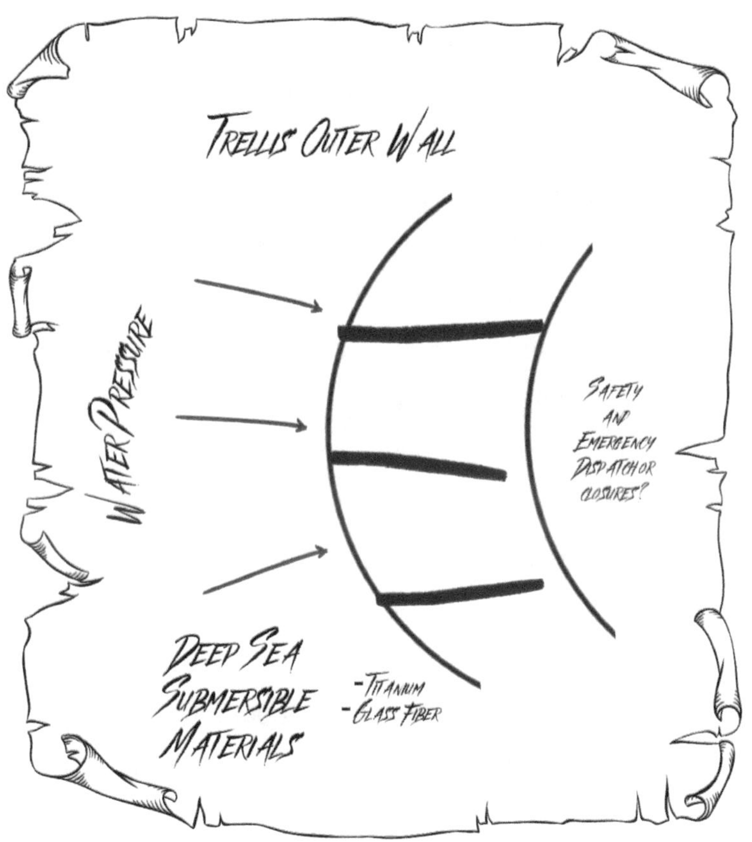

"I've made a huge mistake," Eddi pants as we run through the straight corridor which leads to the connecting point between Phrame 20 and 22. "It's not a command to the physical mechanism."

Trellis

"What's going on?" Jarret asks as he runs directly behind Eddi and me.

A line of others from the room trails behind.

"The turbine was never going to break," Eddi says, talking to me and not Jarret.

"What turbine?" Jarret butts in.

"I was searching to stop the mechanical malfunction of the turbine, but nothing was there—"

"Nothing was where?" Jarret speaks louder.

"Shut up, Jarret," I turn my head toward Eddi.

"There were no commands to disrupt the function of the turbine," Eddi says to me.

"What does that mean?" I ask. "The turbine isn't actually going to break?"

"Exactly," says Eddi.

"So that's good news," I say, "right?"

"No," Eddi responds, "it's not good news. Instead of physically breaking the turbines, the computer was simply communicating to our charts that the turbine was going to break."

"Computer?" I say, peeking over my shoulder to see if everyone from the room is still trailing behind. They are— even Jarret, who is pleasantly silent.

"I mean— sorry—" Eddi shakes his head. "It's an old word. I just mean the system. The virtual system miscommunicated the information to our charts so it only looks like the turbine would break."

"I don't see why that's bad news," I say.

"Because it means I can't stop the turbine!" Eddi throws his hands in the air, which seems like a lot of effort for someone who is in a full-speed run. "The turbine was only a front— a smoke screen. It was never going to break, but the phrame is still going to flood. I don't know how it's going to flood or where the water is going to come from, so I can't stop it."

Jogging straight ahead, I can't turn toward Eddi as I try to understand what he's saying. There's something I don't perceive, but I don't know what questions to ask. In some faint memory, I hear the sound of a roaring wave crashing through hallways. Not in the present moment, but in similar halls, I remember hearing pounding footsteps, then screams. Plangon found me in the corridor and told me that my mother was gone. I heard what he said, but I couldn't really perceive it.

That same confusion is what I feel as Eddi's explanation passes through my mind and I search for understanding. If we can't stop the corridors from flooding, is he saying…. Does that mean Leal is gone?

A blur covers my vision as I step forward and my chest tightens. I barely have control of my body as I try to step forward. That's a lot to convince my body to do— step, breathe in slow, step, breathe out slow, step, look straight ahead and ignore the blur in my vision, step. But where am I stepping to? I have to find Leal. I lose control of my right leg as I step and stumble.

"Woah!" Jarret tries not to trip over me as I stoop halfway to the ground.

I catch myself before falling and stand straight, trying to take another step, but it fails and I sink to the ground. Jarret grabs my arm before I hit the floor. Eddi turns around, instructs the crowd to keep moving past him, and grabs my other arm.

"Gia," Eddi says, "What's going on?"

"Leal," that's the only thing I can make myself say.

"We're going to find him," Eddi assures.

"Where is he?" I can't make sense of all the information coming in. That's what I kept asking when I lost my mom— where is she? But she wasn't anywhere. It's like my mind is trying to make itself understand the same thing about Leal. Maybe he isn't anywhere anymore.

"He's somewhere," Eddi says. "We need to find him."

My brain snaps back. Leal is somewhere. There is something we can do. I shake my head and stand straighter as the two let go of my arms.

"Sorry," I take slow steps forward, trying to assure everyone, including myself, that I'm fine.

"It's okay," Eddi says, "but we have to keep moving. We're almost to where Desman broke off to find Ara. Leal would most likely be in that direction." He looks to the floor, maybe ashamed he didn't go this route in the first place.

"I'm sorry," Jarret says as we pick up the pace and progress through the corridor. "But what's going on? What about an accident and a turbine?"

"There's going to be an accident," I explain.

"Like, an *accident*, accident?"

"Yeah," I say, "the only kind of accident there ever is."

"Okay," Jarret prolongs his words, "so it's alright for you to ask questions about turbines and stuff, but I can't ask what's going on?"

"Fine," maybe I have been impatient with him. "This entire Phrame is going to flood and be closed off just like Phrame 21. The accidents aren't real, but manufactured."

"Manufactured?" Jarret asks. "Why? Who would do that?"

I jog forward in silence. Who? My dad maybe. Possibly Plangon and Gaines Cyro are involved. Why? I can't be sure.

"We aren't sure," Eddi responds to the question.

I look over to Eddi as we turn left, down the walkway where we last saw Desman. What does Eddi know? Has he known about the accidents all these years?

"We need to take the next right," I say, seeing our connecting corridor just ahead.

Trellis

Pivoting fast to the right, I crash directly into another person and we both topple to the ground. I roll over and look at the person on the ground next to me.

"Oh, my son!" Eddi exclaims, squatting to the ground and wrapping his arms around the scrawny figure sitting on the floor.

"'Leal!" I say as I sit up.

"Great reunion," Jarret announces, "but we all still need to get out of here."

"What's going on?" Leal rubs his head.

"The quickest way out of Phrame 22 is back the way we came," I say, hopping from the ground. "There's a connecting point between Phrame 20 and 22."

"What are you wearing?" Leal asks, still sitting on the floor. Then he gasps, yanking his hands from the floor and looking at them like they're strange creatures.

A stinging cold touches my feet and I jump a little. Looking down to the floor, water trickles beneath my feet.

"Leal, get up!" I yell, grabbing his wrist to yank him up.

"Run, son!" Eddi says as he shoves us back in the direction we came.

Jarret slips on his first step, then bolts down the walkway with the other three of us sprinting behind. Splashes fill the walkway with each frantic step and the frigid air creeps through the space as more water trickles in.

With the connection point in sight, we run straight on, hoping the corridor doesn't close. Keeping my gaze straight to the connection point, running as fast as my body can carry, Desman comes into sight. From the opposite corridor, he runs straight into the connection point and stops abruptly, looking down as he steps in a puddle of water. He looks at his feet, then looks down the corridor, and then sprints toward us.

"What are you doing?" I yell after him.

"I can't find her!" he exclaims as he reaches our group.

"No," I say when he reaches me. I grab his arm and yank him in the other direction, pulling him toward the connection point. "She's not that way. We just came from there."

He gives in and runs with us through the threshold into the connecting point between Phrame 20, 22, and the sealed door to 21. Eddi slows, then puts his hands to his knees, breathing wildly when he passes the threshold. We stand in the connection point, safe from the accident that is supposed to end, but the water still trickles in.

"Let's get away from here," I say moving toward Phrame 20.

"No," says Desman, "Facilitators are that way."

"And?" I demand.

"They were after me, Gia," Desman seems worried. "I don't know where Ara is or if they did something to her."

He bends over with his hands on his knees. "I couldn't find her anywhere!"

"Look!" Leal points down the corridor, toward the flooding walkway. Ara's in the corridor. She takes slow steps toward us, almost as if in a trance.

Desman leaps up and starts toward her.

"Stop!" Ara yells before Desman passes into the corridor. She stops moving, as if threatening something if he comes any closer.

"Wha—" Desman halts, with ripples moving across the water, away from his feet. "What's going on? You're in danger, Ara."

Footsteps sound in the corridor that leads to where we stand. Facilitators are coming toward us—fast.

"We're all in danger," Ara says.

"So let's go," Desman pleads.

"To where?" she asks. "To the Facilitators at the other end of the corridor?" Her voice changes as she speaks, as if there isn't a harsh enough gesture or tone she can conjure to let out the years of pent-up emotion. "Back to our workstations where we force-feed lies that people work together to make a good life? Like there's any meaning to any of this?"

"Meaning?" Desman reaches for her like his hands might be able to stretch far enough to get her safely to the other side of the threshold. "What are you saying, Ara?"

The roar of strong, rushing water sounds behind Ara. In the other corridor, people in grey suits turn down the walkway and sprint toward us. Five… Seven… Ten of them. Ten Facilitators run toward us.

"We're all just like the microbes, right?" Ara's voice is barely louder than the roaring water behind, but she looks directly at me as she speaks. "Some live. Some die. It all goes in a circle. Nothing ever changes."

I shake my head no. We're more than the microbes. We have to be.

I take backward steps, shielding my ears from the sound of the roaring water. I run toward the sealed doorway to Phrame 21 as the flood of water becomes visible and rages in the corridor behind Ara.

She turns to face it.

I turn to the door behind me, slamming against it with my fist. "If anyone is there," I plead, "open the door!"

Ara takes a step toward a towering wave.

"Please!" I beg, hitting the sealed entrance to Phrame 21. "Open the door!"

I push with all my might on the door, then tumble forward into darkness. From my knees, I turn and see Leal rush next to me. Jarret and Eddi drag Desman through puddles and past the entrance by Leal and me. Freezing water drips from my hands and knees as I stand on the other side of a door that's been sealed since I was a child.

Water towers over Ara, but she continues to walk toward the wave in Phrame 22. The doorway to Phrame 22 ravels shut, swift and strong, like lightning. The Facilitators almost reach the threshold, but the door in front of me seals shut before they make it.

My eyes adjust to the dim lighting.

Where are we?

There's darkness all around except for a glow from lights that creep along the tunnel walls. The lights look like veins or something that stretch through a dim corridor.

Desman bangs on the door, but it doesn't open back up.

All goes silent.

Chapter 12: Sanctuary

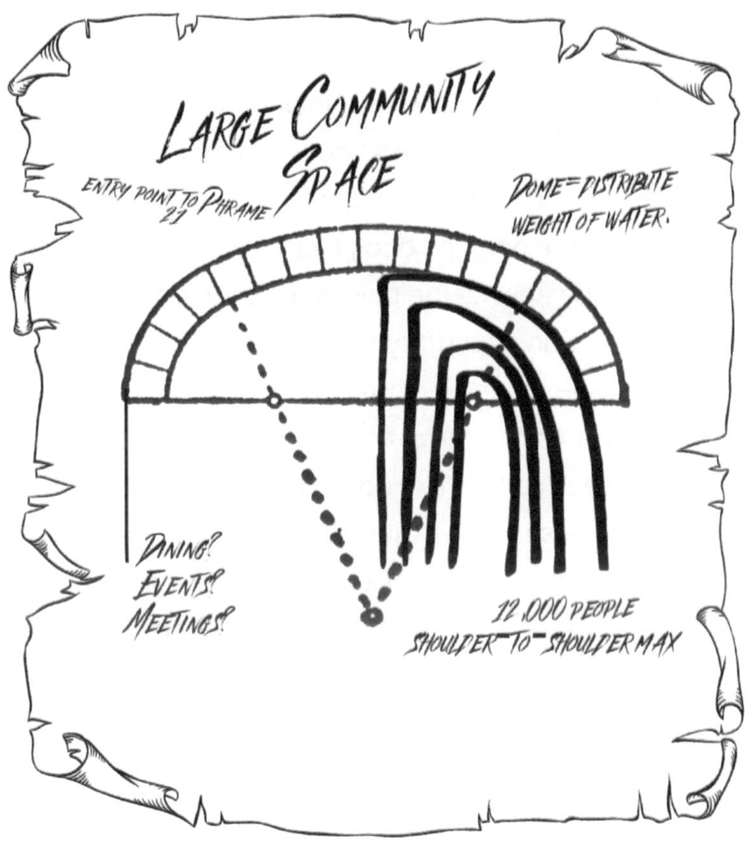

White lights stream along the corridor. The glowing trail reaches farther than I can see. How long do the lights stream? How long does the corridor go?

"Wait!" Desman's voice heaves and his fists bang against the metal doors. The sound of his lungs striving for breath is the only noise breaking the silence of the dim corridor.

"Open back up!" he begs, slamming against the door.

Eddi puts his hand over Desman's shoulder.

Desman leans from the closed door. His gaze wanders down the corridor, as if looking for answers. His breath slows. His brown eyes become almost lifeless. He shoves Eddi's arm from his shoulder and lunges toward the entrance, banging the door, kicking it, then collapsing his whole body against the raveled metallic door.

There's no sound from the other side, only the tense inhales and exhales mixed with Desman's plea. He turns, with his back leaning on the door. A tear streams down his cheek as he sinks down into a puddle of cold water. He covers his face with his hands.

Jarret kneels beside Desman, splashing his knees in the water with a flush-red face. He sticks his hand toward Desman, hesitating for a moment, then reaches his arm around his neck.

Panic rises in my stomach, but I look around, remembering that no cameras watch this moment. No one is going to come around the corner and mark them down for emotional instability. No one is going to tell them to get up. No one will tell them to stop crying and get to work.

Leal kneels to the ground on the other side of Desman, putting his arms around Desman and Jarret. The three sit on the ground. Like breathing oxygen for the first time, the pressure of being watched is released as tears roll over their necks and arms. Sniffling, crying, and sometimes wailing, the group remains in a puddle of water and grief. I want to kneel beside them. I want to comfort and be comforted. But I can't.

The three let go of each other, and gaze through the corridor as they wipe their faces. Desman breathes in, then releases a long exhale.

"Let's go," he says in a solemn tone before putting his hands on the cold, wet floor and pushing himself up.

In silence, we follow the illuminated veins of the corridor. For far too long, there are no light sources ahead and the only noise is our feet splashing in the wet corridor. My feet start to go numb with the cold of the water.

Eddi points to the end of the corridor, "I think there's light."

At first, I can't see it. Then, our footsteps splash along and there's a faint light that suggests there's an exit to the corridor. Getting closer, the dim light reflects off the edge of the tunnel end like a silver lining on the corridor exit. Still, there's no noise except our footsteps moving through the water.

Then I hear murmurs. I can't see anything through the tunnel exit, but there are people ahead. How did people get here? Are these survivors of the accident? Is my mother here?

My heart pounds as we get closer to the exit. Silhouettes stand like shadows peering at us in the corridor. The figures are more defined as I reach the threshold and the shadows turn to people murmuring among themselves and staring at us.

A teenager with straight, brown hair stands in the crowd. I recognize her.

"Wait," I whisper. "You're her." I step toward the girl with brown hair and the gaze of the crowd locks on me.

The girl takes a small step backward, tugging a young boy's shoulder along with her.

"I—" the girl hesitates and looks around the crowd, tensing her shoulders toward her ears. "I don't know you."

"You were out there," I say. She's the girl who disappeared in the security footage.

"I don't—" she stutters.

"I'm sure of it," I interrupt her. "You were in the corridor."

"You were where?" a fierce voice shouts from behind and the crowd parts as a woman steps forward. With red hair and a strong figure, each step the woman takes forward is filled with power and purpose.

"Young lady—" The woman scolds the girl.

The woman's powerful gaze shifts from the teenage girl and toward our company. "Eddi?" The fire leaves her eyes as she tilts her head and her red hair spills over her shoulders. "Edison Fitzgerald," a smile breaks across her face as she walks toward Eddi with her arms open toward him, embracing him in a welcome fit for a returned friend.

"I can't believe it's you!" Eddi halfway exclaims and halfway laughs.

"Do you have something to do with this?" The woman releases Eddi and motions toward the ground where cold water puddles across the floor.

"Partially, I'm afraid," Eddi says.

Murmurs erupt from the crowd.

The woman looks at Eddi, as if demanding more of the story.

"I can answer anything you want to know," Eddi says, "but it will take some time."

The floor beneath seems warmer than the paths through the Trellis corridors. I look at my feet— still covered in a green suit. We follow the woman from the crowd through rows of blankets that are propped on sticks and strung across ropes. Silence hangs in the room as people lean around blanket walls to catch a glance as we walk through a maze of blankets— homes. They are homes.

Desman wears a dark green suit as he struggles to hide a limp and breathe at a normal tempo. Eddi wears a green suit. Jarret's broad shoulders seem to take up the entire space of the pathway between tents. He wears grey. There's a sour feeling in my stomach as we turn down a different row of blanket walls and more people gaze around the corners to look at us in silence. I should be wearing grey. It makes no sense, but I feel far from home. Not that I know what home is, but the only thing that's been consistent is that I wear grey— I am a Facilitator. But here, there is no Facilitator. My world— the Trellis— it's not the only one. This place must have completely different people in charge. A different way of being. If I'm not a Facilitator, what am I? What did I work so hard for?

The woman guiding us wears red. Where did her red suit come from? She stops in front of a large blanket wall. Voices sound from behind the walls. Pulling back a fold of the blanket wall, the woman reveals a large space where figures are seated in a circle.

"Vega, I've been waiting to hear—" a man speaks rapidly, but cuts himself off when he realizes that he doesn't recognize the people who stand in front of the entrance. "And who might these be?" He asks with a tone of cynicism.

"Friends," the woman replies as she enters the tent with her shoulder back and her red hair waving slightly in her high-postured sway.

"Friends?" the man questions.

I have the same question. Friends? We just met. What makes her confident that we're friends?

"Friends, Cloplin," the woman's words are curt, "and they'll be able to tell us what's going on."

"Then take a seat," the man motions to the floor where others sit in a huddled circle.

We trail behind the woman in red as she takes a seat next to another man in a red suit. The man smiles at Eddi and reaches his hand out. Eddi looks sad and grabs the man's hand, shaking it as he takes a seat.

Jarret is like a clumsy giant as his large figure slowly lowers to the ground. He crosses his legs like the others in the circle, then uncrosses them finding that his thick legs don't actually cross. He sticks his legs in front, then tries to shift around, realizing how much more space he takes than everyone else.

I turn, placing my hands over Desman's arm to help him to the ground. He jerks his arm away, lowering himself to the floor in a way to hide his pain. He grunts a little when his body finally makes it to the ground— serves him right. I sit and look around the circle. Faces of people in different colored suits look back at me. Who is in charge? Victoria Menhit was the Trellis leader who supposedly died in this accident. Should she be in a meeting of leaders? I look around at the faces and don't recognize anyone.

"I'll start," says the man in red who sits next to the woman we had followed here, "since these don't know me." He motions to Desman, Jarret, and me. "My name is Arcturo Delphino, this is my wife, Vega," he motions to the woman next to him.

Blood drains from my face. There's a silence next to me as Desman stops breathing. He has the same last name as Ara. These are her parents.

"Vega oversees systems here and I communicate for people," Arcturo continues his explanation. "Around you are delegates who communicate between the sections and facilities in the Sanctuary."

"What's the Sanctuary?" Jarret asks.

Trellis

"This," says Arcturo, "this place is the Sanctuary. We're the survivors from the disaster which was created for Phrame 21, which was stopped by Britannica Hamiltoni 15 years ago. We've been here ever since."

I can't hold in the energy electrifying my mind. I jolt forward. "Is she here?" Maybe there's hope. I look around the circle of people, half-expecting to see a familiar face.

"You're Gia," Vega says with a quiet, sweet voice, "she's not here."

The energy evaporates from my mind. Emotions battle one another inside— a sense of loss as hope drains from my heart; embarrassment that I had hoped; questions over where she is. What happened? Am I childish for hoping she is somewhere after all this time? Maybe it's possible— an entire society survived here, so maybe she could be here.

"We don't exactly know where she is," says Vega.

"Gia," Arcturo's deep, soft voice soothes me, "I know you have a lot of questions."

I fight back tears. It's like he sees the struggle going on in me.

"We will find the answers," he continues, "I promise we will. But right now, we have to sort out what's happening."

He doesn't tell me to be stronger. He doesn't force me to drown my emotions and demand that I find solutions. He doesn't say that *I* need to do anything. He says *we*— we will find the answers.

"I'm Cloplin," says the man who was speaking when we arrived, "and I'm the conversation moderator. Now that introductions are in order, we're interested to know what events have brought you all here."

"Well we are happy to—" Eddi begins to speak.

"Ep— apologies," Cloplin cuts him off, "I wasn't quite finished. Not everyone in this assembly is fully informed on the recent events of the Sanctuary. We were patiently waiting for Vega to give an overview, then we were to make proposals about how to move forward. Further, it would be best for you all to hear what's been going on so that you can know what information is helpful for the assembly to know. I won't have us tarry on frivolous narratives when decisions are to be made."

"Agreed," Eddi responds, "Vega, I'm interested to know what's been going on from this side of the Trellis."

"There's water leaking from the outside!" a voice shouts from the group.

"Some of the kids in our section are sick!" another voice shouts.

The group erupts with shouting voices.

"We need to send someone outside to figure out where the leak is coming from!"

"We can't just send people outside, idiot."

"We need more resources to—"

"My section still needs more space; the one next to ours has—"

"Silence!" Cloplin's voice rings above the others. "We will go through this in an orderly fashion. Vega, share recent events, Edison, you will share the events on the outside, then we will raise up to five propositions on where to go from there."

Cloplin called Eddi by his actual name. I don't think we introduced ourselves. Do they all know each other?

"Thank you, Cloplin," Vega says, calm and unconcerned with the man's rude tone. "All of you know we had a blockage to the siphon a while back which restricted our water and food supply."

"Restricted," a man from the group mumbles in a sarcastic tone.

Vega shoots her eyes toward the man, locking her stare on his shrinking figure.

"It's just," the man's voice quivers slightly, "people in my faction almost starved."

Vega doesn't lift her gaze.

The man shifts, seeming uncomfortable, not knowing how to respond.

"Anything else?"

"No," the man's gaze is at the floor like a scolded boy.

Vega has the attention of the room. All minds hang on her words. "The siphon was blocked from the outside, and I struggled to investigate ways to fix the problem. I sent messages to my outside contacts— Eddi, who you see before you. I'd like you all to show respect and hospitality because this man and his wife risked their lives daily to keep resources coming to us."

Vega shoots her glare to Cloplin. She pauses. Cloplin looks at Eddi, then at Vega. He seems a bit softer, maybe humbled. Vega then turns her gaze to speak to the entire room.

"The same goes for Garridon Hamiltoni, whose daughter is with us today," Vega motions at me.

Eyes turn toward me. I'm suddenly aware of how I'm sitting, uncomfortably hunched on the ground, shifting slightly as if I could shake the stare off me. But maybe more uncomfortable, the role of my father. He was in communication with the Sanctuary? How does he know about this place?"

"This is Gia," Vega continues, "I'm assuming those in this company will have time to explain their role in all of this and how they all came here. For now, know that those with us have been trustworthy friends who may be able to offer aid to our situation. More recently, I have been unsuccessful in communicating with the outside. I'm sure Eddi will be able to inform us what happened from his perspective. On our side, we were unable to contact the outside, and, thus, unable to find the block in our siphon. After a few days passed, the siphon seemed to unblock itself. We don't exactly know how this happened— I have some theories, which are still under investigation."

People in the circle move and fidget increasingly as the explanation draws on. It seems uneasy, like there are inward protests to Vega's account which the assembly members withhold. Vega scans the room with a strong gaze.

Trellis

"Recently," Vega continues, "water began leaking into various parts of the Sanctuary. This is obviously very concerning as we don't know the systematic implications of water coming from the physical structure where we live. At first, the leak was isolated to one section. More places have started to leak, but water came trickling in from the tunnel which leads to the exit to Phrame 21. That was shortly before you five came through the corridor."

The space fills with surprised expressions. Maybe even some muted gasps.

"That's where I will end my explanation," Vega says, "and ask you, Eddi, to explain what you know."

"It's interesting to hear that information," Eddi says with his arms crossed and face toward the floor. "Interesting because I never got your communication attempts, Vega." Seeming to come out of some deep thought, he unravels his arms and looks up at the group. "I never got the comms. But I know that your mother, Norma, was detained not too long back for some attempt to sabotage the Trellis system. She's harmless, I knew she wouldn't be attempting to break any systems. She also never kept her own stuff to herself."

Vega chuckles at hearing this, placing her hand delicately over her mouth.

"You know how she can be," Eddi continues. "She was always ranting about the Alaster ship and her family who were communicating with her from the dead. I didn't doubt that some form of communication was getting to her, but I couldn't investigate in case it was flagged as suspicious by computer algorithms. I couldn't put my family at risk, especially when so few on the outside are capable of receiving communication from the Sanctuary."

"Vega," Cloplin interrupts with a straight posture, "do you know who would have been trying to get ahold of your mother?"

Vega and Arcturo look at one another.

"Lyra, maybe," Vega responds. "She's tried contacting my mother in the past, I think she was ultimately trying to get in touch with her sister."

Lyra— that's the girl from the crowd. The girl who disappeared. She must be Ara's sister. I feel like I have a piece of the puzzle to explain— they don't know she was outside the Trellis. At the same time, I sense that might be one of Vega's "theories" that she is withholding for a purpose.

"Any chance Lyra got in contact with your mother?" Cloplin questions.

I look to Leal who turns back at me. I think he senses it too— there's a reason Vega isn't offering the possibility that Lyra had something to do with this.

"Lyra has tried in the past," Arcturo says, "but Norma could never understand morse code and would never respond. Norma would have just seen blinking lights every now and again. She may not have ever known why."

"That's why," Leal whispers.

"You have something to add?" Cloplin asks.

"Uhhh—" Leal stutters, "n-no, no sir. I just noticed that Norma had conspiracy theories about blinking lights and people trying to communicate with her."

"Is that all then?" Cloplin pushes.

"Yes," Leal says, looking to his father as if to ask if he should offer any other information. "That's all."

"Good then," says Cloplin. "Edison, please continue."

"To skip the boring parts," Eddi continues his account, "there were some unusual events which lead to these two coming to my sleeping quarters." He motions to Desman and me. "From there, they warned me of an accident that was planned to take place in Phrame 22. It was supposed to be a broken turbine, which I thought I could fix. Turns out, there was nothing wrong with any turbine."

"What?" Leal's voice shoots over his father's. "The turbine wasn't broken? I was sure— what about the giant squid? It broke it— it was right there next to it— what else could have happened?"

"I'll explain that later," Eddi says with his hand out to comfort his son. "It was no accident. I knew that when it was happening, but I thought they were going to intentionally break a turbine, which I could fix. Turns out the accident never actually had to do with a turbine. They were just going to flood water in from somewhere, but I couldn't tell where. I— I couldn't stop it." Eddi's voice quivers. He chokes on his last words.

"It's okay, Eddi," Arcturo puts his arm around Eddi's shoulders.

"It's not," tears flood over Eddi's face. "It's not okay. I tried, Arcturo. I tried." There's a hush over the assembly. The only sound I hear is loud sniffling as tears pour and bubble from Eddi.

"Hey," Arcturo's calm voice soothes Eddi, "we'll work through it, okay? Let's tell the assembly what they need to know about the accident."

"That's all there is," I'm surprised to hear my own voice cut between the conversation. Eyes shoot toward me in anticipation. I feel nervous, like I'm in a spotlight, but I didn't want Eddi to have to say what he was about to say in front of everyone. I didn't want Arcturo to hear in front of everyone.

"That's all that happened," I continue. "Eddi and I tried to stop the accident, but we couldn't. We met Jarret, Leal, and Desman on the way out. The entrance to Phrame 21 opened for us as Phrame 22 flooded and the door sealed."

"It just—" for the first time in the conversation, Cloplin seems genuinely interested in what someone else has to say. "It just opened?"

"Yes," I say back. Different people in the assembly lean in toward me.

"You didn't enter in some security clearance and get it to open?" Cloplin presses.

"No," I say, "I just asked it to open."

"You asked the door?"

"Yes."

"Oh," Cloplin rolls his eyes. "One of those 'Alaster is in control and will take us to the surface someday' people."

"Alaster?" I say, taking a quick glance at Leal. He also seems surprised.

"Yes," Cloplin replies.

"The submarine?" I ask.

"If there's any other Alaster, let me know," Cloplin replies. "Maybe he knows how to get the door open."

"You mean," Leal speaks up, "no one here can open the door?"

"Except the beloved and supernatural submarine, apparently," answers Cloplin.

"How would a submarine get the door open?" Leal asks.

"You can ask one of his followers. They're the ones who talk to him," says Cloplin.

"Followers?" Leal questions.

"How?" I ask.

"On a screen," Cloplin explains, "you can try it sometime. I don't know how it works. Probably some trick of the Trellis to get into our heads— it can seem alive sometimes, the Trellis can. I don't know how the Alaster computer answers people, but I can assure you that there is a big leap in logic from words on a screen to believing in a submarine that will take us to a surface that we know isn't habitable."

It seems ironic that Cloplin was so adamant about keeping only the most important information in the discussion, and now he rambles about the absurdity of the people's beliefs. It's like he can take a break from discussing the important topics in order to prove that he only believes in facts.

"In any case," Vega breaks into the conversation, "it seems we're at the point to decide what to do next. The pressing issue remains that water is leaking from different places. We now have the information that there was a premeditated accident on the outside, which may have induced leaking in the Sanctuary. With this information, I posit that we look into possible structural causes of the leaking, and figure out how to fix it."

"Nay!" a man's voice shouts above the assembly. "We now know that the door can open. We know we can't stay here forever. I say we go figure out how to open the door."

"We've tried," says an old woman sitting on the ground behind Leal. "There's no sense in getting the door open. And if we did, would we just go back to the heads who are killing us off?"

"It's better than dying in here!" the man says back.

"Maybe we can change things outside!" an optimistic voice says. "It's worth it to get out."

The assembly erupts in arguing voices.

"We have everything we need here. Why go out there?"

"As long as it doesn't get blocked! It's getting harder and harder."

"Quiet! All!" Cloplin yells above the others. "We have two options posited: find the structural issues and try to open the door to the Trellis. They aren't necessarily mutually exclusive, although I believe the door is a waste of time. I posit that Vega and her team look into the leak and Burgy goes to open the door with whoever else wants to. Do I hear any other positions?"

There's silence.

"Are there any nays?" Cloplin asks.

Silence.

"All in favor?"

The group becomes a sea of "yeas."

"Good," Cloplin says, "then that's settled. Now, for the guests. I trust the Delphinos won't mind housing these newcomers and inquiring further for any other useful information?"

"It would be our pleasure," Arcturo says with his arm still around Eddi.

It's hard to see as we exit the assembly. And it's quiet. As my eyes strain to see what's in front of me, they also struggle to stay open. My mind is heavy. It's like a warm blanket covers my body; comforting me, but making it difficult to take each step forward.

"What's going on?" Leal whispers.

"It's nighttime," Vega says quietly as she guides us through the labyrinth of fabric walls. In a single file line, I follow closely behind Leal as he follows Eddi who walks behind Vega. She finally stops in front of a blanket tent where she pulls back the fabric and motions for us to go in. Two people are already inside, but it's too dark to see who it is. All my training for my entire life taught me to keep going; keep being aware of the environment no matter how exhausted I am. But my years of training are in tension with my body that begs me to rest.

Vega says something, but I don't understand it. Her hand grabs mine and she takes me to a pile of folded blankets. I stand in front of it, with all my logic saying to stay awake and present. She puts her hands on my shoulders.

"This is your bed," she says, helping me to the ground.

I sink slowly into the sea of comfort. Safe. I feel safe as my mind lets go and I fall asleep.

Chapter 13: Being

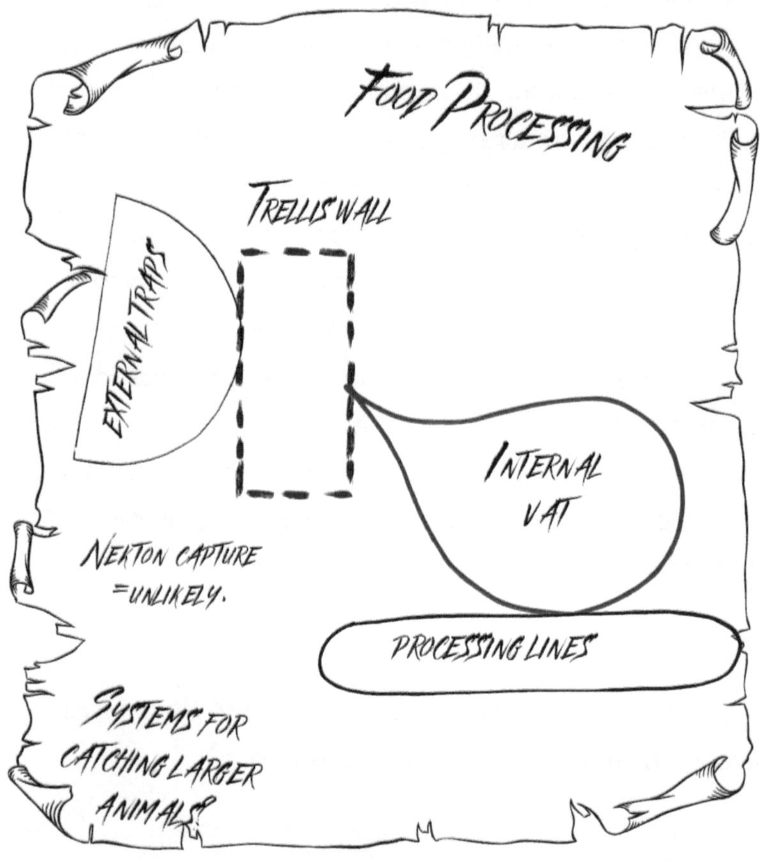

It sounds like a rush of wind as I breathe in. My eyes still closed, it seems lighter. I breathe out. Propping myself up, I open my eyes. Everything is quiet except the sounds of breaths in and out across the room made of blankets. Beside me, it's the girl from the security footage — Lyra, Arcturo and Vega's daughter. I feel my heart sink. She's Ara's sister.

I push myself up further to look across the tent-like room. Desman, Leal, and Jarret sleep in a row on the other side of the tent. Next to them is a boy. It's the one who was beside Lyra when we first entered the Sanctuary.

Am I awake early? There's a sound outside the tent. Someone must be awake already. Will there be a bell or a buzzer? Am I allowed to see what's outside the tent? How does anyone know when to get up?

I sit up on my pile of blankets, looking around. None of the sleepers stir. Outside the tent, I hear a faint voice. It sounds like crying. I stand, tiptoeing to the edge of the tent. The walls of the room are folds of fabric. My hand pushes against a fold in front of me, but it only shifts the fabric and doesn't create an opening. I feel claustrophobic. Which fold can I pull back to find the exit? How do I get out of here? With my fingers running over the fabric, I step over the piles of blankets until my hand finds the edge of the blanket wall. I sigh in relief. I've found the exit. I push between the folds of the blankets and stick my head out of the tent.

It's brighter than when we fell asleep. I can see the rows of blanket tents clearly draped on either side of a path. I hear a single sniffle. The citizens of the tent city slumber in piles of blankets— except me. There's another sniffle. Well, me and one other person. I leave the tent, walking toward the sound of the sniffle.

There's an edge to the city of blankets. The rows of tents end a few meters from the edge of the giant, domed room. Glowing vines crawl across the walls of the domed room. The vines are bright, but not too bright to look at. They illuminate the silhouette of a single figure who sits on something and stares toward the wall. I walk to the figure, who turns toward me.

"Gia—" Arcturo's voice says my name quietly before I recognize his face. "I—" he sniffles, "I didn't hear you come. I'm sorry if I woke you." He wipes his tear-soaked cheeks, but without much benefit. His face is red, glistening with tears.

"It's okay," I say, not knowing exactly what I'm supposed to do. I remember the group who sat with Desman when the doors shut and he couldn't save Ara. Maybe that's the thing to do— sit with someone. I walk to Arcturo and eyeball the long metal box where he sits. It seems stable. I take a seat next to him.

"You don't have to stay here," he says, staring at the wall.

Looking at the wall in front of us, I don't say anything. I just grip the metal box, rubbing it with my thumb. I open my mouth, as if the right words will show up, but nothing comes out.

"Gia," Arcturo sighs, "it's not your job to carry the weight of my grief."

It sounds like he's about to excuse me to leave. But it's like there's something here for me— like I can be honest, out loud, to another person.

"I'm learning," I say.

"What?" he turns toward me.

"I think," I don't know how to phrase the words, "it's like I'm learning how to be human."

"What do you mean?"

"Mabel Fitzgerald tried to hug me…" I say, "I guess you know her since you know Eddi."

Arcturo smiles, but doesn't say anything.

"It's like she reached to my memories and brought up this feeling of being held. By my mom— she must have held me because I don't know how else I'd know the feeling." I pause for a moment. How do I explain this?

"But then I remembered my dad," I finally say. "Every touch meant pain would come. I learned that I need to be able to protect myself. At the same time, I feel like I'm missing something. Like, protection is isolation. But I want to learn…"

"How to be human," Arcturo finishes my sentence. He looks at the wall before speaking again, like he's thinking about something far away. "It sounds like fear has gotten the best of Garridon Hamiltoni." Arcturo looks down as if he's found a new level of grief. "What a loss that you grew up without knowing."

"Knowing what?" I ask when he pauses.

"How much he loves you," Arcturo looks directly at me.

My mouth feels tight, like it's locking itself in case any words or cries try to come out. Is this what it is to be human? To let out the pain and not worry about what the other person does about the mess?

"He was trying to protect you," Arcturo says, "but it's a lesson on being human." His voice quakes. "The purpose of life isn't to protect ourselves from losing what we love. Sometimes we do lose— it wouldn't hurt so bad if the thing we lost wasn't so…" he takes a few breaths, trying to keep his shaking voice level. "I guess grief shows that what we had must have been truly beautiful." He puts his hand over his mouth, like he can't handle the words coming out. He heaves in and out. "And I'm grateful that her beauty is something I've had the pleasure to know."

Arcturo shields his face with his hands and weeps. One of Leal's songs comes to my mind. A melody joins the sound of Arcturo's cries. It's my own voice— I've never heard myself sing. It's scratchier and higher-pitched than Leal's voice, but it's comforting to feel the song reverberate throughout my own body:

"Can you hear it as the rain hits the ocean?
It's the sound of becoming one.
Can you smell it in the flames of the campfire?
It's the scent of your memories ignited.
Can you see it in the beauty of the stars?
It's in lessons of our ancestors.
Oh, how magnificent our stories pierce the dark,
even long after we depart."

Still crying, Arcturo puts his arm around my shoulders as if to thank me. I wrap both arms around him. He puts his other arm around me. And we cry.

There are voices coming from the tent when Arcturo leads me back to the fabric-draped space where I had slept.

"I'll go speak with Vega for a moment," Arcturo says before departing. "We'll figure out the most important… Ummm…" His words trail off, like his thoughts are in some sort of fog and he's trying to make them out.

I feel it too— worn, a sense of exhaustion I've never known. It's like my energy had escaped with every tear that left my eyes.

"Sorry," he said, trying to pull his mind from the fog, "we'll figure out the most important steps for today. I'll leave you here for now, but we'll be back shortly."

I look up at him, both of us with drained spirits reflecting in our eyes. He puts his hands on my shoulders, looking at me like he sees something precious. Then he lets go and walks down the path.

I pull back the fold of the tent and see familiar faces inside, huddled in a circle.

"Gia!" Leal exclaims with a bowl in his hands.

"You're back!" Jarret says, looking like a giant as he sits between Lyra and a young boy.

"Where were you off to?" Desman asks, with his arms crossed.

"Hi!" the boy next to Jarret yells. "I'm Pictor!"

"Hi Pictor," I give a slight wave as I lower myself to sit between Desman and Leal where there is space. "I'm Gia."

Trellis

"Hi Gia!" he yells back. "This is my sister, Lyra!"

I look at the thin girl seated next to Jarret. "Hi, Lyra." I smile.

"Hi," she says quietly, looking at the floor and tucking her hair behind her ear.

"What do you have?" I ask Leal, turning to him. I don't bother to answer Desman's question, though I feel the weight of his skeptical gaze on me.

"A mole!" Jarret answers my questions excitedly.

"A bowl!" Pictor laughs with so much power that he struggles to control his body. He places his tiny hand on Jarret's knee to stabilize himself and continues to laugh.

"Oh," Jarret chuckles at the boy, "it's a bowl."

"I can see that," I smile at the sight of the boy's enjoyment of Jarret's mistake. "What's in the bowl?"

"Wait," Jarret says, "how do you know what a bowl is?"

"I just know," I respond. I feel too tired to think of where I learned about bowls.

"Why does everyone here know what a bowl is?" Jarret throws his hands in the air.

Pictor laughs harder, slapping Jarret's knee this time.

"It's an ancient cultural artifact," Desman responds.

"Except," Lyra chuckles a bit, "not ancient."

Desman straightens his posture and seems to fold his arms even tighter.

Lyra's chuckle evaporates instantly.

"So," I say, "what's in the bowl?"

"Food!" replies Pictor. "And Leal is going to try it first." He giggles more.

"Pictor," Lyra says, "be polite."

"I can't," Pictor stretches his whole body over Jarret's lap, "he's never had food before!"

"Correction," Leal says, "I've never had *this* food before."

"Eat it! Eat it! Eat it!" Pictor yells.

Leal puts the bowl to his mouth and tips it back to eat some of the food. Leal spits back with so much force it surprises him.

"What is that?" Leal exclaims.

Pictor bursts back into a fit of laughter.

"It's food," Lyra responds. "And you can't waste it."

"What is this food made of?" Desman asks.

"Same thing as your food is made of," Lyra says back.

We all look at each other.

"Uhhhh—" Jarret rubs Pictor's side to try and calm the boy down as he remains stretched across Jarret's lap in a whirlwind of uncontrollable giggles. "What is our food made of?"

"Sea creatures," Leal responds. "But puréed into a fine liquid."

"Then coated in a shell made of a seaweed and algae blend," Lyra finishes the explanation. "I've been told your food is served in a ball. I haven't seen one or eaten one, but I've replicated the shell in my lab."

"Your lab?" Leal questions.

"Then what is this, exactly?" Desman cuts off Leal's question and eyes the bowl.

"Your food is made in stages in an assembly," Lyra says. "Machines on the outside catch sea animals. People in the Trellis cut up the pieces that are edible and put them in a large vat with water. The vat leads to a machine that blends it all and coats portions of the liquid to make the food pods. This here," she pulls out a bucket from behind her, "is our food. It's siphoned from the vat of your food which has chunks of sea animals and water. More importantly, it grows bacteria quite quickly after leaving the siphon and mixing with the air. This means we need to eat it before it goes bad, or we'll get sick. And we need to eat it all. We each get a bowl full."

Leal looks at the bowl in his hands, turning pale at the thought of eating it. He takes a deep breath, then puts the bowl to his mouth. In one gulp he takes in the entire contents, then lowers the bowl and chews with his cheeks bloating full of food. His eyes water. Involuntary sounds come from his throat— like gagging. Finally swallowing, he lets out a breath with his arms limp at his side as if the escapade stole every ounce of power in his body.

Pictor points at Leal, giggling quietly. Lyra smiles slightly as she puts the bucket in the middle of the circle.

"Who's next?" she asks.

Desman takes the bowl from Leal, dips it in the bucket, and puts the bowl to his mouth. Taking a solid gulp, he tries to hold back his disgust, not lowering his posture for a second. But his whole face scrunches as he chews the food, then swallows— maybe prematurely because he coughs and hits his chest with his fists like he's trying to get a piece down. Finally swallowing it all, he tosses the bowl in my lap.

Leaning over the bucket, I see different colored pieces floating in a blackish liquid.

"Why isn't the liquid clear?" I ask. "Water should be clear."

Lyra shrugs. "Just from blood or ink from different animal pieces, I guess."

Dipping the bowl into the bucket, I pull out a serving of the chunky liquid. It's cold in my hands. I close my eyes, as if it will help, and pour the cold food into my mouth. I chew— but it doesn't disintegrate like the sustenance packets would. I feel like throwing up as the sharp, oily flavor hits the back of my throat. I chew more. Again and again, I chomp down on the meaty, squishy pieces in the food. It gets warm by the time it's all blended together in my mouth. I finally swallow, but it's like my mouth is still coated in an oily, fish taste. I force my limp arm to hand the bowl to Jarret.

Pictor watches Jarret closely as he takes the food. Maybe Jarret learned from watching us not to take the whole serving at one time. He sips in a small portion of the food and chews it.

"That's terrible," Jarret says with his mouth full.

Pictor cracks up.

"And it's cold," Jarret smiles at Pictor, who laughs even harder. Jarret eats the rest of the serving with less difficulty than the rest of us. He hands the bowl to Lyra, who eats a portion without much effort.

"Finally!" Pictor says enthusiastically when Lyra hands him the bowl. "I'm starving!" He refuses the bowl and aggressively picks up the entire bucket. Then he gulps the rest of the food from the bucket.

"Lyra," a voice says from outside the tent. Vega's head peers through the folds of the blankets. "Lyra, we have something important to talk to you about."

Lyra puts her head down. Pictor looks at her sympathetically.

"You're not in trouble," Vega says. "Although we will be discussing what you've been up to lately, that's not what we need to talk about now."

"Okay?" Lyra sounds confused as she stands.

"What should we do, mom?" Pictor asks with full energy.

"You," Vega smiles at the boy, "I'd like you to show our new friends around."

"Okay!" Pictor yells back. He grabs Jarret's large arm with both of his hands. "We're going to have so much fun."

A high pitched-sound breaks through the atmosphere around the blanket tents. The sound continues as Pictor skips through the maze of homes while pulling Jarret along by his hand.

"What is that?" I yell toward the front of our single file line at Pictor.

"Where did it come from?" Desman sounds cautious.

"It's a whi—" Pictor yells back, but I can't hear his entire sentence as he faces ahead with Jarret, Desman, and Leal between us.

"A what?" I say back.

"A whistle," Leal turns his head and says to me.

"For what?" Desman asks.

"What do you mean 'for what?'" Leal asks.

"What does it do? Is it like a drill or something?" Desman is curt.

"You'll see," Pictor turns his head back to answer Desman, "when we reach the court."

"What's the court?" Desman inquires.

"It's a designated open area," Pictor says, "for activities!"

"As in," questions Desman, "activities for training or education?"

"No," Pictor yells loudly, not slowing his skip or releasing Jarret's hand. "It's just for fun."

A clear melody sings over the tents as we get closer to the court. A deep, smooth voice runs over the Sanctuary:

Trellis

"My memory is like a daydream,
my friend."
Arriving at the court, I look around the edge of the
tent city and try to find the voice as it sings another line:
"Coming back where I've been,
once again."
Adults and children are scattered across the
circular opening among the city of tents. The voice
continues to sing:
"I travel by the morning light,
longing for those I once held tight."
A smile stretches across Leal's face as the figure
becomes clear. Eddi shifts through the small crowd,
singing directly to his son:
"Until I'm home with you."
With a broad smile, Leal opens his mouth and
sings the next line:
"Never forget us, though you journey far beyond
our home."
The melody continues as Eddi's line interrupts
Leal's:
"How could I forget my only hope?"
Pictor grabs both of Jarret's hands and swings
them back and forth.
Leal continues with the next line: "Reminisce of the
times we sang at dinner time."
Eddi sings a line: "I remember the times we
danced all night."

People in the crowd pair up and hold one another as Leal and Eddi sing the next verse together:

"Remember, we laughed and sang beneath the tree.

Remember, what it was like to be family.

Now apart I truly know,

the reason you need roots to grow."

A small girl tugs at my wrist, offering her other hand as if asking to dance. I clasp her hands and sway back and forth. Her brown eyes looking up at me, I feel a sense of joy. Like I'm smiling from the inside.

Leal sings his next line: "Come, and I'll splash you with the cold water from our stream."

Eddi sings his line: "Soon, and I'll push you on our tire swing."

The room swirls and sways with dancers as Leal and Eddi sing in unison:

"Summer evenings and Autumn walks in the park

Winter home and Spring with a brand new start.

Let's dance and let's sing at the change in weather.

Let's hope and let's pray that we'll soon be together."

The crowd unleashes applause as Eddi and Leal end their song.

Laughing, Eddi puts one arm around Leal.

"My son," Eddi beams proudly at Leal and wraps his other arm around him.

Gazing across the crowd of smiles and laughs, tears well in my eyes. It's as if I'm seeing some glimpse of what humans were meant to be. Up on the surface, before the Trellis, before social groups, it's like a shadow of what we could be.

But I feel like I'm pulled back underwater as I notice a girl walking through one of the pathways toward us. Her shoulders hunched, she sticks to the side of the court.

"Hey, Lyra!" Pictor waves at the girl, recognizing that it's his sister. "We're singing! Come sing us that song about all the animals and flowers in the forest!"

Lyra doesn't look at him. She remains near the court edge with her focus on an exit pathway.

"Pfff," Pictor says to Jarret, "Girls— one minute they're eating breakfast with you, the next they're running away from you."

I keep my eyes on Lyra as she exits the court at one of the pathways. I wonder what happened. I wonder where she's going with so much urgency.

"Hey, Leal," I say quietly.

"Yeah?" he responds, laughing as he releases from his dad.

"I'll be right back," I say, "but don't wait up for me."

Chapter 14: Alaster

I nearly lose sight of Lyra as I follow her to an edge of the Sanctuary where I can see the wall of the domed room. She's just out of sight, but I see her slip through an archway. It must have been a corridor that connected to this phrame long ago. My footsteps don't make a sound since they are padded with the bottom of my green suit. I walk toward the archway to find a tunnel lined with the vine-like lights. Lyra's silhouette just barely slips beyond my sight as I walk through the tunnel.

Trellis

Reaching the end of the tunnel, there's a closed door— not one of the raveled doorways like those around the Trellis. It looks like it's made of panels of metal. As I approach, it opens upward into the ceiling and reveals a world I've never seen. A huge expanse of space as I walk through the threshold, it looks like I'm at the base of a massive, metal sphere. To my right side is a vast, curved wall. Along my left side is a system of ladders and hanging platforms that lead to closed doors beyond number. Maybe the most surprising thing is a huge circle that hangs far above my head. A bridge leads to the circular platform that looks like it could be some sort of control center. Is there a way up there? I scan the left side and see steps that lead to the first raised platform where the system of metal scaffolding begins. A creak and small crash sounds from somewhere along the platform. I walk up the steps and along the metal scaffolding, looking through the doors and halls which connect to the platform where I walk.

One of the doors is open— I peek into it. The large room is filled with metal instruments, containers of liquids, devices with wires sticking out, and misshaped objects I've never seen. I take a step into the room. Lyra sits in a chair with her hands covering her face like a tiny creature in a nest of metal and wire.

"Hi," I say quietly.

She looks up at me, the dim light reflecting off her pale cheeks. Her light blue eyes glimmer. She sniffles, wipes her face, and straightens in her chair.

"Hi," she says back.

"What's going on?" I ask.

"It's nothing," she says back with a soft tone.

I look at her. She must have heard the news about Ara. She clearly doesn't want to talk about it. I don't feel equipped to bring it up. What am I supposed to do in this situation?

"What's all this?" I ask after a long pause.

"It's my lab," she answers.

Silence hangs in the room. We don't have anything to talk about. Do I leave? Do I keep asking questions?

"What—" I start forming a question to end the silence, but I have so many that I don't know which to ask. "What do you do in here?"

"I make things," she says. "And learn things. Answer questions."

"Like what sort of questions?" I ask.

"Like, what things are made of," she responds. "Why things are the way they are. Where we came from. Where we're going, maybe."

I don't know what more to say. She shifts in her chair and shuffles objects in front of her.

"This is chlorine," she says, picking up a glass container with liquid in it.

"It looks like water."

"It's not. You wouldn't want to drink it. I'm pretty sure it could kill someone."

"How would someone know the difference?" I ask. I feel concerned. What if someone drank it by accident?

Trellis

She pulls off the lid on the glass container and pushes it toward me.

I jerk back, trying to control my instinct to fight.

"Smell it," she says, holding it toward me.

There's a sense of vulnerability. I'm used to defending myself from things that I can see. It feels like I have no control, like some invisible enemy could get inside me as I lean toward the container. I jerk back again the moment the strong smell reaches my nostrils. I cough, trying not to be dramatic, but like I can somehow get rid of invisible death creatures that got in my body from sniffing the liquid.

"It's perfectly fine," Lyra says, pulling it back toward her. "I'm around it all the time and it hasn't hurt me. I've read a lot about it and it should be harmless as long as no one drinks it. But I don't think anyone would mistake this for water."

"You've read about it?"

"Yeah," Lyra puts the lid back on the chlorine container and picks up an electronic tablet. I notice a few trowels scattered across her desk where she picks up the tablet. Where did she get these? Does she know what they do?

"I read from the same information as you do," she says, handing me the tablet. "Except I stick to the original sources."

"Original sources?" I question. "What is that supposed to mean?"

"Things written on the surface," she explains. "The scientist who made the Trellis, she kept a journal of the things happening before she got down here. More importantly, she made notes on how she made everything: the Trellis, the lights, the doors— everything. From the chemical materials to the machinery, it's all in there."

I look at the tablet and skim through the information on the screen. I always knew these notes were accessible from the tablets, I knew about the head scientist on the Trellis project— we learned about it in educational training. I've read these journal entries before...well... at least I skimmed them once... I think. But everything we needed to know about the journal entries was in our educational trainings. Or at least I thought so.

"Did you learn how to make this liquid from these journal notes?" I ask, my eyes still on the screen.

"Yes," Lyra replies, "it's made from brine, we have a lot of that available here."

"Why?"

"Why is brine available?" Lyra seems confused.

"No," I say, "why did you make the liquid?"

"Oh," Lyra says, "the lead scientist— her name was Symphony— she said it might be a sustainable solution for killing off bacteria that makes people sick in the underwater facilities." Lyra shuffles around the shelves. She grabs a glowing, blue container and a small glass dish.

Did she say *facilities*? As in, there is more than one facility?

Trellis

"This is what your lights are made of," Lyra says, holding up the glowing container. She takes the lid from the container and pours the glowing, blue liquid into the small dish. It looks like a magic potion.

"Ah—" I yell, covering my nose. "It stinks!"

"Yeah, it must be a thing you get used to."

"Are you used to it?"

"No," Lyra smiles at the dish. "You must. You all smelled faintly like this when you showed up in the Sanctuary."

I feel a little embarrassed. We smelled like that? Maybe we don't smell it as strongly since the lights are always contained in the ceiling.

"Watch," Lyra picks up the container of chlorine from her desk. "The lights are made of bacteria, just like some things that make us sick are made of bacteria." She pours the chlorine into the glowing, blue dish. Rapidly, the glowing blue dissipates and turns into a transparent liquid. "The chlorine kills all the bacteria. If I can figure out how to make the chlorine safe, it might be able to save a lot of people from getting sick."

"Is that a big problem?" I ask.

"Is what a problem?"

"People getting sick. Do people get sick a lot?"

"Oh, yes," Lyra seems surprised that I asked the question. "Yes, it's a problem."

There's silence hanging over the room of containers, wires, and gizmos. I sense there are many mysteries Lyra wants to solve and I might be able to provide information. But I also have so many unanswered questions, I don't even know where to start. We both remain in the quiet of the cluttered lab.

"I was wondering—"

"So do you—"

We both start speaking at the same time to break the silence.

"You go first," says Lyra.

"No," I say, "I've been asking a lot of questions."

She waits for a moment to make sure it's okay to start asking her question.

"I mentioned the lead scientist on the Trellis project," Lyra looks in the corner of the floor as she speaks. "Her name was Symphony."

"Yes?" I question as she pauses.

"Symphony Hamiltoni," Lyra looks up at me.

I don't know what she is trying to imply.

"It's a long shot," she shakes her head.

"What is?"

"There's this box," Lyra explains. "A locked box."

"I don't know anything about a box," I say.

"I know. I don't expect you to. I'm wondering if you can open it."

"How am I supposed to—" I don't want to disappoint her, but I don't know how I could open it. "I don't have any sort of key, or code, or anything."

"I know," Lyra sighs, "it's a long shot, but I've been waiting so long."

"For what?"

Trellis

"I found the box when I was exploring the Alaster submarine," she explains. "Years ago, and I've always wanted to know what's inside. The lock isn't like anything I've seen. After reading through the journal notes, I think the box is triggered somehow by DNA."

She pauses, like she's embarrassed about what she's about to ask. But the desperation to know the answers is more than enough to overcome the embarrassment.

"Will you," she pauses again. "Will you try to open it? I know it isn't likely to work, after all this time, but maybe you will have enough of the DNA sequence to open the box."

I don't say anything. Is this lock anything like the door to my father's office?

She sighs and drops her head a bit.

"Show me the box," I say.

From beneath her desk, Lyra pulls up a rectangular container, thick and heavy. It looks like a hefty box that could be covered in vines, but a dark, matte skin covers the vines. It's like there are veins beneath a metal skin. Is it living somehow?

"I think it's made from the same thing as the doors in the Trellis," Lyra says.

"What do you mean?"

"I mean that Symphony Hamiltoni used the same technology to lock this box as what she used to open and close doors."

"I understand that," I say. "I mean, what are the doors made of?"

"Oh," says Lyra. "Something that's alive, but also not."

"Like a plant?" I stare at the box which Lyra places on the desk.

"Almost," she rubs her hand on the box. "It's some sort of organism, but it's also sort of like a machine."

"How does that work?"

"I'm not totally sure," she says. "The journal notes talk about the different experiments she used to make the material. On the exterior, she used something she called squami. When I looked into it more, it seemed like she used an animal called Chrysomallon squamiferum, which is also called a scaly-foot sea snail. Symphony Hamiltoni replicated this deep sea snail, then mixed the genetics with different plants so that the organism would grow on its own to certain sizes and shapes."

"So this box and the doors in the Trellis are made of a sea snail and plants?"

"I guess, but it doesn't totally end there. She chose the genetics of certain plants and organisms that would respond to stimulus. So the doors would open when they sensed movement, just like a Venus fly trap might have closed when it was triggered by an insect."

"What's a Venus fly trap?"

"Doesn't matter," Lyra isn't annoyed or curt, but she seems very involved in her explanation and almost like she can't slow down until she's explained it all. She reminds me of Leal when he's discovered something he's excited about and needs to say everything he knows. "The doors all respond to certain stimuli, and they grow— like something living— but they are comprised mostly of metals. Able to withstand heat and pressure, the material she made is like an organism, but also a machine."

"It is dangerous?" I've never thought about the things I live with being actually alive. Maybe they could develop their own ideas and become malicious.

"Not in the way you might think," Lyra says. "There are parameters on their genetics, and the things grow by themselves, but can't reproduce."

"What do you mean, parameters?"

"I mean, she engineered each thing so that it could only grow to a certain size and be used for a certain purpose. It can't physically go outside of that. And they can't breed or make more of themselves, so there isn't a chance of them changing genetically. Also, they don't have brains, not even simple ones. So they can't do anything outside of what they are programmed to do. In that sense, they are like computers."

That's the word Eddi used in the Trellis. What exactly is a computer? I guess that doesn't really matter.

"What might make them dangerous?" I ask.

"People," she says. "If a different person knew how to use the same technology, they could change the purpose of the technology and use it for something different."

"Like what?"

"I don't know," Lyra stops and contemplates. "This thing is like a shield, not a weapon. So it's not directly malicious, but all good technology can be used for something bad. I think the more puzzling thing is that the doors can be controlled by technology as well as movement."

"Right, like with the trowels."

"Exactly," Lyra seems excited that I was following her train of thought. "You can send a command to electronically open the door if you have a trowel connected to it."

"Is that how you opened the door to Phrame 21 and left the Sanctuary?"

Lyra's eyes widen and then shoot toward the floor.

"It's okay," I say. "I don't want you to get in trouble, I just want to know what happened. How did you leave… and why?"

Lyra remains silent for a moment, staring at the floor.

"We've been trying to open that door for years," she finally says. "We've tried everything. That's why I learned so much about the doors— to try and get that one open. Nothing worked— trowels, chemicals, brute force."

"How did you finally get it open?"

"I asked," she looks up at me.

"Who?"

"Alaster."

"The submarine?" I don't mean to sound so surprised, but she's telling me she talks with a 300-year-old submarine.

"I can show you," Lyra defends herself. "But can we first try to open this box?"

"Oh," I had completely forgotten about the object Lyra now squeezes with her left hand. "Of course."

There's a small opening on the matte, grey box. I put my thumb on the opening. Nothing happens, but I keep my thumb there, remembering what had happened with the door to my father's office.

There's a creak. Then one of the veins beneath the grey skin of the box twitches. Under the metal skin, one vein slinks back. Then another. Each vein twitches, then creeps across the surface of the box, slowly. Lyra's eyes are glued to the object. Surprise? Excitement? Shock? I can't tell what emotion her eyes portray as the box finally moves after years of trying to open it. The veins stop moving, but nothing happens.

"What next?" I ask, removing my thumb from the box.

She puts both hands on the lid of the box and lifts. It opens. It's like a thousand years of questions could break open with the cracking of the lid. I feel like some golden beam should be emitting from the box to bestow us with the knowledge of the universe. But there's nothing. I can't see anything coming from the crack in the lid. Lyra lifts the lid open entirely. There's no light, nothing magical except some plain objects. Plain things from ancient times that I've never seen in person.

Lyra's hands shake as she opens the box and retrieves the thing that caught her attention— a journal. A journal made from paper. Not a screen, not something electronic, but a physical object with physical writing. She opens the journal.

"It's hers," a tear streams down Lyra's face. She wipes it quickly and aggressively. "It's Symphony Hamiltoni's journal. Physically!"

I reach into the box to retrieve the other objects— A shirt, shoes, and two photos. Both photos are of families. The first has a man with wispy, white hair. The smiling man holds a toddler with curly, silver hair and bright, green-blue eyes. The toddler looks like a mythical creature with her light coloring. The man also has his arm around a woman with reddish-brown, curly hair and deep, green eyes. In the second photo— it might be the toddler when she had grown up— there is a woman with curly, silver hair who holds a baby with dark brown hair. The woman and baby are cradled by a man who also has brown hair.

I hand the photos to Lyra, who studies them before she tucks them inside the journal. I pull the shirt from the box and let it unfold to show an image on the front. The image is of kittens— fantasy kittens, some of them flying and some with red beams coming from their eyes. I slip the shirt over my green suit and look down at the image. A flicker of joy grows in my stomach and I let out a little chuckle.

Lyra looks at me with the open notebook in her hand.

"Kittens with laser vision?" she tilts her head.

"Laser kittens," I giggle at the shirt. "I didn't know cats had lasers."

"They didn't," Lyra says, matter-of-fact.

"They might have."

"They didn't."

"How do you know?" I ask.

"How could any animal have that?" she argues.

"I don't know," I say. "But I also didn't think an entire society could be living under my nose as I was a Facilitator in the Trellis."

Lyra murmurs and looks back at the journal. "Cats didn't have lasers."

I roll my eyes and pull the shoes from the box. Black with white laces, I put them over the foot padding on my red suit. Pulling the laces tight, the white strings fall to the side and drape loosely over the shoe.

"Is this how these are supposed to work?" I ask.

"I don't know," Lyra sounds short. "Why are you putting this stuff on?"

"I'm just trying it," I say. "These are what they're for, right?"

"They should be studied," she says. "These are artifacts. They could tell us about life on the surface."

"Well," I say, "it shows us your scientist friend had a sense of humor."

"What makes you say that?"

"Look at this shirt!" I pull the shirt bottom to spread the image. "This is ridiculous."

"It was probably a style," Lyra says.

"Have you seen pictures of anyone wearing anything like this?"

"I'm sure there was a logical reason," Lyra seems offended. "Symphony Hamiltoni was a genius. A professional. She took things seriously. Maybe that was someone else's shirt."

I smirk, but don't say anything else as I look back into the box. There's nothing else. I run my hand all around the edges and bottom of the box to make sure nothing is hidden. How could that be it? After 300 years of being stowed away, why are these the things that we find? Why are they important?

"Are you ready?" Lyra places the photos inside the journal and closes the cover.

"For what?"

"To meet Alaster."

I breathe heavily, following Lyra up the system of ladders in the massive area that's shaped like a sphere. We walk across platforms, past doors and openings to walkways, and climb up ladders to reach even more platforms.

Trellis

"We're almost there," reaching the top of a ladder, Lyra puts her hand on the metal railing.

Her body is so thin and frail, I wonder how difficult it must be for her to climb these ladders. I've physically trained all my life, and it's a bit of effort, even for me— it must be so much worse for her. Lyra's straight hair falls over a red suit. It makes me wonder where they get suits and how they choose colors. Her face looks a bit like Ara's, but thinner. Her body is also less full than Ara's, but maybe it's because she's young. I remember Ara being quite thin during our training days. But her hair was always thick, wavy, and red. Lyra's hair is brown-grey and completely straight. Though Ara's eyes were green and Lyra's are blue, they seem similar. Their eyes aren't particularly brightly colored, like the girl in the photo we found, but there is something striking about them. Like they hold worlds of beauty and wonder. Ara's beauty was always on the surface— like her beauty was an alluring fragrance that was picked up by everyone. But Lyra's seems more hidden— like her beauty is a secret locked in a grey box that can withstand any amount of heat or pressure from a person who isn't meant to open it.

"It's this one," Lyra says as we reach a final platform. It's the one that connects to the platform in the center of the room that looks like a control station.

There's a walkway, like a bridge, from our platforms to the circular one hanging in the center of the room. Lyra walks effortlessly over the bridge. I reach the bridge and look over the edge. It's higher than I've ever seen. Who knew a person could get up this high? I've never been off the ground in my life. I look at my hand. It trembles. I grab the metal railing on either side.

"It's safe," Lyra says, looking back at me. "You can't really fall off unless you try."

"Is it stable?" I ask, with my eyes locked on the walkway in front of me.

"Yeah," says Lyra, "just take it one step at a time. One foot in front of the other."

I try to pick up my foot. I can't get it to move.

"Mind over matter," Lyra walks up to me, "it's what my dad always says. He gets scared too."

"I'm—" I say, trembling, "I'm not scared."

"Have you ever been scared before?" Lyra asks.

I think about my father. All the trainings. The time when I asked questions and he beat it out of me. I was scared then. I wanted to hide, to protect myself. This is entirely different. My body is going limp, not getting tense.

"Yes," I say.

"What do you usually do when you're scared?"

"I fight whoever I need to."

"What if there is no one to fight?"

"What?" I look up at Lyra, still gripping the railing.

"What if the thing you're afraid of isn't a person?" she asks. "Then there's no one to fight."

"There's always someone to fight when you're scared."

"Maybe this is a different kind of scared," Lyra says. "You're not afraid of a person, but a thing."

"What do I do?" I ask, trembling.

"Well, what do you want to do?"

"I don't know! I'm following you."

"Why?"

"What do you mean why?" the railing starts to get warm as I squeeze it.

"I mean, why?" Lyra isn't yelling, but this is the loudest I've heard her speak. "You followed me here. Why?"

I don't say anything.

"It's okay," Lyra says, "we can turn around."

"No!" I say.

"Gia," she says, "you clearly don't want to do this, you don't have to."

"Yes, I do!"

"Why?"

"I want to know," I say.

"Know what?"

"Answers." The railing gets wet in my hands as my sweat pours over it. I feel like I could slip. "I want to know why you were in the Trellis and disappeared. I want to know what's going on in the Trellis. I want to know how the Sanctuary got here and what Gaines Cyro did with Victoria Menhit. I want to know what the Alaster submarine has to do with all of this. I want to know what happened to my mom."

Hot breath leaves my mouth with each word I manage to get out. My eyes remain fixed on the walkway.

"And being here will help you know the answers?" Lyra asks.

"I want to meet Alaster," I can't think of another response. I don't have enough foresight to know how else to answer the questions.

"Then," she says gently, with both hands draped over the rail, "come meet Alaster." She takes steps backward to keep her eyes on me as she moves over the bridge.

My heart pounding, I move one foot forward. Then the next one. I take slow steps down the walkway with both hands gripping the rail. Reaching the other side, I release a long sigh.

"Pictor would have a hay day," Lyra says.

"What do you mean?"

"He laughs every time my dad comes here because he's afraid of heights. But I've never seen anything like that."

"Like what?"

"That much fear of heights."

"Heights?"

"Yeah," says Lyra, "fear of being high-up."

"Why would I be afraid of that?" I ask, trying to release my grip on the railing.

"I don't know," she walks to the center of the circular platform. "You tell me."

There's a semi-circle control panel at the front of the platform. It has buttons and levers like I haven't seen before, and two chairs situated in front. Lyra looks behind her as she walks toward the panel.

"You can come too," she says. "Nothing bad will happen. It's perfectly safe."

I take small steps out to the center of the platform, trying not to think of how high we are raised above the ground.

"I don't see anyone," I say. "How am I going to meet Alaster?"

"You're in it," she puts her arms out wide and motions to the entire area.

"In…" I look around, "Alaster?"

"Yes."

"We're in a submarine?"

"Yes."

"If that's true," I say, feeling a bit annoyed that we've been in it the whole time and she made me walk across that walkway of terror, "and the Surfacers are correct about the earth being habitable, what stops everyone in the Sanctuary from driving away?"

"That's a great question," Lyra says. "And you can ask."

"Ask who?"

"Alaster."

"Lyra," I clench my fists, "you took me all the way — how am I supposed to—"

"Just," she motions to the empty space in front of the control panel, "ask."

I walk toward the front of the space. At least my irritation is enough to distract me from how high up we are.

"Ummmm," I start saying to the empty space. "This is stupid," I say under my breath. I feel like Norma talking to lights in her room. But, then again, Norma was right.

"Go ahead," says Lyra.

"Excuse me, Mr. Submarine," I say, "I was wondering what stops us from driving away from the Trellis?"

The metal wall before the control panel illuminates. It turns to a lighter grey or white light, almost like a screen switches on across the entire thing. I lean on the control panel and grip the edge. Words type out across the area in front of me:

"Hello, Gia."

The words erase. Then another phrase types itself across the screen:

"It's good to finally meet you."

Chapter 15: Tumultuous Seas of Questions

"How—" I gape at the words typed across the massive wall in front of me. "How is that happening? Who is typing?"

"I'm Alaster," the words type themselves across the wall.

I look at Lyra. How do I know someone isn't sitting in some room typing the words and tricking me? I've lived my entire life in a place of deceit. I don't see why it would change now.

"And," more words type, "to answer your question, I decide when we leave."

"What do you mean?" confused, I can't find any other words.

"You asked what keeps us from driving away from the Trellis," the words type. "The answer is, I decide when it's right to leave."

"Wait," Lyra seems taken aback by the answer. "When is it right to leave?"

"When everyone who wants to come is here," types Alaster.

My brain can't process the information typed across the glowing wall. I interrupt with the first question that formed when the submarine introduced itself. "How do you know my name?"

The screen flashes to show security footage of me. A section on the screen shows an image of me in the workstation. Leal sits in the chair beside me and hums. Another section shows me in training with my father drilling me. Another shows me in the questioning room with Ara.

"I see everything," the words type across the screen.

I feel vulnerable— invaded, even. I'm used to the feeling that someone might watch me on a screen, but it feels almost like someone can see something deeper. How could this person have access to all this footage and be showing it to me now? If this Alaster has control over the Trellis system, is he in charge of everything? The training programs? The lies? The accidents? I'm calling it a *him*. What even is this? What am I talking to?

"Are you in control of all this?" that's the question I manage to get out.

"In one sense, yes," the words type. "In another sense, no."

"I don't know what that's supposed to mean," I say.

"I see everything," the words say. "But I can't change everything."

"You can't change things or you won't?" I demand. "If you have the code to override security like this and see everything that happens, surely you have the capacity to stop bad things. So you're either enabling Gaines Cyro, or you're the one doing it all." I struggle to keep my voice level as anger tries to spill out.

"I see everything," Alaster repeats, "but I can only operate where people choose me."

"What does that mean?" I ask.

"If people choose to have me in a certain place, then I can be there."

A video plays across the wall. The footage shows different angles of the Sanctuary— but back when it was just Phrame 21. People shuffle around the magnificent room and are free to move between the corridors to enter and exit the phrame. There are no blankets. Just space. Then, the footage shows a woman running through a corridor with a trowel. She looks powerful and focused. She halts in front of a panel and inserts the trowel. Water trickles at her feet. I realize who it is— Britannica Hamiltoni.

It's my mom.

My heart races. I lean over the control panel, like I could talk to her and tell her to get out of the area.

A tower of water builds in the walkway. It's about to swallow her, just as the wave that took Ara.

"No!" I scream.

In the footage, my mom looks straight at me like she could hear me, but she looks away. The door to the corridor shuts as fast as lightning. The tower of water stops building upward and crashes down. Then it floods the corridor, but only up to my mom's waist. She lets out a scream as the water comes toward her, but stops when she realizes the water isn't high enough to harm or drown her.

"It's cold!" she yells. She sounds desperate.

"Go down the walkway," a voice resonates throughout the corridor. There's no other person there; just a voice.

Shivering with damp hair, she wades through the walkway.

"Turn left," says the voice.

Trellis

She's almost helpless as the freezing water steals her power. After turning left, the walkway comes to an end.

"What now?" she looks up and asks the ceiling.

"Look to the right," says the voice.

Along the right wall are pieces of piping that form something like a ladder.

"Climb those," says the voice.

As she climbs, a circle opens on the ceiling much like the doorways which unravel all over the Trellis. But this one is in the ceiling. I've never seen that. Have I seen that? I don't typically look up.

My mom pulls herself through the hole in the ceiling and it closes again.

The footage ends. The screen goes blank.

"Wait!" I cry. "What happened?"

"That was a door to a maintenance pod. She made it out." The words show across the screen. "She's with me. Safe."

"What do you mean?" I feel myself slumping to the floor. The more Alaster answers, the more questions swirl in my mind.

"You saw the trowel in your mother's hand?" Alaster asks by typing across the screen.

"Yes," I say.

"I gave it to her. It contained a code that would let me infiltrate the system in that area. That's why I have control of this area instead of Gaines Cyro."

"So where did she go?" I plead.

"There was nowhere to go except up here," Alaster says.

"Where is *up here*?"

"The surface."

Anger replaces my desperation. Is this a joke?

"You're telling me," I clench my fists, "that I'm supposed to believe my mother is on the surface? She magically got to some place that might as well be imaginary?"

Alaster types.

"Yes."

Emotions erupt inside me— anger, grief, confusion, frustration, hatred, hope. I barely even notice the clamor below and behind me as I hear frightened voices. I turn and see others crossing the bridge toward me. I take a defensive stance. Then I recognize who it is.

"Just one step at a time, son," Eddi grips both sides of the railing and says to Leal who walks behind him.

"I'm okay," Leal says with a tremble. His pace across the bridge shows he has less fear than those behind.

Pictor pulls Jarret to the bridge, whose legs visibly shake as he steps onto the metal platform suspended in the air.

"Can this thing hold this many people?" Desman shouts from the back.

"Only one way to find out!" Pictor giggles.

"He's kidding," Lyra shouts. "It's meant to hold a lot of weight."

"But," Jarret quivers, "I mean, this has been sitting here for a few hundred years. Can we be sure it will hold?"

Lyra turns to look at the wall, then back toward the group crossing the bridge.

"Yes," Lyra says.

I look back at the words typed across the screen: "It's safe."

"My, my, my" Eddi puts his hands on his hips after crossing the bridge and making his way toward the screen. "After all this time. All my generation with Victoria Menhit trying to hide the Alaster ship, now with Gaines Cyro trying to get us further and further from finding it, here it is."

"Here I am," the words type on the wall.

"Woah!" Eddi jumps. "I wasn't expecting that!"

"What did you expect?" the words on the screen type. It's like I can read a chuckling tone in the typed words.

"You're— How did you—" Eddi struggles to find the words. "You're a machine." He turns around in a circle as if looking for something. "Is someone somewhere controlling the software?"

"In a sense," Alaster says. "I'm on the surface..."

Leal gasps as he stands next to his father.

"...and also down here." The words finish typing.

"What?" Leal says in a quiet voice.

"What are you wearing?" Pictor looks at me and giggles as he pulls Jarret behind.

Desman steps beside me. I look at his hands— he tries to hide the trembling.

"I was a man," Alaster types. "In a sense, I still feel like I am since I have a physical being. But I'm now in this machine. You could say my consciousness is in this machine, but it feels like me."

"Wha— how?" Eddi asks.

"Read the journal," says Alaster.

"Journal?" Desman says.

"Hello, Desman," Alaster says.

Desman stands straight as a metal sheet. He barely breathes.

"Hello," Desman says, shifting his eyes like he's looking for a camera, person, or something to address.

"I've been wanting to talk to you," Alaster says.

"Me?" Desman can't seem to find the words. "With regards to what?" His shoulders shift back slightly.

"I want to introduce myself," Alaster says.

"Okay?" Desman questions.

"I want to introduce myself to all of you, actually. But Desman alone."

"What?" Leal erupts. "I have so many questions! We can't leave now. What about the surface? Where does the extra oxygen come from down here? Why is that giant squid outside the Trellis? How do the accidents happen?"

"The surface exists," types Alaster, "I live here. There's enough oxygen because I, this ship, am connected to the surface and provide extra air. That's also why Cyro can't close me off entirely. Everyone will die if he does. The squid is just a squid. It lives by the Trellis because there's a lot of food near the brine. It is not responsible for the accidents, except for what you've seen when Cyro sent a maintenance pod in that area."

The entire paragraph sits on a screen for a moment, then erases itself.

"Leal," Alaster types. "I know exploration of truth is important to you. Take a tablet from Lyra and you can access me anytime. Read through the journal; it will explain a lot. Then ask your questions."

Leal gapes at the screen with longing in his eyes. He turns to Lyra, who holds the journal in her hands. She puts another hand on top of it, like she's unwilling to give up the physical copy.

"Come on," Lyra says motioning to Leal, "we'll get you a tablet."

"The squid didn't cause any accidents?" Leal murmurs as he walks toward Lyra.

"Eddi," the name type across the screen. "I hope to see you back up here."

"You will," Eddi says, following behind Leal.

"That was quick!" Pictor shouts.

Is this our queue to leave? There's still so much I don't understand.

Pictor grabs my hand when he sees I'm not following, and he pulls Jarret and I toward the bridge.

"Gia," a voice booms across the entire room.

I jump. Then turn back toward Desman and the screen.

Words type on the screen: "Your mother misses you."

I feel waves of grief, love, and confusion.

"And," the words type again. "You don't have to find these answers on your own. Rely on your friends and come back here when you can."

I turn toward the bridge. Come back here? My face gets hot with anger. He only gave me more questions. He showed me footage of my mom almost drowning, then leaving. Then he leaves me with all these questions and wants to talk to Desman alone. And he wants *me* to come back *here*? Why should I trust these words on a screen anyway? I don't have any reason to believe some person is typing the words and this isn't some trick.

My shoes make noise as I step. *Tap tap*. I look at my shoes. *Tap*. I walk beside Leal as the entire group exits the corridor that links Alaster with the Sanctuary. *Tap tap tap*. Eddi comes to a stop at the head of the group.

"I thought I might find you here," Arcturo's voice is clear as I watch the group cluster around him.

"Yeah, Eddi wanted to see it," Pictor says, "but we didn't stay very long."

"Is that so?" Arcturo has a faint smile as he looks at his son.

"Yeah, and now I'm going to show Jarret how to play *poltyball*."

"I actually came here to borrow you for a moment," Arcturo says to Pictor.

"Can Jarret come?" Pictor asks, holding Jarret's hand.

"Not this time," Arcturo says. "Your mother and I want to talk to you."

Beside me, Lyra rubs her arm.

"Am I in trouble?" Pictor asks.

"No, you're not in trouble."

"Then why can't Jarret come?"

"We just have something important," Arcturo responds.

"Don't you think that it would be good for me to have a buddy with me to hear important news?" Pictor debates in a suave voice.

Arcturo chuckles a bit. "Do you think it would be?"

"Yes," Pictor says.

"Even if it's not good news?"

"All the more reason to have a friend."

"Well," Arcturo starts to give in, "only if he wants to come."

Pictor hangs on Jarret's arm and looks up at him.

"If you need a buddy," Jarret says, "I'll be there."

"Okay," Arcturo surrenders. "Follow me, then. Lyra, do you mind taking everyone else back to the house?"

"Actually," Eddi says, "I was hoping I could go on a walk with my boy. There's a lot to catch up on."

Arcturo smiles at his friend. "Of course." He looks over to Lyra and me.

Lyra's skin looks pale. Her eyes seem tired and worn.

"You don't mind going back to the house?" Arcturo asks.

Lyra shakes her head.

"Gia?" Arcturo looks at me.

"That's okay with me," I say.

Tap tap tap tap. Not paying attention to the direction we walk, I look between my shoes and Lyra's in front of me. I can feel each step as my foot hits the ground and makes a sound. It feels like I step with authority. Like the noise from my shoe powerfully announces my presence. Soft padding on Lyra's suit mutes her steps. I never thought how a difference in material could make you feel different. Maybe this is why people in earth's past had more than one pair of everything. Did each pair of shoes make a different sound? Did different shoes make people feel more powerful than other shoes? The shirt ruffles over the fabric on my suit. I smile at the image of a kitten with laser vision. It's funny. I wonder how many shirts my mom has. Is she really up there? Does she wear shoes? Childish— I shouldn't be wondering these things. I should be figuring out what this Alaster thing is.

"Can you tell me about Alaster?" I ask, looking ahead.

"What do you want to know?" Lyra sounds tired and doesn't look back as she guides through the single-person wide walkway through the blanket tents.

"What's the gimmick?"

"The what?" she sounds more awake.

"The trick," I say. "What does he get out of this?"

"Nothing," Lyra again sounds like she doesn't have enough energy to answer.

"Nothing?" I ask.

"I think he wants to bring as many people as he can to the surface."

"So he's just nice?" am I supposed to believe that someone doesn't have a self-protective motive?

"I don't know," Lyra shrugs, "he just seems like a good person— or whatever he is." Lyra stops in front of a blanket tent and pulls back the flap. How does she know which one is hers from the outside? Crawling into the tent, the blankets are arrayed in the same fashion that we left them after eating. It's definitely the right tent. I just wonder how she can tell them apart.

Lyra lets out a sigh as she sits near a pile of blankets. Still holding the journal, she rubs it with one hand. Then she opens it and takes out one of the pictures of the families.

"What are you thinking?" I ask after a long time.

Lyra's tired eyes pierce my heart with a weight of longing and grief.

"I wish I had a picture," she says.

"Of what?"

"Us," she puts the picture back in the journal. "My parents, me, and Ara. Of when we were little. I want to remember us together. Pictor too, although he was born later and never met Ara."

She looks to the corner of the room. It's like tears try to form in the corner of her eyes, but her body is too tired to actually make any tears.

"Do you remember her?" I ask.

"Not really," says Lyra. "And," her voice breaks as she speaks, "I feel embarrassed." Tears finally form and crash down onto the journal. "It's almost like I know her, but maybe I just invented it all. My whole life—it's like I've made stories in my head— I imagined what she's like and what we could be like. I just— I just wanted a sister."

"Well," I'm surprised to find that tears fall down my own cheeks. "Tell me about her."

"What?" she sniffles and looks at me.

"You said it's like you know her," I say, "so tell me about her."

Her eyes glisten as she looks at me thoughtfully.

"She's kind of like me," Lyra says after moments of silence. "Inside we're similar, but outside, she's more bold — I think. Maybe we would fight because she's too emotional and I'm too much of a thinker." Lyra chuckles a little bit. "But I look up to her. She can fight for things that she cares about and act on them in the moment. I take a long time with things. I sit in my lab, thinking, playing with bacteria, and wishing that I could be the kind of person who speaks up when things happen. I wish she could teach me how to be that kind of person. But now—" more tears come. "It will only ever be in my head."

I shuffle over to Lyra and put my arm around her.

"She would be proud of you," I rub my hand over her head. "She would be proud of who you are."

Lyra's tears drench the side of my kitten shirt.

Neither of us speaks anymore. I try to think of what Lyra must be feeling— missing someone who she doesn't remember. Like my mom. Except, maybe Alaster is telling the truth and my mom is on the surface. Maybe the hope of meeting her someday could be real. But how? I wonder. Can I get there? How do I know if Alaster tells the truth and there is a surface? My mind drifts to a rolling sea of questions.

Lyra's tears become quieter.

What did Alaster want to talk to Desman about?

What kinds of stories are in the journal that I don't know about?

Like a ship drifting further from the shore, my mind floats away and I lose sight of questions and the search for answers. My mind quiets and floats away.

Chapter 16: Hope or Delusion?

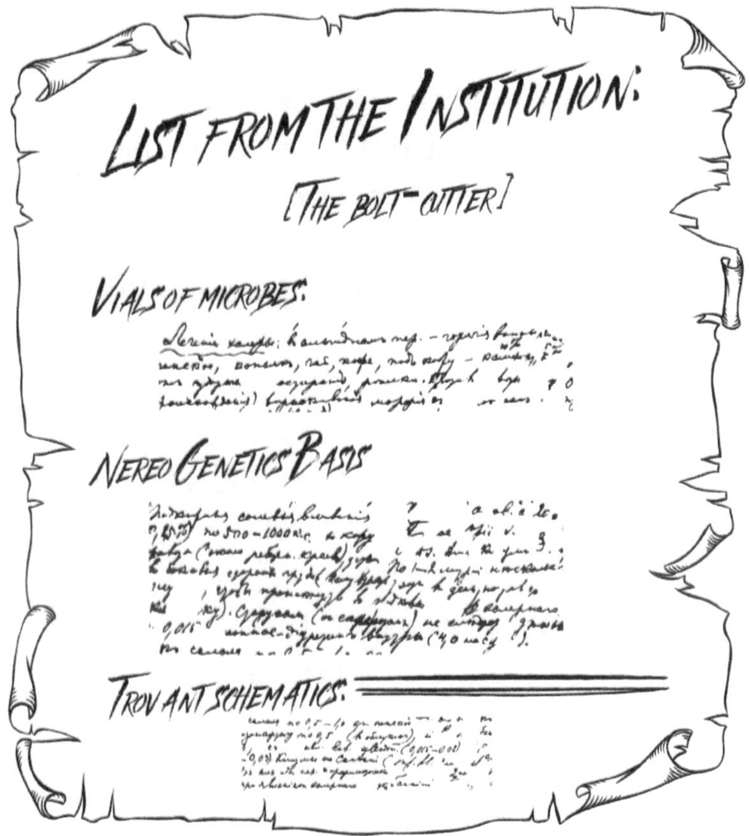

A flush of warm air fills my lungs. As I push myself up and rub my eyes, Lyra situates herself on the floor instead of my shoulder. There's a rustling in the blanket home. Someone is in here with us, but it's too dark to see who.

"It's just me," a voice whispers, as if it could read my mind.

"Me who?" I whisper back. Looking around, there are lumps across the floor. They're too big to be piles of blankets. People must have come in while we were sleeping.

"Desman," whispers the voice.

"Where've you been?" I ask quietly. My mind is sleepy, not entirely able to think of where everyone is and who is in the tent with us.

"You know where," Desman whispers. "The same as where you left me."

"You were there a long time." I don't actually know what time it is or how long he had been there.

Desman doesn't respond, but I hear him moving around and laying beside one of the other lumps on the floor.

"What did you talk about?" I ask.

"I'm tired, Gia," says Desman, laying on the ground.

Tired? I've never heard him say anything like that. It almost sounds like he's admitting to a weakness.

"Okay," I relent instead of pushing him for answers.

I lay back down. It seems quiet at first, except for Desman's slow, intentional breaths in and out. Loudly, he takes in small amounts of air at a time, probably to ensure his ribs don't take on too much strain because of his injuries. Listening to Desman's breath, I become aware of the other sounds across the tent. Some deep, smooth breaths. Some short and quick. Someone shuffling to change sleeping positions.

Trying to fall back to sleep, my senses start to wake up. I'm aware of people crowded around me, though I don't know how many. I could assume it's my friends who have been there this whole time— but I can't see anything to be sure. It's hot. I throw off the blanket on my feet, but it doesn't help. Breathing. We're breathing each other's air. I try not to panic. I want to leave the tent, but I might wake everyone. My arm feels squished against the blanket-covered ground. I move it, but feel like I might disrupt all the sleepers around me. My body stiffens. My heart feels fast. And my stomach is empty. It hurts.

I realize that, since I can remember, last night and tonight are the only times I've slept with other people near me. I'm used to quiet. My room is usually lit so that I sleep and wake to different colors. My bed is usually spongy and padded. The ground here is hard beneath my body. Slowly, I shift around, trying to accommodate the pressure on my limbs without waking my tent-mates.

I try to think of something else. But my mind floods again with questions. I try to take them one at a time— what did Alaster have to talk to Desman about? Is the surface real? What's in the journal? Topics cluttered my mind— my mother, Ara, Desman, Alaster, the Sanctuary, Victoria Menhit, giant squid, accidents— my brain runs like a machine trying to find a solution that unites and explains every disaggregated piece of information.

But it's not working. I try to calm my mind. But I hear breathing. Their exhales filling my inhales. The sounds fill my ears. I put my hand over my ears and turn on my side. I lie there— uncomfortable, tired, annoyed. I can't just wish them to stop breathing, but I wish they weren't here. Is this what it would have been like to grow up in the Cultivator Phrames? Leal lived with his parents in a small space. Is this what he's used to? What do people do when they don't want to be around anyone anymore?

I shift back and forth. Trying to forget about the heat, the strangling blankets, the loud breathing, the close bodies. A low gargling comes from my stomach. It hurts. Is this... is this hunger?

I don't remember falling asleep, but I must have because I wake up and it's light in the tent. Leal lies on his back holding a tablet above his face. I push myself up and look around. No one else is in the room. Everyone else woke up and left without me realizing it.

I lay back down, smashing my face against a blanket. Just Leal and me— that's how it's supposed to be. It feels right.

"There are higher oxygen levels and atmospheric pressure," Leal says.

"Huh?" I push myself to my forearms.

"And biomass in the ocean," Leal doesn't look away from the tablet.

"What are you talking about?" Something in me feels like smiling. Leal doesn't make sense, but it feels normal.

"It's why the squid is so big," says Leal. "Squid didn't use to get so big when the surface of the earth was habitable. All our information about sea creatures is from ancient textbooks of when the surface was habited. There used to be scientific research— a lot of it. It used to be people's jobs to just ask questions about the earth and try to find the answers."

Leal puts his arms at his side and looks at the blanket ceiling. A beam of light comes in through a hole in the blanket home and shines on Leal's face. He closes his eyes and takes a deep breath in and out.

"You okay?" I ask.

"I just feel like," Leal pauses. He turns on his side and faces me, propping his head on his hand. "All of this — it feels like there's something more out there."

"Like what?"

"I don't know," Leal lies back down and folds his hands on his chest. "You know that I've always hoped the surface was real. The more I read in the journal, the more I think maybe it is real. Maybe we can go back up there."

"What does the journal say?" I ask.

"It's a lot of notes on scientific research," Leal smiles. "But it also tells a story. It's written by a scientist who made all this— and more."

"More?" I sit up completely.

Leal pushes himself to a seat.

"Gia," he almost whispers, "I don't even know if I can believe it. There are other facilities."

Trellis

"What?" as if shock moves through my spine, I sit completely straight and my eyes widen.

"The Trellis was a government-sponsored experiment to protect people from impending devastation," Leal explains. "The lead scientist thought there wouldn't be enough space for everyone in the Trellis. So she secretly made other facilities."

"Other Trellises?" I lean toward him.

"Kind of," says Leal. "But they're different. There are two of them. You know how the Trellis is made of metal walls with some biotechnology integrated?"

I nod. The real answer is no— I never actually took the time to think about what the Trellis is made of.

"The Trellis is like a machine," Leal says. "But these other two— they're like organisms."

"What do you mean?"

"I mean, one of them is made mostly of rock and the other is like a plant or something."

"I'm not following," I picture a rock and plant like the ones I've seen in pictures. I can't imagine how facilities could be those objects.

"I don't totally understand it," says Leal. "I'm just piecing it together from the field notes and what Alaster said. Basically, both facilities actually grow to support more peop—"

"Wait, what?" I butt in.

"I know! The facilities can grow!"

"No," I respond. "I mean about Alaster. What did he say?"

"Oh, right. It's like I can message him or something on this thing. But I asked about the other facilities— if they exist and if we can go to them."

"And?"

"And, we can."

I'm stunned.

"In fact," Leal continues, "we are."

Still stunned, I can't think of what questions to ask. I just sit straight up, staring at Leal.

"I mean, according to Alaster, we are." Leal seems uncomfortable by my silence. "He said he plans to go there once we leave here."

"What?" I basically yell at Leal.

Leal clutches the tablet, putting it in front of him like it's a shield.

"What do you mean leave?" I raise my voice. "I'm not even sure this Alaster isn't some guy in a hidden room typing things. I don't know if this isn't some trick of Gaines Cyro. We have no reason to believe the surface is habitable or that there are other facilities. We can't just leave!"

Leal lowers the tablet when he realizes my rant is over.

A sense of guilt settled in my stomach. I feel like the version of myself that attacked him during training.

"Leal," I say.

He doesn't say anything back.

"I'm sorry."

"It's okay," he says, with his eyes toward the floor.

Trellis

I lean over to meet his eyes.

He looks at me.

"Lea, I'm—" Sitting across from my closest friend, I still have trouble getting the words out. "I think I'm afraid."

"Of what?" he asks.

"Of being wrong."

"About what?"

"Alaster, my mom, everything."

"What do you think is right?"

I pause for a moment. "I guess I have this hope that the surface actually is real and my mom is there and Alaster can get us there."

"Well, what if he's not real?"

"What do you mean?"

"I mean," Leal looks to the corner in thought. "If Alaster isn't real, what would life look like?"

"Ummm," I take a moment to think. "I guess we could either stay in the Sanctuary in these tents for the rest of our lives. Or we'll face the Trellis leaders and our lives will end in some accident."

"I don't know if we can stay in the Sanctuary."

"Why?" I ask.

"My mom is out there," Leal throws one hand in the air. "We can't leave them there. Besides, I've talked to Lyra. She said they have some people on the outside who help siphon the food and resources here. The Trellis leaders are getting better at finding the siphons and the people involved. I'm not sure the Sanctuary can go for much longer. If they find everyone helping from the outside and cut the siphon— well, let's just say the Sanctuary can't survive forever."

"Trellis leaders like my dad?" I ask.

"Nope," Leal smiles. "Trellis leaders like Plangon and Gaines Cyro. Your dad is one of the ones keeping people from getting caught. Ever wonder why we never got caught looking at footage from the past?"

"Because you could bypass the system."

"Yeah," Leal says, "my dad laughed when I told him that. He's sure that Garridon noticed and was covering up for us."

"So, you think my dad was helping us?"

"I'd like to think I'm smart enough to bypass his system, but there's too much evidence to say otherwise."

"Why would he help us?"

"He's your dad," Leal sounds matter-of-fact. Like it's obvious that a father would help his daughter. But, is he forgetting that we're talking about *my* dad?

"Assuming you're right," I say, "with him being so close to Gaines Cyro, his every move is heavily watched. How would he get away with it?"

"My dad has a theory about it."

"What's that?"

"When the accident happened 15 years ago, it was your dad's job to close the doors and seal the phrame with the people drowning in it. When your mom put the trowel in the wall, Alaster took control of the area, shut the door, and turned off Gaines Cyro's access to the security footage. Alaster was sure that the doors closed first."

"Why is that important?"

"It appeared on the outside that your dad closed the doors with your mom inside. My dad's theory is that Garridon gained Cyro's full trust for being willing to sacrifice his wife."

I don't know what to say. I let out a "hmmm."

"And I hope my dad is right instead of my first theory," says Leal.

"What was your first theory?"

"Gaines Cyro knows that your dad is involved with the Sanctuary."

"Why would Cyro keep my dad alive if that was true?"

Leal shrugs. "Maybe Cyro's watching him. What better way to uproot everyone involved with the Sanctuary than to closely watch the guy who's connected to everyone?"

I shift around. The thought of my dad being on my side is already a hard thing to accept. It's even more difficult to imagine he's a piece of some game put on by Gaines Cyro.

"I want to go back to what we were talking about before," Leal speaks after moments of silence.

"What were we talking about?"

"You were explaining what would happen if you were wrong to hope in Alaster."

"What more is there to talk about?"

"What if you were right?"

There's silence again. What if it was right to hope in Alaster? I feel embarrassed at the idea. Like a little kid believing in a fairytale. "I don't know, Leal."

"What would happen?" he presses the question.

"I guess," I fidget with a blanket in my lap. If Alaster was right and we could be on the surface, then we wouldn't really need to be down here. "Maybe we could leave the Trellis."

Leal smiles.

"I didn't say it's true," I smile, feeling light at the thought that it could be real, but also ridiculous that I'm saying something like that out loud.

"It could be," Leal's smile gets bigger.

"Yeah, easy for someone like you to say," I tease him for his attraction to a fantastical idea of life. "You're into things like jazz and romance."

"And those things are real too," Leal says through his smile. He takes a deep breath in, letting out a harmonious, quick rhythm. "You know I can't live without —"

"No," I laugh as my friend puts his arms in the air and breaks into song.

"That lovely thing you've got about…" Leal sings his favorite song from the swing genre.

"Nothing lovely!" laughing, I put my hand out as if to stop him.

"You," he takes my hand and swings it back and forth. "Take it one step at a time—"

"I won't."

"Please say that you're mine!" he throws one hand in the air and looks at the ceiling.

"I still won't," I laugh.

"Oh, yes I believe!" he releases my hand to throw both his hands to the sky.

"I don't!"

"I believe it," with eyes closed, Leal wiggles his hips to dance as best as he can in a seated position. "I believe it, yes I do."

"No, you don't," I smile.

"I believe it should be me and yoooouuu," Leal dances with his eyes closed and both hands on his chest like he's holding his heart.

I burst into laughter as he holds onto the last note with his voice ringing like a trumpet.

The flap to the tent swings open. Lyra crouches in the entryway, with her eyes wide and face frozen.

"Hi," still laughing, I put my hand toward Leal to tell him to shush.

"Ummm," Lyra doesn't come into the tent. "Am I interrupting something?"

"No," I say, calming my chuckles.

"Yes," Leal smiles and grabs my hand again. "I'm trying to bring life to this robot heart and prove there is beauty and truth in romance."

I laugh, knowing he's just playing around— but also uncomfortable that Lyra might think there's actual romance between Leal and me. "He's proving nothing except that he's unrealistic and sentimental."

"And sentiment—" Leal starts a different melody.

"No!" I start laughing again as he begins his song.

"My Dear, nothing on earth is permanent," Leal sings this out of tune as he tries to keep himself from laughing. "But they are as real as you and me—"

I lunge toward him with my hand out and cover his mouth.

My hand mutes Leal's voice as he tries to sing another line through my fingers. Leal pulls my hand from his mouth and we both slump toward the floor with laughter.

"Okay," Lyra says, looking surprised and maybe uncomfortable, "I just came to see if you were awake and wanted to eat."

I shoot up straight. "Yes, I think I need food."

"I've already eaten," says Leal. "I'm going to stay back and keep reading."

"Come with me, then," Lyra says to me.

The twists and turns are more familiar as Lyra guides us through the paths of blanket homes. I can tell we're getting close to the court. We'll likely have to go through it to get wherever we're going since so many pathways seem to connect through the court.

"Ah, Gia," an unfamiliar voice announces as Lyra and I walk into the court.

I look around to find where the voice is coming from. A rope is strung across the court, dividing it. Kids stand on either side of the suspended rope. That is, kids and Jarret. Pictor and Jarret each hold a side of a smaller blanket between them. The kids stand in pairs, holding a small blanket between each pair.

"I was hoping you'd turn up," says the voice.

Scanning away from the peculiar scene of kids and blankets, I see the man who was at the meeting tent when we first arrived in the Sanctuary— Cloplin. He stands next to Desman as if they were in deep conversation.

"I've been speaking with Desman," says Cloplin. "And I'd like to get some information from you as well."

"Okay," I say, looking at Lyra, who seems to want to leave.

Lyra puts her head down slightly as we walk toward Cloplin.

"I have some questions," Cloplin says. "Desman has so kindly given insight into the reason water has leaked into the Sanctuary. Cyro has probably spent his energy covering up after your group ruined his plans for the accident. You created quite a few loose ends." He smirks like he's congratulating me for good work.

The kids yell and laugh. I look over at them, but then quickly back to Cloplin as he keeps speaking.

"Unfortunately, that heightens the problems we have here. With your father and Mabel Fitzgerald on heavier surveillance…"

Cloplin keeps talking, but I struggle to focus as my mind journeys to the kids with the blankets. What are they doing? Each kid holding a side of a blanket, they stand with some distance between each pair. Then, I start to see the object of their cheers and laughs. A blanket wrapped into a ball flies over the rope. The kids screech commands to each other as the blanket ball descends.

"That's you!" says one girl.

"Go right!" a boy says to his partner who holds the other side of the blanket.

The kids shuffle around so that one of the pairs catches the ball in their blanket. Once the ball is caught between them, they catapult the ball back over the rope. I watch the blanket ball as it goes back and forth between the blankets and over the rope. Then, the ball gets catapulted, but flies under the rope instead of over. The kids stop.

"Our point!" Pictor yells. "It's our serve now," he says to Jarret.

Jarret looks like a giant among the group of kids. He looks especially awkward as he tries to keep the blanket at Pictor's level. While putting the ball into the blanket, Jarret and Pictor move to fling the ball from the fabric, but the blanket wraps around itself and traps the ball.

"No," Pictor says to Jarret. "You push up! Remember? Don't tilt the blanket. Just fling it up." He turns to the other kids. "He's new! We get another chance."

"Yeah, okay," says one of the boys.

"That's fine!" some kids from the opposite side of the rope say.

Trying again, Jarret and Pictor manage to get the ball over the rope.

"Is this a game?" I ask, looking at the kids.

"This is real life!" Cloplin exclaims, not realizing that I hadn't been listening to him for some time. "Oh—this—" he notices that my eyes are focused on the kids. "Yes, that's a game. It's called poltyball."

"Can we—" I look between Cloplin and Desman. "Can I play it?"

My stomach makes a gurgling noise. I'm used to eating at the same few-hour intervals. A pain in my stomach reminds me that my body doesn't do well being off that cycle. There were a few times that I had to skip a sustenance time to train. But I've never gone this long without sustenance. I feel weak.

"Gia," says Cloplin, "we need to focus on more pertinent things. I need to know more about the security system. I want to see if we can't infiltrate the system."

"Infiltrate it?" I'm taken by surprise. "What for?"

"To take control," says Cloplin.

Take control of what? I try to hide the skepticism from my face. What does Cloplin want control for? Like I'm confronted with a Trellis leader, my posture straightens and my mind converts back to a mode where I am careful about every word and gesture.

"Explain more," I say.

"It's like I've been trying to explain," Cloplin's posture drops a little, like he notices my skepticism and tries to seem more friendly and approachable. "We can't stay here." He sighs, then looks to Desman. "Maybe Desman can explain better."

"Gia," Desman puts his hand on my shoulder.

I furrow my brows. What game is he playing?

He releases my shoulder.

"You've seen how scarce the resources are," Desman continues. "Cyro is honing in on the network on the outside and, soon enough, the siphon will be blocked permanently with no one on the outside to fix it. We'll starve here— you, me, Leal, the Delphinos— everyone."

The sounds of kids yelling fill the court. There are shrieks and laughs as a team accidentally drops the ball.

"So you think we can overthrow Gaines Cyro?" I ask.

"What other option do we have?" Desman says. "This isn't just about the Sanctuary, either. Think about it. Your dad is still out there. Leal has his mom out there— what do you think will happen to them?"

Arms crossed, I don't respond.

Kids laugh and the ball goes back and forth over the rope.

"Think about them!" Desman says. "What will happen if Cyro stays in power?"

"I don't know," I say back. "But what if we fail?"

Now Desman stands without responding.

"Think about the accidents," I demand. "How many people die?"

"People will die anyway!" says Desman.

"What about Alaster," I say.

Lyra rubs her arm like she's uncomfortable.

"You can't be serious," Desman leans back slightly. "Why?"

"Alaster," Cloplin cuts in, "is an invention. It's a machine. An intelligent one— but still a machine."

"Alaster took control of this area," I argue. "My mom put a trowel in the corridor outside the Sanctuary and stopped it from flooding in here. Maybe we can do it again."

"Gia," Cloplin squeezes his forehead between his fingers. "I know this is hard to hear."

I ground through my body and take a defensive stance.

"I know it's easier to believe that your mom is still out there," Cloplin continues, "and this submarine can take us away from here. But this is it. This life is all we have."

"How did the Sanctuary get here if Alaster isn't controlling the space?" I ask.

"It was some glitch," says Cloplin. "A mistake in Gaines Cyro's system and it saved us all."

Lyra seems to be frozen with discomfort.

"And it continues to save you every day that you aren't given over to Gaines Cyro?" I question.

"Is that harder to believe than some mystical submarine that can communicate with us and take us to the surface?" Cloplin sounds mocking.

"There's footage," I say. "Of my mom. And journal entries of the surface and how we got down here."

"Footage can be fabricated," Cloplin says. "And have you read the journal?"

"No, but Leal has," I try to defend myself.

"Well I have," says Cloplin, "The journal is nothing but a collection of scientific experiments and random thoughts from a scientist who lived 300 years ago."

Lyra has both hands wrapped around her stomach, squeezing tight like she tries to comfort herself. The sounds of kids' laughter contradict the tension in our argument.

"My tummy hurts," Pictor's voice sounds over the laughter and tension.

Lyra's eyes shoot toward her brother while she continues to hug herself with her thin arms.

"We need to consider more options before planning something as detrimental as an overthrow," I say with my arms crossed.

"Honestly," says Desman, "what other option do we have?"

My mind races with possibilities and questions. I need to talk to Desman without Cloplin here.

"I'm open to other ideas," Cloplin says. "I'm all ears." He sounds condescending.

There's a flutter of gasps and kids squealing as splattering sounds near the game. Lyra leaps to the scene where Pictor had thrown up near Jarret.

"Don't touch him!" Cloplin yells reactively and points his finger at Lyra.

Trellis

Lyra stops, with her hands hovering above Pictor, about to comfort her little brother in her arms.

"To the field!" Cloplin commands.

Pictor falls to his hands and knees. Lyra's demeanor sinks into a sea of panic and grief.

"What is *the field*?" I ask Lyra as I trail behind her. Both of us carry blankets in our arms.

"It's a way to make sure we don't spread sickness," Lyra says. "We keep all the sick, dying, and dead in one place."

"Dead?"

Lyra doesn't say anything back. It's like I can feel the pressure of Lyra's bottled emotions as they beg to come out. We exit the labyrinth of tent homes and come to a space near the wall of the Sanctuary. It's a different place than where I found Arcturo my first morning here. I can tell because there isn't the metal box to sit on and because there's much more open space. It's like a large semi-circle was carved out from the tent city. A few single tents litter across the space.

"It smells here," I say, plugging my nose.

Although Lyra sets the blankets down and begins moving things around, her face is frozen and unmoving.

"We need to make a tent," she says.

"For what?" I feel like the cold from her demeanor creeps into my muscles and I tense with concern.

"Pictor."

"He won't sleep in our tent anymore?" I follow Lyra's lead in pulling up the blankets, propping them on poles, and hanging them over rope.

"He's sick. We can't risk all of us getting sick."

"Isn't there anywhere else he can stay? Maybe somewhere closer to his family and that doesn't smell so bad? What is that smell anyway?"

Lyra's pale finger points to a far edge of the room.

"The smell is coming from that tent?"

"No, past the tent."

I look beyond the tent and see a hill of blankets. There's a stack of something with draped blankets to hide whatever is beneath.

"What is it?" I ask.

"The dead."

Chapter 17: A Multi-Faced Lie

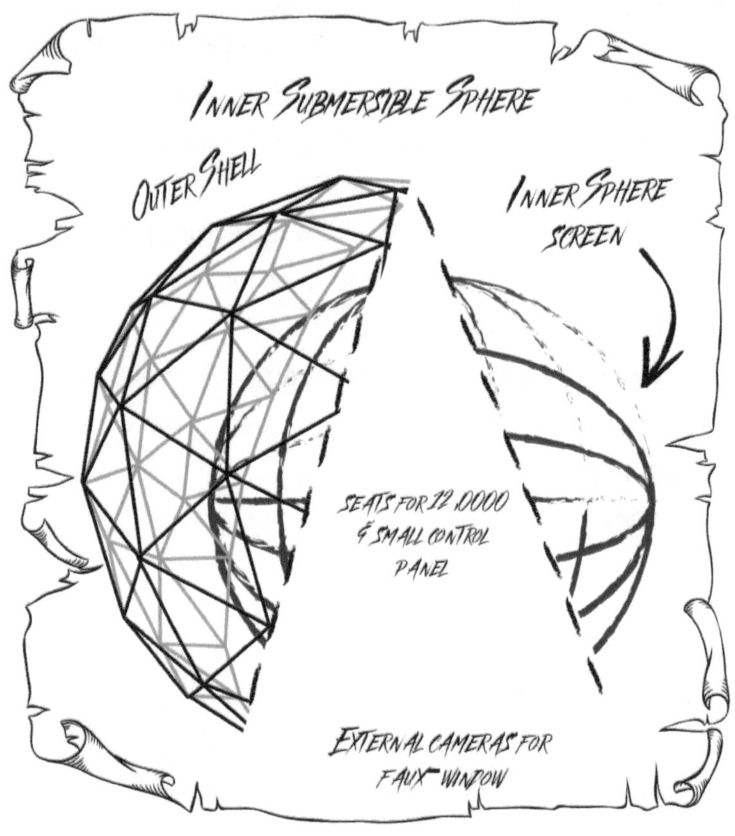

"I'm quite concerned about the others," Cloplin says to the group standing on the edge of the tent city by the field.

"Which others?" asks Arcturo, who looks anxiously at a tent where Vega settles their son into bed.

Arcturo turns back to the circle of us who stand around— me, Cloplin, Eddi, Leal, Lyra, Desman, and, of course, Jarret.

"He's been staying in the same tent as Lyra and the newcomers," says Cloplin. "If he's contagious, he could have spread to the others by now."

Arcturo stands with his arms crossed and one hand rubbing his mouth. "He's been in contact with just as many children who have gone to their families by now. Not to mention his contact with Vega and myself. He's been close enough even to you, Cloplin. We can't put everyone in the field."

"Which is exactly why I suggested tighter social controls months ago," Cloplin says. "If we're going to survive…"

"If we're going to live," Arcturo cuts in with a strong voice, "we need to let people do the things that make up life. That includes socializing."

"You choose entertainment at the expense of people's lives," Cloplin argues back.

"We've had this conversation and I'm not changing my position," says Arcturo. "And, as you're aware, I don't like having these discussions without Vega present."

"We need stricter measures," Cloplin continues. "Imagine if the others are carrying sickness to the rest of the Sanctuary. We can't have another outbreak."

"What we can't have," Vega walks toward our small gathering, "is dissension."

"Vega," Cloplin seems to stiffen, "we were just discussing what measures to take."

"What measures we take," Vega says, "is the protocol previously decided by the assembly: sick individuals are isolated in the field until three days after symptoms desist."

"Vega—" Cloplin tries to interrupt.

"Any further measures," Vega cuts in, "are out of line with assembly decisions and will not be considered."

"Mom," Pictor's weak voice sounds from the tent. "Mama?"

"Be reasonable…" Cloplin tries once more to negotiate a different arrangement.

"You may leave now," Vega's arms are crossed and her stance is firm.

Cloplin stares at Vega. He takes a breath like he prepares to say something, but then sighs, shakes his head, and walks away.

"Mom," Pictor's voice says again.

"He threw up again on the way here," Vega says to Arcturo as she turns toward the tent.

Arcturo rubs his hand over his mouth again. "He'll be dehydrated."

Vega's head seems to hang slightly as she goes again to the tent.

"Mama," Pictor says as Vega pulls back the tent flap.

Vega says something, but I can't quite make out what she says as her soft voice carries from the tent.

"My tummy hurts," Pictor says.

"I know, baby," Vega says.

"I want you to come in here," Pictor whines.

"Remember what I told you?" Vega asks with sympathy in her tone.

"That I can't touch anyone for a little bit?"

"Yes, and that dad and I will move close by so you don't feel so lonely."

"I want you close in here," Pictor weeps.

Arcturo covers his mouth entirely as he watches the tent with an intense stare. It's like I can hear his heart breaking for his son. Not just hear it, but feel it. I sense the magnitude of Arcturo's heartbreak reverberating around us.

Eddi puts his hand on Arcturo's shoulder and rubs. Arcturo grasps his hand over Eddi's, but keeps looking at the tent. Jarret also looks concerned and grieved as his eyes are locked on the tent.

"What does it mean that he's dehydrated?" Jarret asks.

"It just means he needs water," Lyra answers. "and he's probably also losing nutrients. It isn't safe to be malnourished when you're sick."

"Can we give him more food?" Jarret begs.

"No," says Lyra.

"Wait," my head shoots up at the realization that I haven't spoken for a while. "I haven't eaten yet."

"Yeah!" says Leal, "if he has one of Gia's rations, there isn't any extra portion taken from the food. Then, we could take turns giving him each of our portions so he can make up for the nutrients he loses from throwing up."

"Yeah!" says Jarret. "I'll go next! He can have my next portion."

"No," Arcturo shakes his head. "I appreciate your willingness to sacrifice. But it's against the rules."

"Rules?" Jarret sounds offended or even disgusted.

"We've had this sort of situation in the past," Arcturo still doesn't look from the tent. "We ended up losing more people because they were giving up nourishment and becoming too weak to fight off the sickness. We lost people who should have survived."

"But if we choose it—" Jarret panics.

"It's against the rules," Arcturo interrupts. "We had to establish this protocol, trust me."

Lyra's head hangs down. Some memory lingers like a ghost, haunting to remind her why the rule exists in the first place.

The atmosphere feels thick and heavy. So intense that I didn't realize Vega had rejoined us.

"There isn't much else we can do," she says. "Arcturo and I will set up a tent over here for now. Gia, it's time you get food. Lyra, I'll come find you in a few hours to discuss the siphon…" she trails off, looking at each of us. It's like she finds comfort in being able to control a situation, but finds that there isn't anything more to control. Her eyes move to a spot outside of the group, and it looks like her mind goes to a different place.

"The rest of you," Arcturo puts his arm around Vega, "feel free to go about while Vega and I set up a tent. We'll regroup later."

Eddi puts his hand on Leal's shoulder, beckoning his son to follow. The two walk away as Lyra vanishes in the opposite direction.

"Do you know where to get food?" I turn to Desman, knowing he must have gotten food somehow today.

"Yeah," he says, "follow me."

Desman and I walk toward a path that leads to the field. As we reach the path, I turn back to see the Delphinos.

Arcturo's broad arms are wrapped around Vega's body and her face is pressed against his chest. Vega trembles as tears flow onto her husband's microbial suit.

"Arcturo," Vega's voice is so weak, I can hardly tell it's her. "I'm scared."

"I know," he puts his large hand on the back of her head and holds her close. "I'm right here."

"Can we talk?" I ask Desman after walking in silence.

"About what?"

"You, Alaster, Cloplin— everything."

"What specifically?"

"What did Alaster want to talk to you about?" I ask.

Trellis

Desman takes a moment before answering. He starts to say something, then stops. It's like he wrestles with himself about what to say.

"*Alaster*," he says with a tone of sarcasm, "told me to ask my questions."

"You could have done that with everyone else around. There must have been something else."

Desman is quiet. I can tell there's something else he doesn't want to say. "What does it matter anyway?"

"It just might help me understand what's going on."

"What's going on," Desman raises his voice slightly, "is that we live in a colony under the sea with nowhere to go and a bunch of hopeless fanatics is trying to get to a mythical surface to cope with the dismal reality that we're stuck down here."

I can't see his face, but the back of Desman's neck gets red as I walk behind him through the pathway. In the larger paths, I try to stand beside him, but most of the paths are too narrow to walk side-by-side.

"We can defeat this, you know," Desman speaks in a calmer voice. "If everyone just cooperates."

"Defeat what?"

"Disease," he says. "Death, maybe."

"What do you mean we can defeat death?"

"Maybe not now," Desman says, "but we have the technology to keep people from getting sick. We have the systems to keep the Trellis going. We can keep inventing new ways and pull ourselves out of the social tension, the lies, and the decay. We don't have to live the way we have been living."

"So," I try to hold back my skepticism, but it doesn't quite work. "You think, if we work hard enough, we can solve all these issues and not have to see this decay anymore?"

"Yeah," he says, "if we collaborate. It's like Cloplin says. If we think of ourselves as one entire organism, then all people will naturally be cared for and supported. Just as we tend to an aching part of a body, we'd care for broken parts of society if we saw each other as the same creature."

"What if…" I think of the argument between the Delphinos and Cloplin only a few minutes ago. "What if some people's idea of what's best doesn't align with what you imagine?"

"We'd just have to make sure there was quality education in place to inform people why certain ideas are the best ones."

"And what if some people just don't want to cooperate?"

"Well," Desman takes a moment to think. "I think people would want to participate if they knew the reasons why it works the way it does."

"And if they still don't?" I press.

"We'll have structures in place," Desman tries to explain his position. "With a healthy system in place, we can make different roles so people can participate in the way that seems best to them."

Trellis

"Healthy system?" the terms leave a bad taste in my mouth. "Roles? Proper education?"

"Gia," Desman tries to cut in.

"And I assume there can be three social classes that work together to form a proper community to keep the Trellis community alive?"

"Gia," he cuts in again, "it's not like that."

"And if we defeat disease and death, then what?"

"What do you mean 'then what?' Then we survive."

"What happens when there are too many people for the resources we have?"

He doesn't say anything.

"What happens when we can't feed everyone? Do the highest groups in the social hierarchy get food first?"

"There aren't higher groups."

"Sure," I say, "and Cultivators are treated the same as Facilitators."

"You're not thinking about this the right way."

"You still didn't answer my question."

"You're asking the wrong questions!"

"What happens when there aren't enough resources? We will never be able to support a bigger population. Will there be someone to decide who lives, then? Will there be accidents?"

Desman spins around and points his finger in my face. "You've gone too far."

"No," I say, "you have."

Almost reactively, he puts his hand on my shoulder, grasping tight like he's setting up to do a take-down move by pinching my top half to distract me as he knocks my legs from beneath me. He refrains from completing the take-down move, like it was some sort of instinct and he stopped himself before it got too bad. But I grab his wrist, flipping his arm the opposite way and putting him in a shoulder hold.

"And what about Cloplin?" I say, holding him in the position.

"Gia," he says, "drop the subject." He flips his body the other way and spins me into a headlock. I can feel his stressed breathing still struggling from his injuries. He must know he can't win this fight physically.

"Why do you think he wants control so bad?" I say, holding Desman's arms, but letting him keep me in a headlock.

"He wants what's best for the community."

"I'm sure Gaines Cyro does, too."

"You know he's not the same as Cyro."

"Do I?" curling my body, I flip him over my head and slam him into the ground below. Unfortunately, the pathway is too narrow and I slam him directly into a tent, tumbling a wall of blankets on top of both of us. Pushing a tangle of blankets from me, I sit up and look around. No one had been in the tents that we destroyed.

"Gia," Desman sits up, panting and holding his side. "I want to work with you, not against you."

Looking around, people start to peek from different tents and come around the corner to see what happened.

"Sorry," I put my hand up to wave at different people.

"We're sorry," Desman does the same.

I feel bad, but after building the tent with Lyra, at least I know it's not too difficult to put back up.

Desman and I look at each other and around at the people, who stare for a bit before walking away.

"Do we fix it?" I ask.

"I don't think we'll put it back the right way," he says.

"Let's just do the best we can."

Desman grunts as he pushes himself from the ground. We make our best attempt at putting the blankets back on the ropes and sticks laying around.

"Things are created when we work together," Desman says as he throws a blanket over a rope. "And they're destroyed when we fight."

"Yeah, but not very good things are created," I take a step back and see that our tent is much more droopy than the others around it.

Desman smiles slightly. "Gia," he sighs, putting his hand on my shoulder. This time his touch is gentle. "I care about you."

I feel stunned. I stand frozen in front of the tent I just wrestled him into.

"I know it doesn't always seem like it," he continues. "But I think we can make a difference here. You also don't know this, but you have a lot of people on your side."

"My side?" I ask, surprised at the idea that there are sides. And, if there were sides, why would anyone be on mine? Why do *I* have a side? Not Leal or the Delphinos, but *my* side.

"A lot of people will follow you," he says.

Follow me? Into what?

"Just," Desman sighs, "think about it. And you're skeptical about most things— stay skeptical of this Alaster thing. And promise me you'll think about what I said."

"Okay," I say, looking wide-eyed at him.

"The food's over there," he points to the end of a path that leads to a part of the rounded wall of the Sanctuary. "Bowls are over there too."

I walk to the path's edge as Desman takes off in the other direction. Looking back and forth, I notice where we are. It's right next to the corridor where I had followed Lyra into her lab— into the Alaster ship. A large tube runs along the wall and ends close to me. I walk to the tube and notice a lever at the end and a stack of bowls.

How do I do this? Lyra had a bucket. Is that a normal thing, or did she just do that to bring the food to us on our first day? I look up and down the pathway along the wall. There aren't any buckets. I pick up a bowl, putting it under the tube. I pull the lever slightly. Nothing comes out. I pull it further and food pours forcefully from it.

"No!" I say, pushing the lever back to close the tube. The bowl overflows and some spills on the floor. The smell reminds me of that oily fish taste. My stomach

churns at the idea of eating it again. I take a sip from the
bowl. Despite my growling stomach, my throat struggles
to let me swallow the awful flavor— and I haven't even got
any chunks yet. I take another sip, gulping in some of the
cut-up sea creatures and chewing them, then forcing
myself to swallow. I let out a huge sigh when I finish. The
pain in my stomach starts to go away as it fills with food.
What do I do with the bowl now? I look around. There's no
pile of used-looking bowls. Maybe this was a used bowl.
Do they clean them? Looking around, my focus locks to
the corridor that leads to Alaster. Will Lyra be there?
Maybe she can tell me what to do with the bowl.

      The metal platforms creak as I climb the ladders to
where we had met with Alaster. I had heard Lyra's voice up
here when I entered the large room, so I began climbing
without checking to see if she was in the lab. Lyra turns to
see who's there. I grasp the railing in each of my hands,
preparing to cross the suspended platform. My heart
races, but I remember from the last time that I survived
crossing the platform before. Mind over matter, I inch my
way across and toward Lyra, who sits in a chair and turns
back to look at the giant screen. There were words on it,
but they erased before I was close enough to see what the
screen said.

      "Lyra?" I say, walking toward her chair. I sit in the
chair next to her so I can be beside her.

"Yes?" she sniffles, looking straight ahead and wiping her eyes. In the chair she sits with both legs pulled to her chest, hugging her knees.

"I—" I try to think of a good reason to be disturbing her. "I was wondering where to put the bowl when I'm done with it. I left it at the bottom because I couldn't climb with it."

"Oh," she says gently, still not looking at me. "I can take care of it."

That wasn't the real reason I came up here. I don't care that much where the bowl goes. Why did I feel the need to find Lyra?

"I guess," I start trying to answer my own question out loud. "I was wondering how you are doing."

"I'm okay," Lyra answers.

"You don't seem okay."

She looks ahead with both arms wrapped around her legs. "I just..." she bows her head to her knees as her voice quivers. "I just want to know what to do."

"Do about what?"

"I can't lose Pictor," Lyra sobs in her lap. "I thought maybe there was something I could do to fix it."

"Did you come up here to ask Alaster what to do?"

"I didn't know what else to do."

"What do you think he could do to help?"

The light of the screen flickers on Lyra's face. I look ahead to the screen where a sentence types out: "You could ask."

Trellis

A piece of me feels annoyed. I'm tired of asking Alaster. I'm not even sure I think it's a real— submarine? person?— whatever it is.

"Okay, Alaster," I say with a small amount of sarcasm. "What do we do?"

"About what?" types the screen.

I roll my eyes. "Pictor, the Sanctuary, everything."

"You need to ask the right question," says Alaster.

"Which is what?" I demand.

"How you can be a part of what I'm already doing."

"And what exactly are you doing?" I feel a flicker of annoyance.

"Go on," types the words. "Say what you're thinking."

The flicker turns to a fire of anger. "Why do you speak like I'm supposed to believe that the surface exists and you're some hero that can take us up there?"

There's a moment's pause before Alaster answers.

"Because," the screen types, "I am."

Like the answer slapped me in the face, I feel stunned and can't find words to respond.

"So," I finally say, "you expect me to just take your word for it?"

"How do you normally decide who to trust?" Alaster asks.

I thought about it. The only person I really trusted was Leal. I guess trust was built because I'd seen him respond in certain ways. I don't know how to see if someone was trustworthy without there being opportunities for it.

"How did you know you could leave the Sanctuary?" I turn to Lyra.

"After I read about it."

"About what?"

"Alaster," she says, "and what he's capable of."

"And what is that?"

"It's more than any person is, that's for sure."

"So, Alaster gave you instructions on how to leave the Sanctuary?"

"No," she responds.

"Then how did you open the door?"

"I asked."

Just then, I hear the creaks of people climbing on the metal platforms. I can't see them yet, but I hear voices below.

"Oh," says Eddi's voice as his head peers above the ladder to see onto the platform, "I didn't realize anyone was up here."

"Who's up there?" Leal's voice asks the question, but I can't see his face yet.

"I can't see very well," Eddi says looking down the stairs. "Who's there?" he yells toward Lyra and me.

"It's Gia and Lyra," I say.

"Hi, Gia!" Leal's voice yells enthusiastically from below the platform.

"Hi, Leal," a smile creeps up my face as I yell back to my friend.

Trellis

Lyra shifts uncomfortably in her chair. She releases both feet to the ground and wipes her face to get rid of any tears.

"What are you doing up here?" I yell toward them.

"Probably the same as you two," says Eddi who helps Leal from the ladder and onto the platform. "To talk to Alaster."

· Both of them slowly make their way across the walkway to reach the circular platform where Lyra and I sit. Eddi moves to the control panel, standing next to me while Leal stands slightly behind.

"This seems weird," Leal smiles.

"What does?" I ask.

"You never sit there," he points to my chair. "That's my side."

I smile, remembering that we spent every day of work together. Facing the screen, I always sat on the left and he would sit on the right. For the first time in my memory, I'm facing a screen and sitting in a chair on the right side. "Do you want your chair?"

"No," he chuckles and then moves between Lyra and me to put his arm on the back of my chair and leans on it.

Lyra looks ahead, but this time like she's completely frozen. Not sad or angry. I can't even read what emotion is on her face. She almost looks stunned.

"Hello, Alaster," Leal says like he's talking to a friend.

"Hello, Leal," says the screen.

"I've got some questions for you," Leal sounds a bit suave as he leans on the back of my seat and speaks to the screen. "And I'd be willing to bet you've got the answers."

It's not possible to hear a tone of voice from words on a screen, but it feels almost like Alaster and Leal are good friends and Alaster might laugh a bit as he types: "Ask away."

"Victoria Menhit," Leal says, "she obviously isn't in the Sanctuary. What happened to her?"

"Victoria Menhit isn't what you think," says Alaster.

"Okay," Leal seems confused. "But is she alive?"

"She's alive in the same sense that an idea is alive."

We all glance at one another, as if asking each other if anyone knows what that is supposed to mean.

"What..." Eddi seems he's formulating a question. "What idea exactly?"

"The same one Cloplin believes," says Alaster.

I remain still in my seat, trying not to give away how tense I feel at the mention of Cloplin's name.

"And," says Eddi, "what is that?"

"That people can live down here and solve all the problems without my help."

"Solve?" Leal remarks. "What might we try to solve?"

"Oxygen, food, space, disease, death," Alaster types. "Since the beginning, the same lie has been reborn with different faces, but it's always the same thing."

Trellis

I lean forward in my seat. "And what exactly do you do to help?"

"Anywhere people will let me," types the screen, "I can take control. When I'm fully allowed everywhere, I can take everyone who wishes to the surface."

I remember the footage of my mom putting the trowel into the side of the Trellis. She was able to put Alaster in that space, and it made it so he had control of the area. What would happen if Alaster had control of the whole Trellis? What if he had access from the control panel in Gaines Cyro's living quarters?

I stare at the screen but don't say anything.

Chapter 18: Blocked Siphon

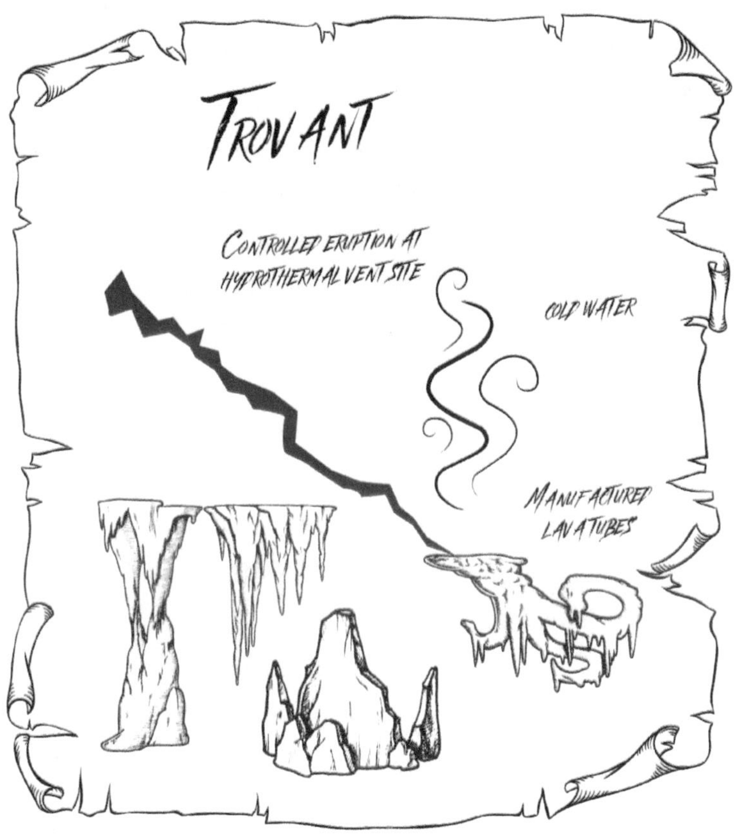

The lights are dim in Lyra's lab as we stand in silence, thinking about the gravity of our discussion. Lyra, Eddi, and Leal stand on the opposite side of the room as I stare at a glowing container on the desk. I had proposed an option for getting people from the Trellis to Alaster, but it was risky.

Escape— that's what's on our minds. I feel a crushing weight over me. What if this all went wrong?

Trellis

"Britannica put the trowel in the corridor just outside the Sanctuary," says Eddi. "That has a code on it which gives Alaster access to everything in that area. That's how we can give Alaster control over Gaines Cyro's quarters."

"The only thing is," Leal says, "once we take the trowel from the wall to move it, Alaster no longer has control of this area. We lose control of the Sanctuary."

"That's where the rest of the plan comes in," I say.

"Do you think it will work?" asks Leal.

"We need to consider the consequences," Eddi says after a long silence. "What could happen if we're wrong?"

I think about the escape pod which was destroyed by the squid. I think about the accidents.

"We could be killed," I reply.

"But," says Leal, "what happens if we don't try?"

"It's only a matter of time before Cyro shuts down the siphon for good," says Lyra. "If we stay here, we'll starve."

"We're missing one option," I say.

"What's that?" asks Eddi.

"Desman wants to overthrow Gaines Cyro and take control of the Trellis."

"Desman wants that?" Eddi asks.

"And Cloplin," I say.

"I thought so," Eddi replies. "But it's just like Alaster says, the lie that keeps us down here is that we can survive without his help."

"That's assuming," I say, "that Alaster isn't some trick and that the surface isn't a myth."

"You're right," says Eddi, "that is an assumption. Do you think it's a trick?"

"I don't know," I say, wanting Alaster to be true, but also remembering my promise to Desman to stay skeptical.

"Well," Eddi says, "if it is a trick, who would be behind it?"

"Gaines Cyro?" Leal asks.

"Maybe," I say. "He could be luring us to his living quarters so he can trap us."

"But," Lyra cuts in, "if Gaines Cyro had control over this area the way Alaster does, he wouldn't need to trick us— he already would have us. It doesn't make sense for Alaster to be controlled by Cyro."

"You're right," Eddi strokes his chin.

"Unless," I say, "Alaster is someone worse than Gaines Cyro and needs our help to take control of the Trellis."

"Maybe," Eddi still strokes his chin. "It's not impossible. Does it seem likely to you?"

I think about the things I know of Alaster. Really, I don't know that much. He's shown me footage where he saved my mom. That could indicate he's good, but it also could have been manipulated footage to trick me.

"No," Lyra speaks up after I don't answer.

"From everything I've read on the tablets," Leal says, "Alaster the human sacrificed himself to save everyone else. I'll be honest, I don't understand how he is some sort of conscious person inside a mechanical thing. But, from what I do understand, he's only ever saved people."

"And what if it's a trick?" I have a hard time believing this weird submarine would do anything for us. He might be able to show footage of me, but what reason do I have to believe that he cares about us enough to help?

"Then," Leal says, "we die. And if we stay here, we die. And if we try to overthrow Cyro ourselves, we'll end up making another Sanctuary where people are still sick, hungry, and dying— or we'll just die in the attempt."

None of us say anything as we contemplate the possible outcomes of our options.

"Gia," Eddi sighs, "you have the best chance of getting into Gaines Cyro's living quarters. If you're in, the plan can work. If you're not, our chances are almost nothing."

"We at least have the Sanctuary," I think of the singing, games, and time spent together. It's the first time I've felt free. "I don't want to lose it."

"We'll lose it either way," Lyra sounds certain.

"Maybe we can protect it," I say.

"This has been my mom's and my role since I can remember," Lyra argues. "I know every physical connection from the Trellis to the Sanctuary. I know where every drop of food, jex of energy, and strand of blanket comes from. Trust me when I say there's no way we will survive much longer."

"I just need some time to think about it," I say.

"I don't want to have to put this on your shoulders," Eddi sounds comforting, "but I'm afraid we don't have much time left."

I lean against Lyra's desk with my arms crossed.

Eddi sighs, like he feels a sincere burden for leaving this decision to me. "How much time do you need?"

"I don't know," I stare at the ground with my arms still crossed.

"How about this," says Eddi. "I'll take some time to talk to Vega and Arcturo. I'll gather some people and we'll be ready for whatever you decide."

I look up at Eddi, considering how different a conversation with him is than with my father. Why is he giving me time? My father would give me consequences for taking 47.2 seconds to make a decision. I don't know what is true right now. But maybe a man as kind as Eddi can decipher when someone else is also kind— even if it is some talking submarine.

"Okay," I finally say. "I'll think about it."

I can't see anything as I lay in the pile of blankets— but it feels emptier. Slow breaths resonate across the warm tent, but one is missing. I can't see it, but I can feel it— Pictor's absence. Although the tent feels safe, there's a sense of loss looming in the air. Maybe I'm the only one who feels it. The others seem to sleep soundly. Except for the person next to me. I don't know why, but I can sense that Lyra is awake beside me. I remember the pain when I thought Leal would be lost in the accident. Does she feel something similar, wondering if Pictor will survive? Eddi said he didn't want this choice to be on me— but it is. Do I hold in my hands the potential to save her brother, but delay the choice?

I turn to my side, eyes open though I see only black.

What if Alaster is not true? Then is it worth the risk? My mind drifts to what Leal said about other facilities. Can we get to them? Even if Alaster can't get us to the surface, it's still a submarine. Maybe it could bring us to a different facility.

I turn to my other side.

But the journal entries were written 300 years ago. Maybe the facilities are gone or never existed. All my years in the Trellis— I never could have imagined a place like the Sanctuary right under my nose.

"Gia?" Lyra's voice whispers. "Are you awake?"

"Yeah," I whisper back.

"Do you think Pictor will be okay?"

I reach my hand into the darkness to where Lyra should be sleeping. I put my hand on her head and rub it with my thumb.

"I hope so," I wish I could come up with something more assuring, but the truth is that I don't know if he will be okay.

"Do you think there's something we can do?"

Like gears in an old, overworked machine, my mind clanks through the risks of leaving the Sanctuary.

"Maybe," I say, "but try to get some sleep and we can figure it out in the morning."

I don't sleep as the opening in the top of the blanket tent lets the light in. It might be like the way a sunrise works, with the light slowly coming through a window. But the light comes from glowing vines along the Sanctuary wall instead of the sun. I don't know how these lights work, but it's like magic. Can I take the chance on Alaster and destroy everything that's here?

The tent flap swings open and more light pours in.

"Lyra," a voice tries to whisper, but also tries to be loud enough to wake the sleeping girl.

I turn to the tent opening and see Cloplin's face. Pushing myself up, I shake Lyra slightly to wake her.

"Lyra," I whisper gently. I don't want to wake her too harshly, but the tone in Cloplin's voice sounded urgent.

"Hmmm?" Lyra stirs awake and rubs her eye.

"Come quickly," Cloplin whispers when he sees her awake.

Trellis

I don't say anything, but sit up with Lyra and follow her through the tent door even though Cloplin didn't invite me along.

"Siphon's blocked," Cloplin says as he steps with authority through the maze of blanket homes.

"Already?" Lyra says with a sleepy voice.

"It's time you tell us everything you know," Cloplin says without looking behind at us. "Both of you."

Neither Lyra nor I respond as we come to a massive blanket tent. I recognize it. The tent is the first place we came to in the Sanctuary, where we were taken to the assembly.

Cloplin opens the flap, to reveal people sitting around in a circle. Arcturo, Vega, and Eddi are among the faces I recognize. And... and Desman. How did he get here? I didn't even notice that he was gone from the tent where we slept.

As we enter the tent, eyes lock on Lyra's small frame.

"What's going on here?" a woman demands.

I'm immediately defensive. Why does the woman sound like she's accusing Lyra?

"We've had two people fall ill in my section and we can't—" a man starts ranting, but Cloplin cuts him off.

"We all want answers," Cloplin says, "so we'll do the best we can to keep this orderly and to the point."

Lyra and I take a seat next to Vega, who looks pale with grey under her eyes.

"What we know so far," Cloplin continues, "is that the siphon is blocked. This was the quickest ever that Cyro found the siphons after our outside people helped set it up. This could be because some of our outside people are now in here. It could be that our outside network has been found out. We don't have all the details, but we will follow protocol:

"Half portions for everyone in each 24-hour period.

"Emergency measures are taken at 48 hours after blockage. That includes halting portions given for the sick. Today will be the last portion given to the sick until we—"

"Wait, what?" I nearly jump from where I sit. "Why would you stop portions for the sick? Shouldn't they be cared for first?"

"We need to make decisions," Cloplin says, "we can't waste portions on people with a low chance of survivability."

"Waste?" I raise my voice. "What do you mean waste? We are talking about people's lives!"

"Exactly!" Cloplin yells back. "This is life or death, Gia Hamiltoni, and we don't have the luxury of pretending like we have enough resources to save everyone."

"There must be something else we can do," I assert.

"Fix the siphon," says Cloplin. "And we can accomplish that by working together."

Trellis

The man across the circle situates himself. "You're not the only one who has a sick person."

I look at him, thinking about the pain he must also be carrying.

"What happens after the emergency measures on the 48-hour mark?" I ask with a level tone.

"The next mark is at 72 hours after blockage," Cloplin explains, but he doesn't say what measure we take.

"What happens then?" I ask.

"A prayer that we survive," Arcturo speaks up.

No one says anything as the reality of that possibility hangs in the air.

"What time did the block occur?" Vega asks with a firm voice, hiding the exhaustion implied by the bags under her eyes.

"It's unsure," Cloplin looks over to Lyra. "Some of you know that Lyra installed a device that monitors the intake and output of the tanks. It should be able to tell us when food stopped coming in."

"Well?" the woman who spoke up previously looks at Lyra expectantly.

"I need a tablet," Lyra says. "The one in my lab is connected to the monitor and can give me the information."

"Great," Cloplin says, "then you can get that data for us as soon as—"

"I want to know what else is going on with the siphon," the woman interrupts Cloplin.

"We are doing our best to—" Cloplin speaks up, but the woman interrupts him again.

"I'm tired of how this girl runs up, down, and all around with no supervisor to decide if she's doing the right thing," the woman says.

"You don't have a supervisor," Lyra mumbles and looks at the ground.

"Excuse me, young la—" the woman's voice raises, but Vega cuts in.

"What she means is, " Vega raises her eyebrow as if to scold Lyra for disrespecting someone, but then she looks at the woman with a sense of power and anger. "We, as the council, voted in heads of sections and fields who are accountable to one another but are not supervised. Just as you and I were voted as heads of a section and Sanctuary systems, Lyra was voted as head of food distribution. If you have a problem, you're welcome to go through the necessary measures to vote for a new person or change our rules on accountability for heads. Until then, the regulations for heads remain and Lyra will be free to do her job."

Cloplin remains quiet until Vega finishes, as if he fears whatever fury will follow if he interrupts.

"Now," Cloplin finally says, "back to the order of things. We do need to know, Lyra, what happened when you left the Sanctuary. Why and how did you do it? And what did you find out?"

Vega looks to Lyra with a firm, but sympathetic look, as if encouraging Lyra that it's okay to say all she knows.

"As you know," Lyra starts, "the siphon was blocked not long ago."

"Tell us something we don't know," the woman says, with her arms crossed.

"Apologies, Lyra," Vega sits up straighter. "I have to briefly interrupt your explanation." Vega turns to the woman. "Is there something you have to add or questions you have that will edify our knowledge of the situation?"

"No," the woman says, with her head cocked and her stare directly into Vega's eyes.

"Then you may listen and get answers with the rest of us," Vega says, "or you're welcome to leave."

The woman doesn't say anything back, but she keeps her arms crossed and stare on Vega.

"Lyra," Vega says, "please continue."

"Ummm, yeah, okay," Lyra's voice is quiet and shaky as she starts speaking again. "The siphon was blocked and our communication got shut down. I couldn't get a hold of the people on the outside, so I couldn't figure out how to fix the blockage. So that's why I left— so that I could fix the source of the block."

"And do you know if we have communication with the outside now?" Cloplin asks.

"I'm not sure," says Lyra. "I need to go to the lab to check that."

The woman interrupts again. "So the information for the siphon is in your lab and the communication with the outside is also in your lab?"

"Yes?" Lyra responds with a tone of uncertainty.

"And no one else has access to this information?" the woman demands.

"Well," Lyra rubs her arm, "anyone technically has access—"

"*Does* anyone else access it?" asks the woman.

"Not really," says Lyra.

"Would you like to?" this time, Arcturo speaks with his arms crossed and his strong figure looming toward the woman.

"I might like to see it," says the woman, "yes."

"Then go ahead," Arcturo says. "The information is available to anyone with a tablet. Go get one and read the information."

"Well," says the woman, "I don't know how to access that information."

"If it's so important to you," Arcturo struggles to keep his voice calm, "then you're welcome to find out all the information for yourself."

"I told you already," the woman raises her voice, "I don't know how. I'm not trained in that technical stuff."

"If this is so imperative," says Arcturo, "why don't you train yourself to get the information?"

"That's not part of my job," says the woman. "It should be someone else's to know that sort of thing."

"Someone like Lyra?" Arcturo's biceps bulge as he squeezes his crossed arms.

"Someone else," says the woman, "someone who is responsible and has a bit more experience."

"Do you think you could do a better job?" Arcturo demands.

"I think I could be more responsible with such a big task," the woman responds.

"Then go," Arcturo points to the exit. "Go fix the siphon. Go communicate with outside people. Go invent ways to eliminate bacteria in the food process. Go reduce the death rate by half in one year. By all means, go be more responsible than my daughter."

The woman keeps eye contact with Arcturo as she stands and walks toward the exit. Then she shoots an angry glance toward Lyra as she pulls back the tent flap and leaves.

"Lyra," Arcturo says, "please continue your explanation."

"Okay," Lyra's voice is quiet and she seems scared as she looks toward her dad for safety.

"I understand why you left," Cloplin says. "Now what we all need to know is how."

"I asked," Lyra says.

"Asked who?" questions Cloplin.

"Alaster," she says.

Cloplin sighs. People around the assembly fidget and let out grumbles.

"Why can't you just tell us?" the man across the circle from me puts his hands out as if pleading. "Listen, I'm with Arcturo in that you've done a good job keeping more people alive, but you are a secretive person. Why not just tell us the truth?" The man looks at Lyra while he speaks, but keeps glancing at Vega and Arcturo like he's afraid of some imminent attack.

"I'm telling the truth," says Lyra. "I don't know how the doors open on a mechanical level— I've tried everything. We reached a dire place the last time the siphon was blocked, and so I just asked."

"Well," the man says, "just *ask* again." The man gestures quotation marks with his hands to suggest that she's still withholding information.

"Going out there could be detrimental to us and our outside people," Lyra speaks quickly, like she needs to get out a stream of information before anyone cuts her off again. "We need to check the comms first and troubleshoot any problems with the internal mechanisms before attempting to go outside."

"It sounds like she's stalling," a woman says in the circle.

"Why would I be stalling?" Lyra pleads. "What do I have to gain?"

Grumbles and rebuttals sound through the tent as the people in the assembly start to vocalize their irritation.

"She has a sick brother," Desman speaks up for the first time and his voice cuts through the murmurs. "If her track record isn't enough to make us believe she wants the people to survive, let that be a reason. If nothing else, she'll be working harder than anyone to get the siphon unblocked so her brother won't have to go without sustenance. Let the scientists do their jobs." Desman looks at both Lyra and me as he says the last sentence.

Scientist? I'm not a scientist. Lyra— and maybe Leal— know about this kind of thing, but I can't see why this would be in my hands.

Cloplin lets out a long sigh.

"I hoped we could spend this meeting getting all the information we need from the both of you," he says to Lyra and me, "but it appears we have more urgent fire to extinguish and the assembly is itching to move forward in action, not discussion. I make a proposition: we let Lyra gather information on the siphon and communication; troubleshooting internal problems—as Lyra put it— and we will decide our course of action once we have a chance to assess all information. Let's assemble four hours from now, giving enough time for Lyra to get all the information we need."

"Just Lyra?" a man in the circle asks. "With all respect to the order, shouldn't there be someone to go along and make sure she's doing the right work?"

"Right," Cloplin doesn't shut down the proposition, but also doesn't seem to think it's reasonable. "Would any of you like to go along?"

There's silence.

"Anyone?" Cloplin asks.

"I would," says the man who has proposed the idea, "but there are matters in my section that need taking care of."

"Are the matters in your section more important than fixing a blocked siphon?" Cloplin sounds almost like he's now defending Lyra and what she needs to do. Whose side is Cloplin on?

Maybe there aren't sides. Maybe everyone is just doing what they think needs to happen to help us all survive. I look around the circle with less frustration. They probably aren't meaning to attack Lyra, she just happens to be the person in charge of the thing that's broken and they're panicked to fix it.

"I'll go," I speak up.

"Fine with me," Cloplin scans the circle as if asking people to give their opinions.

"Can't we send someone from one of the sections to verify that these two are looking at the right things?" a man from the assembly reasons.

"Do you know what to look for?" I question the man.

"Pardon me?" he turns away from Cloplin to look at me.

"If you came along with Lyra and me, would you know how to verify that we are looking at the right things?"

"No," says the man.

"Do any of you know what to look for," I scan the circle, "to verify that Lyra is doing her job?"

No one answers.

I feel powerful, but a bit of a fraud to act like I know what Lyra does. I probably can't verify her work any more than any of these people.

"If there's no one else," I say after some silence, "then I will go with Lyra to make sure we're on track, and you can all get back to your sections."

"Are there any other propositions?" Cloplin asks.

People remain still in the assembly; no one speaks up with a better idea.

"Anyone opposed to Lyra and Gia troubleshooting and meeting again in four hours?" Cloplin asks.

No one opposes.

"All in favor?"

Without enthusiasm, the people of the assembly speak some half-hearted "yeas."

"The yeas have it then," says Cloplin, "we'll meet again in four hours to reassess. Dismissed."

"It's not good," Lyra says as she walks toward me with a tablet in her hands.

I had waited by the siphon as she grabbed a tablet from her lab and came back.

"What is it?" I ask, looking away from the long tube which stretches along the Sanctuary wall.

"Comms are down," she says, "and the blockage started six hours ago." She looks up from the tablet.

"That's a lot of time. I didn't expect it to have been that long ago."

"Why doesn't the monitor have an alarm or something to say when there's an issue with the siphon?"

"There is, but the notifications sound on this tablet." Lyra holds up the tablet. "I left it in the lab."

She lowers the tablet, staring at the floor.

"What's wrong?" I ask.

"I just—" her voice quivers as she speaks, "I just didn't expect a blockage. I should have had this on me while I slept. I should always have this with me." She covers her face with the tablet. "What will I tell them when they find out how long there was a blockage and I didn't know?" I hear sobs from behind the tablet. "They're right. I'm not the right person for this job. Someone who is more responsible should be doing this."

"Hey," I put my hand on the tablet and lower it to uncover her face. "How long did it take to detect blocks before you were in charge?"

"Umm," her face is streaked with tears, "I don't know. There weren't blocks before. They gave me this job because I found the first block and fixed it."

"And what might have happened if you didn't?"

"I don't know."

"This might not be here," I motion around the Sanctuary. "We all might not be here."

Lyra sniffles and wipes the tears from her cheeks.

"It doesn't matter what they say," I put a hand on her shoulder. "No one else knows how this system works and no one else can fix this. We'll figure something out. I promise."

She smiles, looking at the ground as I compliment her on being the only person who knows the system.

"So," I say after a few moments, "what's the first thing to do in order to troubleshoot the problems?"

"I already started," she lifts the tablet. "The assembly wants to know the time of the blockage and the status of the external comms. We have both of those. My devices are running diagnostics for virtual problems, but my guess is that the issue is physical."

"What does that mean?"

"What does what mean?"

"Virtual and physical problems?"

"Oh, ummm," Lyra looks at the tablet. "Virtual problems are like the coding and stuff. Physical is the stuff on the outside. If there was a problem with something in here, it would be with the coding and I could fix it. But it's more likely that Cyro found the siphon and physically blocked it from the outside."

"How can we fix it if that's the problem?"

"Typically, we'd talk to the people on the outside and come up with a plan to fix it."

"But the comms are down," I finish her explanation.

"Right. And on top of that, since you all came here, there's a higher likelihood that Cyro was able to find out who else is a part of the network. Even if the comms weren't down, I'm not sure we could contact them."

"You think something happened to them?"

"Six hours is a long time," says Lyra. "Cyro can do a lot in a few minutes once he has a plan."

I don't know everyone in the network, but I think of Leal's family. His parents definitely were in the network. What would happen to his mom?

"What are our options?" I ask.

"Go outside and try to fix it," Lyra says. "Or starve."

"Until the assembly, I mean. Can we make a plan or get more information while we wait to meet with the assembly again?"

"I can't think of much we can do other than to run these diagnostics for the virtual side."

"Cyro can do so much more in four hours. Can we wait while he might be hunting other parts of the network?"

"Do you have a better idea?" Lyra asks.

I look away, remembering the debate that kept me up all night— *can I trust Alaster?*

"Did you really get out of the Sanctuary by asking Alaster?" I ask.

"Yes," she says.

"Do you know for sure you can get to the outside again or is it up to him?"

"It's completely up to him."

I take in a deep breath. No matter what happens, it seems like our fate depends on a human-submarine thing.

Trellis

"In the meantime," Lyra says, "can we check on Pictor?"

"Are we allowed to?"

"Only the caregiver can get in close proximity," she explains. "That's my mom. But, as long as we keep some distance, we can just see how he is doing."

It seems tense as we get closer to the Field. Turning from pathway to pathway, Lyra takes us to the edge of the tent city where Arcturo and Eddi stand facing Pictor's tent. Eddi rubs his hand over Arcturo's back.

"I thought I might find you here," Desman appears from a pathway and walks toward me. "Never mind the fact that you aren't fixing the siphon. I need to talk to you. Things are getting serious."

Lyra doesn't even acknowledge Desman's accusation that she wasn't doing her job. Her eyes fixate on her father and she stands frozen by the gravity of her father's concerned look.

"Is he okay?" Lyra nearly screams. "Is Pictor okay?" Her ribs move in and out violently as she forces herself to breathe.

Arcturo jumps, like he was shocked out of some trance.

"It's okay," Arcturo puts both hands out toward Lyra, "he's alright." He puts his large hands on her tiny shoulders and pulls her close. "He's very dehydrated, and he passed out."

"No!" Lyra's cry is muffled, her face against her dad's chest, but her breath gets louder and louder as she hyperventilates.

"Shh, shh, shh," Arcturo puts one hand on the back of her head and sways her back and forth. "He's still breathing okay, and he's still allowed one portion. As soon as he wakes up, he can have sustenance and it will be alright."

"Mom," there's a small cry from the tent.

Lyra pushes away from her dad to see what's happening.

"Oh, thank goodness," Eddi's shoulders drop.

"Hi, sweet boy," Vega's muffled voice speaks to her son.

We all sigh in relief at the sounds of voices from the tent.

"I need to talk to you," Desman stands close to me and whispers in my ear.

We hear the sound of gagging from the tent.

My heart races.

"How long?" Lyra says.

Arcturo looks at his daughter.

"How long has he been dry-heaving?" Lyra demands.

"Since last night," Arcturo says.

"He's really depleted," Lyra puts both hands on her head. "He's dehydrated." She loses control of her breathing again. "I don't know how much longer he can survive this."

Arcturo reaches out again and takes both of her hands in his.

"Shh," he holds her hands and bends over to look into her eyes. "It's okay." He sounds reassuring as he tries to calm Lyra, but it seems like there's a haze of fear that he tries to hide from his daughter.

Arcturo can't know that Pictor will survive. He's already lost one of his children. How must he actually be feeling? When I met Arcturo and Vega, it was like I saw two people who were stronger than the ocean and wiser than the stars. As I think of Vega's pale face and see Arcturo's crouched body now, I see two people whose strength is weathered down.

Overwhelmed by waves of panic and fear, it's like the sea of questions finally spit me out on a shore. I know what's right.

"Eddi," I say.

He turns his head toward me.

I bend over, reaching to my feet. I don't know how easy it will be to run in shoes, but I do know that it'll be loud.

"It's time," I say to Eddi as I kick off my shoes.

Chapter 19: Fight and Flight

"Gia!" Desman yells after me as I run full speed away from the field. "Cloplin!" He yells down a different path.

Sprinting through a maze of blanket homes, I don't know exactly the way to go, but I know the right direction. Toward the wall which connects to the corridor. The one where my mom inserted the trowel 15 years ago.

Trellis

The air feels fresh. It feels like an eternity since I've felt the rush of adrenaline. As I move toward the Sanctuary wall, I see the arched doorway to the corridor.

I come to a full stop in front of a closed door.

It's the place that has been closed for 15 years. The place where my mom inserted the trowel and closed off the Sanctuary— closed herself off from the Trellis.

I look up and down the edge of the archway.

"Please," I don't know where to look while I'm doing this. "Alaster—" I feel ridiculous— "please open the door."

I jolt back slightly surprised. I've never seen a door open so quickly. It doesn't even seem to slink into the wall, it just shoots open.

Wasn't this place flooded? I expected there to be a flood of water coming from the corridor, but it's dry.

I take flight again down the corridor. I see it— the trowel is still there.

"What's that?" a voice asks.

I turn to look down the corridor as I reach the trowel. Desman and Cloplin run after me.

"Gia!" Cloplin yells. "No!"

With my hands on the trowel, I feel a weight in my stomach. Alaster will no longer have control of the area. The Sanctuary will be gone.

Cloplin and Desman get closer.

I pull the trowel from the wall.

"What are you doing?" Desman yells as he and Cloplin get closer to me.

The door to the Sanctuary slams shut. There's no way back in.

"What have you done?" Cloplin turns to me.

"Put it back!" Desman lunges toward me.

An alarm sounds. It's not the buzzer to switch tasks. It's not a practice alarm. It's the one that means all Facilitators are ready. They're coming after us.

I slip the trowel down my kitten shirt and into my green suit.

"Run!" I sprint down the corridor.

Desman and Cloplin follow me.

"Where are we going?" Desman yells.

Where do these corridors connect? I've been in the Trellis my whole life, but I don't know my way around this section because it has been closed.

"This way!" Cloplin yells and takes a left.

I look up at the ceiling. It's the spot where Alaster showed the footage of my mom crawling through the doorway. Alaster can't open it anymore. Even if he could, would the escape pod be gone?

We keep running. Two figures in grey suits approach the walkway.

"Gia?" says one of the figures. "What are you wearing?"

It's Zade Traverson, a guy who used to be in the same training cluster as me.

"Zade!" says the girl in a grey suit. I haven't met her, but I know her from security footage. Her name is Koa Burns. "Those are the defectors!"

"Gia?" he scratches his head. "Defective?"

Koa's arm shoots out to close-line me as I run past. I duck under her arm, but I don't see her front leg as she sticks it out to kick my back foot.

"Oof," I crumple to one knee— Koa is pretty good.

I swing my back leg to knock her down, but she jumps over my leg and forces her weight on top of me.

"Koa," I say, "Listen—"

"Koa?" Cloplin says.

Koa looks up at him.

"Uncle Cloplin?" she's surprised. "You've been— you're dead."

"We need to keep moving," Desman says.

"To where?" Cloplin demands. "There's nowhere to go."

"Gia," says Desman, "what's your plan?"

"Buy time," I say. I try to muffle my voice as much as I can while still getting the point across. Cyro can hear me now.

"Before what?" asks Desman.

"What's going on?" Koa asks.

"Koa, we can't reason with defectors!" yells Zade. "We have orders!"

"We can question a person who's been dead for 15 years!" she yells back.

"No," says Zade. "I'm taking them in." He puts his hand on the back of Desman's neck.

I cross my arm over to Koa's shoulder and close one of my legs around her. Contracting my muscles, I throw her off of me and she slams against the floor.

Desman slams Zade against the wall and he sinks to the floor in pain.

Footsteps sound down the corridor.

"This way!" I say turning in the opposite direction.

"Wait!" Koa springs to her feet and runs after me, Desman, and Cloplin.

I brace myself to take her down.

"Where are you going?" Koa doesn't seem like she is running after us to stop us.

"Get to Phrame 21," I say to her, "and bring as many people as you can with you."

"21 is flooded," she says.

"No, it's not!" Cloplin yells as we turn down a corridor to the right.

Koa slows to a jog and leaves my sight as we turn.

I don't hear footsteps behind us.

"Do you think she's keeping the others off our backs?" Desman asks.

"She can't for long," says Cloplin.

"Gia, tell us what's going on."

I slow to a jog, listening. There's no noise other than the sound of our padded feet hitting the floor. The audio surveillance will pick up anything I say… maybe I should have worn the shoes.

"Trust me," I say.

"No," Cloplin responds without hesitation.

Trellis

"Then," I pick up my speed, "go do something else." Not regarding his comment, I listen to the sounds around us and keep attention to the physical surroundings. If trainings taught me anything, it's to pay attention to what is happening and suppress panic instincts until it's definitely time to fight.

"Give the trowel to me," says Cloplin with a breathy voice.

"No," I sound more cavalier than the situation probably deserves.

"Then we'll have to take it from you," he says, panting as he runs.

"By all means," I say, still paying more attention to my surroundings than to Cloplin. The lighting is turquoise, probably changing from blue to green. The air is colder than in the Sanctuary. And I see what Lyra meant about the smell. My nose fills with an alarming odor. How do I even describe it? Did it always smell like this?

"Desman," says Cloplin, "do what you need."

Down the corridor, I see a door seal shut.

"This way!" I yell, guiding us down a different corridor.

Keeping sight on where we're going, I don't worry too much about Desman overtaking me. He can't overthrow me even when he's not injured.

Another doorway slams shut. This one is still down a corridor, but a bit closer to us so that Desman and Cloplin notice it too.

"He's shutting us in!" Desman yells.

I turn down a different corridor. The shuffle of footsteps resonates. If only we can make it to the next intersection, we can make a turn away from the pursuers.

"Left!" I say as we reach the next intersection.

The three of us make a hard left turn. Then I halt immediately at a doorway. It slams shut.

"Trapped!" Cloplin yells. "He's trapping us!"

"Keep going!" I say turning around and going down the opposite path.

"Where are we going?" Desman is breathless. He must be in a lot of pain. A piece of me feels sympathy for him even though he's trying to stop me.

"This way," I say, turning to the right.

We run straight into a massive person in a grey suit.

It's Baeden Lester. He's about Jarret's size and hopefully Jarret's wit as well. I've never trained with Baeden, so I'm not sure.

Baeden reaches his hand toward Desman who runs behind me. He chose to focus on the larger figure instead of the closer one— he might be of less wit than Jarret.

I leap and flash my hands toward his face to break his attention, then kick his waist. He folds over to the floor, trying to grab my feet. But I clutch his shoulder and use his momentum to flip him to his back. He lands just in front of Desman.

The next turn is within arm's length. We can make it.

Trellis

As I cross the threshold, the door starts to close, catching my foot on the fold of the material that rises from the ground. I trip through the doorway. It seals closed before Desman and Cloplin can get through.

"No!" I yell, looking back at the closed door.

"Gia!" Desman's muted voice sounds on the other side.

What do I do? I can't leave them, but I can't get the door open.

I think of the trowel in my suit.

No— not yet. I can't put it in this wall here. Facilitators might grab it and I'll lose it forever. It needs to make it to Gaines Cyro's quarters.

Footsteps sound again from a corridor down and to the right. I take off sprinting again.

Guilt stings my heart as I jog through the walkway that's lit up in a green-yellow color. Will they be alright? I may have sacrificed two people with hopes to save the facility. Is this the same as making a decision to sacrifice a few to save the whole? Is this why Gaines Cyro has the accidents? Am I like him?

I try to wall up the floods of doubt coming into my mind.

I turn to the left. Figures in grey catch sight of me.

Have I done the right thing?

There's a connecting corridor just ahead. The doorway begins to close. Sprinting full speed, I take a leap to make it through as the plant-like material slinks closed.

My front leg makes it through. My upper body flies through the closing doorway. My momentum jerks to a stop. With my hands and front leg toward the ground, I hang slightly as the door closes around my back calf.

I put my fingertips on the ground, trying to pull away from the door. I swing all my force from the doorway and try to wedge from its grip around my leg. As best I can, I pull my upper body toward the folds over my calf. It looks like black fabric with metallic reflection is twisted around my leg. As I claw at the twisted door, my fingernails break. It's too hard to breathe while crunching myself up toward my leg. I swing back down to catch a breath. With all my strength, I pull back up and pound, scratch, and yank at the door around my leg. My body releases to catch another breath. Panting, I dangle in the doorway.

The entire weight of my body rests on the thin slice of metal around my calf. It stings. My leg on the other side of the door starts to go numb. I hear shuffles on the other side. Something touches my foot. I feel exposed. What might they do to the part of my leg that has no ability to defend itself?

Frantically, I try to swing my back leg and foot around. I kick something, but not very hard. My knee makes a cracking noise. A sharp pain fills my leg.

I recall Lyra's description of the doors— some sort of alive-but-dead material made from a plant. Maybe it has a weakness. Letting out a grunt, I pull the upper half of my body again, feeling around the door for some weakness. There are folds and veins in the door and I press them, trying to hurt it or signal it to release. Nothing works. It feels like solid, cold metal.

Footsteps echo through the corridor in front of me. I release my upper body and dangle upside down. Figures in grey suits fill the area. Letting my arms go limp, I breathe out and try to catch my breath.

The door releases. There's a thud as my body hits the ground. I curl into the fetal position, laying limp as grey-suited feet surround me.

"She's hurt," says a voice.

Eight feet— there are only four people.

"We'll have to drag her off," says another voice.

My hand shoots toward someone's shin as my legs power back and knock someone's ankles. As the person behind trips, I pull my hand back and slam another person to the floor. Jumping to my feet, a man standing in front of me moves to punch me in the stomach. I maneuver to his side with my hands on his shoulders and push his force so he runs into the wall. As he's shocked, I take his shoulders again and push his wobbly body toward the girl behind me. The man's body folds as I push him and his weight crashes against the girl so she crumples under him.

Running with a slight limp, I search for open corridors. Is there anywhere to go? How much longer can I do this? There's a hissing sound. It's familiar, but only from simulations— it's gas. Wisps of steam rise from the floor. I hold my breath, running as fast as I can. At each connection, I look left and right, frantically looking for a way out. I keep my mouth sealed, trying to keep myself from what my body screams at me to do— take a breath. I see an entrance in a corridor to the right. As I turn, the door shuts. I slam right into it. The force of the slam pushes the air from my lungs. I gasp in. It's like a warm tide rushes over my mind. I fight to stay present, hitting the door with my fist to get it to open. The tide in my mind pulls me out to sea. My body sinks to the floor. My mind sinks into the ocean. It all goes dark.

Chapter 20: Gaines Cyro

I gasp as my eyes shoot open.

"What do you have to say for yourself?" Cloplin yells as he paces the holding cell.

Red light reflects off Desman's still, crouched body. Laying on the other side of the room from Desman, I push my heavy body to a seat. I grab my knee. It's slightly warm and tender. I move it back and forth and push on it with my thumb. Nothing is broken.

Desman sits on the opposite side of the holding cell. He looks mad. It's like the lights decided to align with Desman's mood as he boils silently across the room.

"You've doomed the Sanctuary," Cloplin says.

I keep my focus on Desman.

"Maybe we can fix this," Cloplin whispers. "We can make a plan to escape. Then we can get into Cyro's office and—"

"What were you?" I look at Cloplin.

"What?" he seems taken off guard by the question.

"What were you?" I ask again. "Promotor?" He must not know very much about the Trellis if he thinks we can openly come up with a plan and not have it overheard by security. Cloplin's suit is green, but I don't know how suit colors work in the Sanctuary. He seems to have the arrogant demeanor of some Promotors I know.

"I— a Cultivator," Cloplin responds.

"Leave him alone," Desman says.

"What?" I ask.

"I said," Desman says slower, "leave him alone." He's fuming. "It's your fault we're in here. Don't go questioning him about things that don't matter."

"I never said it—" I try to defend myself.

"You Facilitators, always thinking you're better than everyone else," Desman continues.

"Desman," I interrupt before he starts a monologue, "I didn't say anyone is better than anyone else."

"You think it," he says. "You've thought it every day since assignment day when we were separated into jobs. You think it at every training when you beat everyone to a pulp."

"Desman—" I try to interject.

"And now, look at us," he stands and motions around the room. "This is because of you. *You* think you had a better plan than anyone else. *You* think you can run a facility better than anyone else. And now we're here. I asked you to be on my side one time!"

"There aren't sides," I say.

"Of course, there are!" he says back. "Maybe you don't notice because you always have your own side and people follow you around in it."

"I've been trying to get us out of this mess, just like everyone else."

"Yeah," he says, "*You*. All by yourself, strong Gia is going to come out and defeat all the bad people."

"Desman," I tilt my head, "what is this really about?"

"Don't play your dumb negotiation tricks on me," he throws one hand in the air. "This isn't about anything other than how much you care for your own plan being the one we choose instead of doing what's best for the community."

"Oh, I'm the one who only cares about my own ideas?"

"Yeah," Desman says.

"So going behind the backs of all the assembly members to overthrow Gaines Cyro isn't caring about your own ideas?"

"We at least had time to present the idea to others before going and making the decision to destroy our homes."

"Maybe by then we'd all be dead from a blocked siphon and the network on the outside would all end up in another accident."

"Well, now we will all be dead!" Desman yells. "Thanks for taking out the uncertainty!"

"No problem!" I yell back.

The sound of metal clanks somewhere outside the holding cell.

"They're coming in for questioning," Desman puts his hand out as if to shush us. "Don't give them any answers. Gia, you know their mind games. Maybe there's a chance and you can negotiate some way out of this."

"There is nothing outside of this," says Cloplin. "They have the Sanctuary already. They have us. There's nothing we have that they could want."

"Maybe allegiance or something," Desman speaks with panic. "Tell them, we can convince the Sanctuary people to obey without a fight, and then we can organize an uprising."

Trellis

"Do you still not understand audio surveillance?" I look at Desman.

"Is that seriously all you're thinking about right now?"

"I'm just saying, no plan is going to work if we say it out loud right now."

I hear footsteps.

"We're out of options," Cloplin hangs his head. "Hold out as long as you can and don't give in to the questioning if you can help it."

The door to the holding cell slinks open.

A figure in a grey suit stands at the entrance.

"Leal?" Desman exclaims.

"Hi," Leal gives his awkward wave at the three of us in the holding cell.

"Hi, Leal," I smile.

Leal waves to the corner at a small bubble in the wall where a surveillance camera is located.

"Thanks, Minji!" Leal says to the bubble.

"What's going on?" Cloplin says.

"The plan," Leal replies. "But we need to hurry. Minji can't deflect surveillance forever."

My heart pounds in my chest as we sprint through the Facilitator's quarters. We're getting closer. The doors will stay open as long as Minji sends commands to deflect surveillance and tell Facilitators to go toward Phrame 21. I'm not as afraid of getting caught, but my mind pulses as

I try to suppress the panic from being in this area. We're getting closer— closer to our fate.

Eddi told me not to worry about it. He trusted this moment, but I don't.

"We're almost there," Leal runs beside me through the walkway. "Minji's workstation is down this corridor. I'll leave you here and take Minji back to Phrame 21. Gia, you have five minutes. Be safe."

"Okay," I feel like a whimpering child as my best friend needs to leave my side at my weakest moment.

"What do we do?" Cloplin asks.

"Umm, you weren't supposed to be here," Leal turns beside us then turns to the corridor on the left. "So do whatever you want!"

"Gia?" Cloplin asks as Leal breaks off and Desman runs straight beside me. It seems like Cloplin has quickly forgiven me for taking the trowel and now trusts whatever plan we have in motion.

"Just," I can't think of what they should do. "Go to Phrame 21."

"No," Desman pumps his arms hard and tries to keep a straight posture to hide the fact that he struggles to keep up. "Where are you going?"

"Cyro's quarters," I run at full speed ahead. Faster than I've run in any simulation. Pushing myself to focus on the situation I've never trained for— to face my father.

We stop in front of the office.

Trellis

"Remember to hold your thumb down for a moment," Desman looks at the thumbprint scanner in front of my dad's office.

It's the only way to Gaines Cyro's office. Eddi told me it's almost certain that my dad would be there to keep guard so no one can get into the office.

My thumb trembles as I put it on the scanner. Holding my thumb there, the alarm sounds. It doesn't turn off as the door creeps open. Either Minji and Leal have left already or Minji doesn't think it's worth turning off at this point. Or— I don't like to think of an alternative. I hope they make it out.

I take a breath through my nose and step through the threshold.

The dark walkway to the office feels like a walk to my own grave. I remember Lyra's voice walking me across the platform toward Alaster. Just one foot in front of the other.

I see him hovering over the control podium in the center of the domed room. A shaky breath leaves my mouth as I step toward my fate. I try to control my tells that give away my fear: my left thumb rubs my pinky finger, my breath gets shaky, my jaw clenches— he knows them all, maybe even better than I do.

"Gia," my father's shoulders droop at the sight of me.

What is he thinking?

"Stand back," I command.

He puts his hand on the podium.

"I said," I take a step forward, "Stand back."

He pushes a button on the podium. Then shoots both hands in the air to surrender and takes a step back.

A door in the side of the domed room shoots open. It's the doorway to Cyro's office.

Eddi was right— my dad is letting us in.

"Garridon Hamiltoni," a voice says from the doorway.

"Plangon," my dad's voice sounds shaky.

Is this a trap? Did he know Plangon would be there?

"Gaines Cyro worried that you might come to this," Plangon walks forward into my father's office. "I have to say, I thought the best of you. After everything with Britannica, I didn't believe you would turn on Cyro now, but he judged you better than I did."

My dad stands for a split second, rubbing his finger with his thumb. Still facing Plangon, he walks slowly in front of me and takes a defensive stance.

Minji had commanded all Facilitators to Phrame 21. No one else will come. It's all of us against Plangon.

I take a step beside my dad and firm my stance, ready to fight.

"Please," Plangon puts his hand up, "let's be more civilized, shall we? Cyro wants to speak with you."

Both my father and I drop the defensive stance. Plangon doesn't try to fight back— it's a good sign. Cyro wouldn't talk to us unless he knew we had the upper hand.

Trellis

"I have to say," Plangon clasps his arms behind his back as we follow him through the entrance to Cyro's office, "you have caused quite a commotion, Gia Hamiltoni. But Gaines Cyro wants the best for us all and is a gracious man."

Entering the room, a massive screen hangs above a control panel. Beside the control panel is something I've only seen in pictures— a sofa. Looking around, the room is furnished with luxuries from earth's surface— an end table with an electric lamp on top, a rug, and glass cups next to a decanter. A light fixture on the ceiling illuminates the whole room. Something feels off. The warm light in the center of the room makes an eerie contrast as the rest of the room feels sterile and cold. It's like nothing has been touched in a long time.

"Why would he negotiate with us?" Desman whispers as he follows me into the living quarters.

"Great question," the massive screen flickers and a white smile flashes. Gaines Cyro's unmistakable, strong face appears above the sofa. "Plangon, you put it well. You have caused a commotion, Gia. I'd be lying if I said I wasn't impressed." He smiles wide, then takes a pause. "But, I also have to say that my patience is quite thin. I will make one offer, which you may take, or you and all your friends can pay the consequence for the disruption of our functioning community."

"Functioning," Desman scoffs, "maybe tyrannical."

"Say what you may, Desman," Cyro smiles, "but I've been around a long time and this is the best way to keep the greatest amount of people alive and healthy. You'd see if your precious Sanctuary lasted much longer." The eyes on the screen move to me. "Now, Gia, about your disruption. Here's my deal. You turn the cameras back on and I'll let you all go back to your jobs and integrate the survivors of the Phrame 21 accident back into our supportive community."

"Cameras?" Plangon stands behind me and tries to piece together the elements of a plan he wasn't a part of.

"Indeed," Cyro's smile stretches on the screen. "All the cameras in the Trellis, up until the Facilitator Phrames, slowly dimmed and then turned off completely. I've searched every strip of code and can't find how you managed to turn them off. Is it your friend's safety that you were trying to ensure? I am a reasonable man, and I never had malicious intent. But I can promise the safety of your friends if you're willing to let order back into our community."

"Reasonable?" Desman speaks up before I have a chance to answer. "You're a coward! You don't even show yourself in person because you can see you're outnumbered. You are no reasonable man. You've murdered to get where you are."

"Have I?" Cyro smiles.

"In every accident!" Desman argues.

"Or maybe," Cyro has a smirk on his face, "the Sanctuary was an experiment and I never intended accidents to hurt anyone."

"What about Menhit?" Desman makes a fist and steps one foot forward. "She wasn't in the Sanctuary. You killed her so you could take power."

"Oh," Cyro leans back, "Did I now?"

The screen flickers. Victoria Menhit's face appears on the screen. Except, it's a younger version of her.

"Or maybe," Victoria Menhit smiles on the screen, "things aren't as they seem."

The screen flashes again. The face of an older man shows on the screen. I've seen him in the history lessons. It's the leader from before Victoria Menhit. The screen flickers between faces. Each one is a former leader of the Trellis community. He gets to the last one. It's the first Trellis Head after when people came down to the Trellis. He must have somehow put his conscience into the system the same way Alaster was a physical person who put himself into a submarine.

"It's like I said," Cyro's face appears on the screen again, "I've been here a long time."

"As for the negotiation," Victoria Menhit's kind voice speaks from Gaines Cyro's face. It switches, Cyro's voice comes from Menhit's face. "Turn the cameras on, and give me the trowel."

I clutch the trowel tucked under my kitten t-shirt.

"Gia," Desman's eyes are serious as he looks at me. He may even be scared. "I don't see a way out of this."

"Like I said," Cyro shows himself in his face and voice, "I am a reasonable man. Gracious, even. And I have an even more tempting offer."

The screen flashes to show a flooded corridor. A limp body floats in the water.

"Ara!" Desman cries.

"Life and death," Cyro's face shows again. "It's a weird thing. Those temperatures are near freezing. Her body and brain are gone, but her consciousness is still available."

"What are you saying?" Desman yells.

"I'm saying," Cyro switches his face to the first head of the Trellis Facility. "You see before you a dead man, but an alive person. She can live, Desman, within the Trellis system. And even better, this beautiful soul will have equal command over the Trellis as me. If you don't trust me to run this place, surely you'd all trust her."

"Gia," Desman looks at me, "we have to."

"Desman," I clutch the trowel, "it's not possible. Her body is completely gone, her consciousness can't be there without the physical. He's lying."

"No!" Desman yells, "I'm tired of following your plans! If there's any chance she could live, we need to take it!"

"There's no chance!" I take a step away from him and guard the trowel. "He's a liar! Alaster is the only way we make it out of this!"

"Can't you see?" Desman swings his hand out to the screen. "He is Alaster!"

Trellis

I pull the trowel from my suit, keeping my eyes on Desman, and walk to the control panel.

"I won't be counted among the people who end up on the wrong side of this!" Desman yells and then lunges toward me. "We take the offer!"

I jolt away from Desman. Plangon lunges toward me, but my dad slams into him in mid-air and knocks him to the ground.

Swinging the metal away from the control panel, I put the trowel toward Cyro's main control station. Desman's hand squeezes my wrist and he pushes his weight on me to push me to the floor. Grabbing the back of Desman's head, I use his weight to slam his forehead into the control panel. Blood rushing from his fingers as he grasps his forehead, he muscles his other hand around to search for some part of me to grab and stop me. He grabs my hair and pulls back as hard as he can, but I keep my hands where they are and stick the trowel into the command center. I release when I'm sure the trowel is in, sending me and Desman flying to the floor from the power of him pulling me back.

He pushes himself up and reaches for the trowel, but I pull him back to the ground.

The screen flickers.

Cyro screams.

The screen goes blank.

Cyro laughs on a flickering screen.

There's a blank screen. Then words type across the screen: "run"

Cyro laughs on the screen again.

A shock of cold jolts through my body.

Desman shoots a worried look into my eyes, then looks at the ground. Water trickles around us.

"He's trying to drown you," words on the screen say. "Run."

Chapter 21: Abandon Ship

    There's ringing in my ear. Shock across my body. Stay present. Fight the cold shooting through my veins from the water. I jump to my feet, but crumble back to my knees with my arms splashing in the water.

    Strong hands grab each of my arms. My kitten shirt is heavy, dripping with cold water as I'm pulled to my feet. I look to each side. Desman holds one of my arms and my dad holds the other. A hand touches my face.

"Gia," my dad grabs my chin to push my face up toward him. "Are you okay?"

"Come on, Gia," Desman tugs at my arm.

I shake my head. The ringing in my head turns into alarms sounding all around me. The emergency alarm, the training bell, the switch buzzer— every sound that comes from the Trellis Facility plays at one time. The electrical light shuts off and the screen flickers between a typed word and different faces— *run*, Cyro's smile, *run*, Menhit with furrowed eyebrows, Cyro's laugh, *run*.

"I'm fine," I push the hands that clutch each of my arms. "Let's go."

Sprinting toward the exit, my injured knee fumbles with each step. We make it through to my father's office, then run through the hallway to the door at the end.

"It's shut!" Desman yells as he reaches the exit first.

I push through and see Plangon beside the control console.

"Open the door!" Desman shouts at Plangon.

"It's what's best," Plangon replies.

"Aren't you the only one who can open and close the door?" Desman asks my dad.

"Not from the inside," my father responds as he lunges for Plangon.

"You know it's the right thing!" Plangon shouts as he's tackled to the ground. "I won't!" Plangon struggles to get words out. "I won't end up on the wrong side of an accident!" Water splashes as my father and Plangon wrestle on the floor.

"Hold him here!" my dad shouts at Cloplin who hovers over them, trying to help.

Cloplin sits on top of Plangon and holds his arms in the water as my father leaps to the control podium and types.

"You know this is a mistake!" Plangon yells. "He needs people alive to keep the facility running. Choose allegiance now, and we can survive."

"Go now!" my dad finishes typing and looks from the podium.

"I'm saving you!" Plangon muscles his way toward the podium with Cloplin on top of him.

Slowly rising, the water is around my shins. Desman and I splash through the hallway without staying to see the battle between Plangon and Cloplin. The doorway is open. Running through it, I look behind to see my father hesitate in the walkway and look back into the office.

"I'll hold him!" Cloplin's voice yells from the office.

My dad breaks his gaze from the office and turns toward me. His eyes seem to sink. He takes another look toward the office.

"Gia! Keep going!" my dad looks resolutely at me and runs out of the hallway.

"Which way do we go?" Desman shouts.

"This way!" I run down a corridor, taking a glance back to the office.

The door shuts.

"Cloplin!" I shout, but can barely hear my voice over the alarms. I pivot back toward the office.

"No!" my father grabs my shoulders and stops my sprint to the door. "Please, Gia."

"But Cloplin," I say.

"Please, keep going!" my dad's face seems tense as both his hands grip my shoulders.

"I can't!" I can still barely hear myself over the blasting buzzer and alarms.

"Why are the lights dimming?" Desman shouts.

All around, the lighting that was bright blue starts to fade.

"We are supposed to be farther along," I try to shout above the noise.

"Where?" Desman shouts back.

I look back and forth. Others are waiting for us. If we don't keep going, people might die as the water rises.

I motion to Desman to follow and run down the corridor. The lights go down further. I won't be able to see anyone. Will we get lost? What if we don't make it? They can't keep waiting for us. They'll drown.

I hear a distant voice above the Trellis noises yell, "Gia!"

I can barely see the silhouette of the person as the light dims around us and water rises past my knees.

"Eddi!" I yell back.

"Thank goodness," Eddi is still distant, but a bit louder.

The alarms stop.

"What does that mean?" Desman's voice asks beside me.

"I don't know." I look around. There isn't much left I can see.

"Everyone," Eddi says as his figure wades through the water toward us. "Grab hands."

I reach out toward Eddi's, but Desman grabs my hand first and then Eddi's. My dad grabs my other hand. My stomach cringes as his hand tightens around mine.

Leading the line of us holding hands, Eddi pulls us forward through a darkening walkway. The water rises up to my hips and the cold starts to numb the pain in my knee.

Water drips down a door as it starts to close in front of Eddi. The door stops, then reopens.

The alarm sounds, then turns off.

"What's happening?" Desman asks.

"I think they're fighting over control of the Trellis," Eddi says.

"Alaster and Cyro?" Desman asks.

"Yeah," says Eddi. "We need to move fast. The others are waiting."

"Why are the lights turning off?" Desman asks as we wade through a nearly black hallway. "Aren't they, like, bacteria or something? I thought you couldn't turn them on and off."

"You can't turn them on and off," Eddi says, pulling the trail of us through a right turn. "We've injected the light panels with bleach. It's spreading and killing the bacteria."

"Ah," my dad says, "I was wondering how you turned off the security cameras. I thought I could hide the code from Cyro, but I couldn't even find it myself. I have to admit, I was impressed."

"We didn't turn off the cameras," Eddi says, "we just made it dark so it appeared they weren't picking up footage. The dimming process worked quickly in the Cultivator Phrames as we used a high concentration of bleach. Then we guided everyone through black hallways to Phrame 21."

"You killed the lights," my dad chuckles.

I don't think I've ever heard that noise from him— a laugh. It seems familiar, like I might have grown up hearing it, but also off-putting, like the laugh doesn't belong to the same man who raised me.

The alarms turn back on, blasting in my ears. As we push further through the frigid water, the lights go completely dim. What if a door closes on us and we can't see? Will we get stuck in one like when the door closed around my leg?

Desman trips, falling into the water and still holding my hand. I inhale at the same time I'm pulled underwater. Icy salt water fills my lungs. Desman releases my hand and I feel around for something to push me up. A reality flashes through my mind— I can't swim. What if the water goes beyond the reach of my neck? From behind, my dad pulls me up and tries to set me back on my feet. The waterline is up to my stomach. I cough water from my lungs and grope around for Desman's hand.

"Desman?" maybe it's the cold, but my voice sounds like a desperate cry as I search for his hand.

"I'm here!" he yells over the sounds of the alarms and grips my hand.

"We're almost there!" Eddi shouts as he pulls us forward once again.

Coughing, my body starts shaking. My teeth clamor together. My chest starts to tighten, as if my ribs reject the command to keep moving in and out in the freezing water. Desman's hand shakes in mine. My dad grips my shoulder as Eddi pulls us forward.

A very dim streak of light is just above my head. Eddi guides us along the light streak, which brightens as we follow it until I can tell that it's a glowing vine. We're almost to the Sanctuary. The water is up to my chest. How far away is it? Can we make it?

Still rising, the water reaches to my chin as we exit a long corridor. Dim vines trace the outline of the massive, domed room. We just have to make it to the other side of the Sanctuary. On my toes, I struggle to keep the pace with the others as Desman's hand pulls me forward faster than I can tiptoe through the water.

Gulps of salty, cold water fill my throat as I stretch my neck to stay above. I feel my dad's hand touch my back and push me forward. My feet no longer make contact with the ground as he lifts me slightly so that I'm not in the water. He guides me left, then right, following Eddi's tug through the blanket maze and toward the Alaster ship.

I see the corridor that leads to the submarine. We're so close. I hear gargles and chokes from ahead. Eddi is shorter than both my father and Desman. His arms splash in the water while he tries to keep his head up. As we make our way slowly through the corridor, I start to hear my dad spit water from his mouth and struggle for breath. Realizing that he can't keep holding me up, I push his hands from me and flap my hands around to stay above water. Gasping in air and water, I struggle to stay up.

It's so close. I can see the open entrance to the submarine just ahead.

I take one huge gasp of air and hold my breath as I sink under the water. The shocking cold rushing over my head nearly knocks the wind out of me. But I keep the breath in my lungs as I sink further until my feet hit the ground. With my feet touching the ground, I lunge forward and out of the water. When I break from the water, I take a quick gasp for breath, then sink back down. It's not quite swimming, but it will do. Again, I touch the bottom, then push myself from the water with my feet, taking a quick breath. Each time I sink to the ground, I force myself with my legs toward the entrance.

Around me, Desman, Eddi, and my dad do the same, bobbing in and out of the water, taking leaps forward, then going under the water to touch the ground and leap forward for another breath.

We splash through the entrance to the submarine, but still aren't out of the water. Voices above shout to help us as we bob toward the ladders that lead to the levitated platforms.

I sink to the ground, then push myself toward the surface to find that the surface is now too high for me to break through. My lungs struggle as I miss my chance to take another breath and sink back down. Hitting the ground with my feet, I use all my might to take a desperate push as far as I can. The top of my head crashes into metal and the air leaves my lungs. I take an instinctual breath in, but only cold water fills my lungs.

A hand grabs my hair. It starts pulling me up. The hand moves around my arms and pulls upward. Water pours from my throat and I gasp for air as arms wrap around my shoulders and waist to pull me up.

Dripping, I collapse when the arms release me to the metal platform. Breathing in and out, I cough more water and push my heavy body up. Desman coughs beside me. Arcturo and Vega kneel toward the edge with their arms around Eddi as they pull him onto the platform. My father grips the metal ladder and tries to pull his way up next to us. Arcturo scoots over to me when Eddi is safely out of the water.

"Gia," Arcturo says, "you okay?"

"Yeah," I struggle to catch my breath as I rise to my feet and feel the water drip from my soggy shirt. I walk down the platform, toward the ladder which leads to the next level.

"Where are you going?" Arcturo asks.

No one tries to stop me as I heave in and out and pull myself up the ladder.

"Gia!" my dad cries when he finally flops onto the platform.

I pull myself up each ladder and stumble onto higher levels. Looking to the left, people crowd in the little rooms which connect to each platform. Different people litter every platform as I climb upward, but I move past them without seeing who they are.

Reaching the top platform, my steps are heavy with water and the weight of exhaustion. I don't hesitate as each step thuds over the levitated walkway that once terrified me. With determination in each stride, I move toward the control panel— toward Alaster.

There's someone in the left seat before the control panel. Leal. He sits in the right chair with his hand covering his mouth and his eyes squinting at the buttons.

"Gia!" Leal exclaims, lowering a tablet in his hand. "I can't figure out how to get this thing started."

I drop into the chair next to him and lean over the control panel.

"Alaster," I say, looking straight ahead at the wall in front of me. "Let's go."

The wall flickers, but words don't appear. Instead of turning into a screen, the wall turns into a window. From the ceiling of the massive ship to the water below, the wall turns transparent and headlights flick on to show the expansive ocean ahead.

Fear grips my lungs. I struggle to breathe in, not because of cold water this time, but from being exposed before the giant, dark ocean. On the white ocean floor, a slimy sea-slug trails through the headlights and then into the darkness. A shark swims slowly into view.

A loud hum sounds. It's from inside the submarine, not outside. The entire ship jerks back and forth. I grip my chair trying to stay stable as the ship moves like an earthquake. Screams fill the air. Leal scrunches with both his feet in his chair, gripping the side of his seat, and looking at me like a cry for help. A shark in front of us moves swiftly away at the loud noise.

As the shaking smooths and the ship presses into the ocean ahead, footsteps sound on the platform behind. A hand, damp with water or sweat, grasps the back of Leal's chair. Eddi hunches over and tries to catch his breath while looking at the open space ahead. Arcturo and Vega follow behind, stopping next to my chair. My dad joins the group with his hand over his mouth. As we gaze at the wonder ahead, Eddi whispers a breathless tune:

"Oh, marvel of mine,

captivating my sight."

Staring straight ahead, Leal finishes the lyrics:

"I see a peril ahead;

you're beautiful, but dark as night."

The ship moves forward at a steady pace, pushing through the darkness and journeying into the unknown.

Epilogue: The Unknown

Garridon Hamiltoni ran his fingers over the railing on the Alaster submarine. The metal railing was cold, but the air felt warm.

Muffled voices sounded behind the various closed doors which ran along the levels of platforms. Down below, water had drained from the bottom of the ship, and people stood on dry ground. Garridon leaned over the railing, toward the cluster of people dressed in green, red, and grey suits. One person stood out from the crowd. Her long, black hair draped over a kitten T-shirt that covered her dark green suit. Gia— she looked so much like Garridon, but her smile, her joy, and her passion were Britannica.

The crowd below was a symphony of claps, songs, and laughter. Standing next to her best friend, Gia danced. Had Garridon ever heard his daughter laugh before? Had he ever seen her smile like that? His heart was like a bound prisoner, sentenced to walk the plank and sink to the bottom of the ocean.

15 years ago, Garridon did not push the button that closed the door and doomed his wife, but it felt like his fault that she was gone. From then, he had vowed to do everything necessary to keep his daughter alive.

Eddi Fitzgerald held his wife's hand, singing while looking into her eyes. Mabel smiled, and grabbed Eddi's other hand, as if accepting his invitation to dance. With a smile, Eddi pulled his wife close, but sang loud enough so all could hear. Leal took Minji's hand and danced next to his parents.

The crowd below was something Garridon had never seen. It was a celebration. Sometimes slow and safe as people held one another and sometimes a whirl of color and joy. It was so beautiful. Maybe Garridon didn't deserve to be a part of it. Garridon didn't let his wife die, but maybe he'd been drowning her for 15 years. Maybe, as he tried to keep his daughter alive, he actually killed an important part of her.

As Garridon gazed at the crowd of celebration and comfort, he finally saw the flicker of Britannica Hamiltoni in the T-shirt-dressed girl who danced below. And he was pounded by a wave of grief and regret. She was there the whole time, and he had never seen her.

A creak in the metal platform informed Garridon that someone was walking toward him.

"Hey," Arcturo had a sweet smile as he walked toward Garridon.

"Arcturo, I—" Garridon hung his head and searched for the right words. Shoulders drooped, blood drained from his face, bags under his eyes, Garridon looked weak. It wasn't a normal look for him.

"Garridon," Arcturo's voice was like a warm blanket covering a worn traveler. He put his hand on Garridon's shoulder. "It's okay."

"It's not," Garridon put his hand over his face. His breath amplified between his fingers as he struggled to keep tears back.

"Look at her," Arcturo motioned toward Gia, who clapped in sync with the new song that Eddi sang. "She's alive, and she might not be if it wasn't for you."

"But what kind of life has she lived?" Garridon wept.

"We all made mistakes," Arcturo grabbed both Garridon's shoulders and looked into his eyes. "But she's here, and that's as much as we could hope for right now." Tears welled in Arcturo's eyes.

"Arcturo," Garridon could see remorse and pain in his friend's eyes, "I'm so sorry." He hung his head once again. "I did what I could to keep Ara alive."

"I know you did," Arcturo pulled Garridon into a hug. "I know you did."

Tears flowed over their necks and suits as the two hugged.

"And we need you again," Arcturo stepped back and wiped his nose. "You know more than anyone else about what is next. We need you to hold a council with us so we can decide what to do."

"No," Garridon shook his hand. "Everything I've ever done has led to pain and more accidents. No one will trust me." He paused. "And no one should."

"We need you," Arcturo stood his ground. "*She* needs you."

Trellis

Garridon looked below at his daughter. She looked young again, like the years of training didn't erode the spirit of a little girl who was so full of wonder. She was wonderful.

She may never accept him. But now that he could fully see her, maybe he could keep her safe. Maybe he could keep Brittanica alive.

"Arcturo," Garridon finally said, "what's ahead could be more dangerous than what's behind."

"All the more reason we need you," Arcturo sounded like a man who welcomed his brother back into the family. "What do you think we should do?"

"It's survival mode right now," Garridon responded without voice inflections. "We take it one step at a time."

The view from the submarine window showed the ship creeping toward the brine pool beside the Trellis Facility's turbines.

"Garridon!" Eddi yelled from the bottom of the metal stairs.

Garridon looked to where Eddi pointed, out the window and toward the brine pool. A tentacle rolled from the brine, slow and smooth, then disappeared back under the pool.

"The first step?" Arcturo asked.

"The first step," Garridon responded.